D1740762

## ALSO BY CAROLYN ARNOLD

### Brandon Fisher FBI Series
*Eleven*  
*Silent Graves*  
*The Defenseless*  
*Blue Baby*  
*Violated*  

*Remnants*  
*On the Count of Three*  
*Past Deeds*  
*One More Kill*  

### Detective Madison Knight Series
*Ties That Bind*  
*Justified*  
*Sacrifice*  
*Found Innocent*  
*Just Cause*  
*Deadly Impulse*  

*In the Line of Duty*  
*Power Struggle*  
*Shades of Justic*  
*What We Bury*  
*Life Sentence*  

### McKinley Mysteries
*The Day Job is Murder*  
*Vacation is Murder*  
*Money is Murder*  
*Politics is Murder*  
*Family is Murder*  
*Shopping is Murder*  

*Christmas is Murder*  
*Valentine's Day is Murder*  
*Coffee is Murder*  
*Skiing is Murder*  
*Halloween is Murder*  
*Exercise is Murder*  

### Detective Amanda Steele Series
*The Little Grave*  
*Stolen Daughters*  

*The Silent Witness*  

### Matthew Connor Adventure Series
*City of Gold*  
*The Secret of the Lost*  
*Pharaoh*  

*The Legend of Gasparilla*  
*and His Treasure*  

### Standalone Title
*Assassination of a Dignitary*  
*Midlife Psychic*

I never expected this change in my forties...

# Midlife Psychic

A Paranormal Women's Fiction Novel

# CAROLYN ARNOLD

HIBBERT & STILES
PUBLISHING INC.

Hibbert & Stiles Publishing Inc.
hspubinc.com

This is a work of fiction. Names, characters, places, and incidents are the products of the author's imagination or are used fictitiously. Any resemblance to actual events, locales, or persons, living or dead, is entirely coincidental.

Names: Arnold, Carolyn
Title: Midlife Psychic / Carolyn Arnold.
Description: 2019 Hibbert & Stiles Publishing Inc. edition.

Identifiers: ISBN (e-book): 978-1-989706-71-8 | ISBN (5 x 8 paperback): 978-1-989706-72-5

# Midlife Psychic

To my sister Sherry,
who helped open my mind to the
power and magic of the universe
and the divinity within myself.

I am blessed to have her as one of
my teachers along this spiritual
journey called life.

# Introduction

**If you told me four days ago that I would be given a vision,** I'd have laughed in your face.

My name is Erin Stone. I'm forty-three, niece, sister, mother, divorcee, friend…psychic? I'm still trying that label on. I work for the Toronto Police Services at the emergency 911 dispatch center. My life was rather ordinary and routine before the psychic bit, and that was just the way I liked it. I had my gorgeous gray tabby cat, Harvey—named after that dreamy character on *Suits*—to keep me company. I drank vodka martinis sometimes but *loved* red wine. Slap a nipple on that bottle some days, and I was good to go. I did yoga at my best friend's studio to offset the wine consumption, and I binged *Grace and Frankie* on Netflix any chance I got. Then again, I could somewhat relate to their situation. At least my husband hadn't dragged our marriage out forty years before coming clean with me. More on that later. But as you can see, my existence was quite ordinary. Peaceful, calm, predictable.

That was about to change.

I'm not talking about the changes expected to hit in your forties—hot flashes, new aches and pains, or the battle with the scale taking on epic proportions. No. I had a dream… One extraordinary dream that would change my life forever and complicate the crap out of it.

You see, clairvoyancy, consulting mediums, foretelling the future, having visions—it all went against everything I'd learned and believed my entire life. I might as well be communing with the Devil. But I couldn't just ignore this dream. As I said, it was extraordinary.

It had felt so real from beginning to end and lingered with me after waking up. Honestly, I thought I was losing my mind. When I found out the events I'd dreamed of had actually happened, I was quite certain I was crazy and headed for a straitjacket and a padded room.

Turns out the universe had other plans for me.

# Chapter One

"I'm going to die."

*The words keep running through my head—over and over. The oxygen mask falls from the ceiling, and I rush to put it on. When I'd watched the flight attendants going through the motions before takeoff, I never in my wildest nightmares thought I might need to know any of their spiel.*

*But now the plane is in a nosedive and shuddering wickedly. Alarms are pinging all around. I'm sitting in the midsection, and when I look forward, I'm also looking down.*

*We're all going to die. Among strangers, yet alone. I don't know one face among the crowd.*

*I gasp out loud, then hold my breath, trying to stay as motionless as possible. As if any movements I make could worsen the situation. There is no worse. And we're all powerless to do anything about our fate. This is the end of the line. Our time is up.*

*People are screaming. Others praying and signing the cross. Others chanting. Making promises and vows. "If I make it out of this alive…"*

*Somewhere behind me a baby cries, and the mother reassures her child that everything will be okay.*

*Warm tears trickle down my cheeks. A lie, but how I would love to believe her.*

*The pinging of the alarms is drilling my skull. Like a woodpecker's beak rapping incessantly. But I've never liked the sound of them, even in smooth flying. Whenever someone flicked on the light to summon an attendant, I'd hold my breath until I realized what the noise was for.*

*I hate flying. I never should have gotten on this plane. I should have stayed home. After all, I had this feeling… This knot in my chest. I knead it now, but the pilot is calling out over the speaker system. It's hard to make out his voice above the din. But everyone starts leaning forward. I follow their lead and glance across the aisle to this mysterious man.*

*He first got my attention at the airport. He's wealthy. The rings on his fingers, the cut of his suit, but there's something else about him—an enigma. He's traveling with three men. One sits beside him, and the other two are in the seats in front and behind him. I get the feeling they are his bodyguards. So who is he? Just someone rich and powerful with enemies to match? The leader of a crime syndicate?*

*But he is calm as he sits there, as if he's prepared for the day of his death and is ready to face it head-on. He holds a small book open in his lap, one hand splayed over the right page, his eyes following the text on the left. His lips move behind his mask as he reads in an undertone. A chant? Scripture? A prayer? All this is hard to reconcile with my fabricated image of a leader of organized crime. His companions don't appear to be equally at peace. Rather their faces are masks of fear.*

*The plane swerves side to side, careening like an out-of-control car skidding on ice, and the nose plunges farther downward.*

*The baby screams louder. No assurances come from the mother this time. I hear her sobs. Despite the racket and cacophony of noises, there's an underlying stillness, quietness—a sense of serenity in our final minutes—and all my senses are highly attuned.*

*"We're all going to die," the woman beside me cries.*

*As if voicing the inevitable makes it more manageable, bearable. Though it doesn't change the fact there is some sort of finality hurtling toward us. But is it an ending or a beginning? We'll soon find out but have no one to tell.*

*I grip my armrest so tightly my fingers go numb.*

*The confident man continues to read. Unfazed. On another plane of existence.*

*The aircraft takes on a violent spin, like a shooting bullet whizzing through the sky on a downward trajectory.*

This is it! *I yell in my head.*

*The woman next to me takes my hand and squeezes. A person I have never met, but with whom I'll be eternally linked. I look down at her hand in mine. Hers so fragile and brittle to the touch, riddled with age spots against my milky flesh and bright-orange nails. I allow my mind to drift away, to try and find some comfort in these final moments. My heart slows. My last inhale becomes caged within my chest forever as we thunder into the ground.*

*I had expected some pain before oblivion, but instead I find myself floating over the crash site. Below me, the plane is in pieces and debris is spread out for miles over a country field. Fireballs shoot from the wreckage and catch the wheat on fire. But there's something unsettling about the flames being licked by the wind… They perform a beautiful dance, but it's one that marks utter devastation and tragedy.*

# Chapter Two

In four days, it will have been twenty-eight years since my parents died in a plane crash. Friday, three days before Thanksgiving. Sometimes it feels like I lost them yesterday. Other times, it's like it happened another lifetime ago. It was probably their crash that caused my nightmare. After all, I'd had other dreams about plane crashes—my shrink told me it was to be expected—but none had been like the one from last night, not even the ones that replayed my parents' deaths. It just felt so incredibly real, like I was actually on the plane and not sleeping in my bed, in my Toronto townhouse. Safe on the ground.

I woke up and went through the motions. The morning constitutional. A long, hot shower. Feeding Harvey, my gorgeous gray tabby cat. Grabbing something to eat and downing coffee. As I waited for another one to brew, I studied my reflection in a compact. The face looking back at me belonged to a forty-three-year-old divorcee and mother of a nineteen-year-old woman. Lines were starting to move in around the eyes and mouth, and the brows were starting to sag—just a little, but I was in denial. I pulled up on my left eyebrow and imagined both eyes the way they'd been in my twenties. No draping skin, perfect for applying eyeshadow, but I would let nature take its course. No Botox for me. I kept my eyebrows plucked and narrow and had full lips my best friend, Trish Gamble, had always envied. My hair went past my shoulders and was blond with highlights from a bottle. The baby hairs framing my face and my roots were gray, but I wasn't ready to let them run wild just yet.

"See you, Harvey." I talked to my cat as if he were a human being. To me, he was as much a part of the family as my daughter, Jenna. Little Harvey and I had become quite close over the last five years. I'd adopted him for Jenna after her father, Chris Pittman, and I had separated, but when she went to university, Harvey stayed. Not that I'd ever regretted the idea. He'd been by my side through the divorce and the move back to Toronto from where I'd lived with Chris in London, Ontario.

I headed out of my townhouse at just after six. If I hit the lights just right, I'd be ten minutes early for my twelve-hour shift that started at seven.

The autumn air was crisp and cool. I burrowed into my coat and watched as my breath ascended in wisps of white, all the while wishing away the scattered imagery from the dream-slash-nightmare. Really, *nightmare* would be a better definition than *dream*. What was more troubling was how it clung to me, like I'd lived through it somehow, more like a memory than a figment of my subconscious.

"Maybe I'm just losing my mind," I said out loud to no one but myself. That fact alone convinced me I might be onto something. After all, only crazy people talked to themselves.

I got into my Ford Focus and let it warm up for a few minutes before driving off. I needed to be at the Toronto Police Service dispatch center in time for the pre-shift "parade" which took place at six forty-five. The parade informed new arrivals of situations in progress. We also found out if we'd be fielding calls or working dispatch.

I had my brother, Jason, to thank for my job as a communications operator. While my divorce netted me a livable sum of money, I needed something to keep me busy and give me purpose. As it turned out, working for the TPS as a communications officer was a blessing, but it wouldn't be a job for everyone. In fact, there was a lot of turnover in staff. The hours were long and the rotating shifts hard, but it was what we faced on a daily basis that tested our character.

Traffic was favorable and so were the lights. It was six thirty when I pulled into the lot for work. By the time I carted myself into the parade-slash-lunchroom, I still had five minutes to spare.

The unit commander heading up the parade today was Jayne Loughlin. She was a civilian, like me. It used to be that each platoon was overseen by a staff sergeant, but about ten years ago, they changed the command structure to a civilian one. At higher levels, we were still overseen by a superintendent and the deputy chief.

Loughlin was a large woman. Five eleven, solid build, and she could probably bench press my five-foot-six, one-hundred-thirty-two-pound frame without breaking a sweat. She was standing at the head of the room and bid me a good morning as I took a seat in the front row, and I replied in kind. We'd never really connected personally, but on the job, we had a mutual respect for each another. In fact, as a group, operators had a very tight sense of comradery. It probably had to do with the fact we could relate to what our fellow colleagues were going through and had been through. Most people were familiar with the term "Thin Blue Line," but as a group, we represented the "Thin Gold Line."

There were already about fifteen people in the room when Lauren Wells dropped into the chair beside me.

"Good morning, Erin." Lauren was smiling, a smile only Lauren could pull off. It immediately lit up the room, and sometimes I wondered how she could always be so happy in spite of the job we did, the things we heard, the situations we dealt with. I loved her cheery disposition, even if she was a morning person—something I couldn't completely relate to. It took me a cup of coffee before I wanted to talk to anyone, and two to be personable. I imagined Lauren hopped out of bed with a bounce in her step and a grin on her face.

"Morning." I smiled back, then took a pull on my third coffee of the day, thankful it was my only real vice. Many of my coworkers struggled with serious addictions.

Lauren swept her long, brown hair over a shoulder and pulled out a notebook and pen.

The room filled up fast after that—approximately another twenty people. At any given time, there was a minimum of seventeen dispatchers and anywhere between twelve and twenty call-takers assigned to each shift.

Loughlin commenced the meeting. The good news was there wasn't a whole lot going on, but the bad news was that might mean a slow shift—though that could change on a dime. Each shift really was like pulling the handle on a slot machine; you never knew if you were going to be passing the time tapping your fingers or hopping with a nonstop barrage of calls and requests from officers in the field.

Loughlin called an end to the parade and doled out our assignments and where we'd be sitting. "Stone, you'll be taking calls today."

At that point, I stopped listening and left the room to get to work. I parked behind my desk, throwing my coat over the back of the chair and tucking my purse next to my feet. We used to have lockers and a real place to put our personal belongings, but with reallocation of square footage and the fact we now shared the building with other police units, we ended up with less space. Another reason our parade room doubled as our lunchroom. Even the room we work in wasn't that expansive. It was L-shaped, and while dispatchers and call-takers didn't necessarily have eye contact, we were able to maintain situational awareness.

I signed into my phone and computer, and not even ten seconds later, my line was ringing. As I answered, I prepared my mind to handle whatever situation might be on the other end. It could be anything on the scale of petty to serious. I'd never forget being on the line with a man who took his last breath and then picking up the next call to someone complaining about a parking ticket he'd received. It certainly took patience, understanding, and strong intuition for this job.

And while my time at work was never routine, my personal life was in fairly good order. It had taken three years after my divorce to get to this point, and it was rather nice having some calm and predictability after leaving here. If only I knew my entire life was soon about to change—to flip upside down, in fact.

# Chapter Three

I'd fielded over fifty calls by the time lunch rolled around, thanks in part to the Automatic Call Distributor (ACD), a computerized system that pumped calls through a queue based on priority. It was set up to siphon calls eight seconds after an operator ended their previous one. Not a lot of time to reset, but it certainly made time fly. Unfortunately, I didn't pack a lunch today, so I headed out to grab something quick. With the twelve-hour shift, I was given two thirty-minute breaks, to be taken one at a time, so I had to hustle. I hopped on the elevator for the main floor, and the doors started to close.

"Can you hold—" Lauren was running toward me, and I stopped the doors. "Thanks." She let out a whoosh of air and leaned against the back of the elevator car.

"Rough morning?" I'd heard that she was assigned dispatch today.

"You could say that. Actually…" She looked me in the eye. "Three words for you. Secret squirrel detail." There was the hint of a smile toying with her lips, but I couldn't miss the irritation in her eyes.

"Secret squirrel detail" was how we referred to officers who acted on their own initiative and got themselves into trouble. "Oh," I said.

"Yeah, oh, and what a mess."

I shared her frustration. As a dispatcher, we were given authority over all radio-equipped police, and our orders were to be received as if they were coming straight from the chief of police, but not everyone on the ground wanted to see it that way. Veteran dispatchers like Lauren would have no problem pointing out the policy in this regard, but that didn't mean it was any less aggravating needing to pull rank. "Sorted out now?"

"As much as possible."

"When will they learn?"

"My guess?" she said. "Never."

We took the elevator to the ground floor and headed for the street in search of a place to eat. We settled on McDonald's—the smell of their fries yanking me in off the sidewalk.

We ordered and found a table next to an indoor children's play area. A man was tossing balls at a young boy, and the kid was squealing with delight.

"Remember when?" Lauren popped a fry into her mouth. "They start off so sweet, loving, innocent. They even like us." Another fry went in.

I was starting to wish I'd just given in and ordered the fries, but I'd been struck by self-judgment and ordered a salad. I plunged my plastic fork into the leafy pile and stabbed one small piece of lettuce. At this rate, I might starve.

I turned to Lauren, picking up what Lauren had said and following a hunch. "Something going on between you and Kaitlyn again?" Kaitlyn was Lauren's sixteen-year-old daughter.

"You could say that. She hates my guts. You know, she actually told me that. Can you believe it? I mean, I know I never liked my mother when I was a teenager, but she's taking this to another level."

"You never told your mother that you hated her? Not once?" I never had the chance to get into the throes of teenage rebellion with my mom, but I could imagine it was the right of passage for most teenagers.

Lauren rolled her eyes. "Maybe once…or twice."

I laughed. "See, and you didn't mean it."

"I did at the time."

"Try not to stress about it. Kids say a lot of things."

"I bet Jenna never gave you a hard time."

Lauren might hate me if I admitted that Jenna had been a golden child—a role model for what every one should be like. But we were also an exception to the standard mother/daughter relationship. We'd always been more like friends. I gave her a lot of free rein, guiding her only when necessary, and she'd never let me down. Lauren was staring at me, obviously seeking out some sort of understanding. "Teenagers are going to be teenagers. There's not much you can do. And I'm sure she doesn't hate you. Teens say a lot of things."

"Uh-huh, so that's a no. Jenna never said that to you."

I shook my head and took another forkful of the salad. This time I lucked out and snatched a piece of chicken. I glanced up at the television mounted on the wall above Lauren's head. It was tuned into *CP24,* a local station that was news all the time with a screen that was split into five sections. Trading numbers scrolled across the bottom. The date stamp and weather were noted in the top right-hand corner with a traffic cam beneath it and text noting any slowdowns. To the left, video was rolling of the current news story, and beneath it was a running ticker tape of other recent news. It was the latter that had my insides turning cold, and I stopped chewing.

*Small        commercial        plane        crashed*
*in      rural      Texas.      83      persons      dead.*

"Erin? Are you okay?"

That depended on the definition of "okay," because I certainly didn't feel that way at the moment. My eyes were frozen on the screen.

The cameraman was panning the wreckage. Flames and debris spreading out for miles. The crash site was exactly what I'd seen in my— *No, this can't be!* I put a hand over my heart, and it was thumping wildly.

"You're white as a ghost." Lauren turned around, following my gaze. "A plane crash? Did you know someone who was on that flight?"

I spit my mouthful of food into a napkin, still in a daze, fixated on the imagery, on the ticker tape.

"Erin?" Lauren touched my hand that was on the table, and I recoiled as if I'd been burnt.

"None of this makes any sense." I was mumbling and barely coherent.

"Erin. You're scaring me. Talk to me. Did you know someone on that plane?"

I slowly shook my head.

"What is it?" Her voice was trembling, the well-assured communications operator crumbling apart.

I met her gaze, and her eyes were filled with tears, mirroring my own. But there was no way I could tell her that I'd seen the crash in a dream—as the plane had been going down. None of this made any sense to me. To verbalize it, she'd have me institutionalized, and I wouldn't blame her.

*It was just a nightmare. Nothing more. Just a dream! Just a dream! Just a dream!*

Maybe if I repeated it enough, I'd believe that—but really, what was the alternative? I had the word "vision" pop into my head, but I dismissed it just as quickly. I'd been raised Catholic, and that sort of thing was tantamount to alignment with the Devil.

Still, I found myself looking closer at the TV, examining the glimpses they were showing of the crash site. It looked much like my parents'—maybe a lot of plane wrecks appeared similar. I had to be making too much out of this. As I'd thought earlier, my nightmare had to be about their deaths and my mind trying to come to grips with it yet again. The grief did have a way of coming up repeatedly and unexpectedly.

"Erin?" Lauren prompted.

I met her gaze and shook my head. "It's nothing… It just made me think of my parents' crash." Not a complete lie, but not the entire truth either.

"Oh, right. Of course. It's coming up on the anniversary of their deaths soon, isn't it?"

I nodded. "Twenty-eight years ago this Friday. Guess just seeing that…" I let my words trail off and flicked a hand toward the TV.

"I can't imagine what that must have been like…them dying that way."

She couldn't. Not that I'd say that when she was doing her best to be sympathetic and caring.

Lauren glanced back at the TV, then faced me again. "Eighty-three dead. How sad. How many on your parents' flight?"

"Theirs was a Boeing 747. Five hundred twenty-three." As I stated the facts, there was no way the crashes could look anywhere near identical. I laid a hand over my stomach, and my skin felt clammy.

"You're looking like hell. Maybe you should take the rest of the day off?"

I wished it were an option, but I was off tomorrow and then again during the upcoming Thanksgiving weekend from Saturday through Monday. "No, I'll be fine." What would I say anyway? *Please let me go home. I'm losing my mind.*

Lauren angled her head as if to question my stand; I was doing so myself.

"I really am fine." I tried to sound convincing and pasted on a smile, but I wasn't sure if either came across.

"Well, it's up to you, but you don't do anyone an ounce of good if you're compromised emotionally, Erin. Especially in this job."

She had a point. Going home early really wasn't a choice for me though. I'd just have to push the stupid nightmare out of my mind and carry on with life. After all, the alternative was checking myself into a mental hospital.

# Chapter Four

After my shift, I went straight home to a date with the bottle of merlot I'd opened last night. Then again, maybe I should stay away from alcohol. *Nah.* They say drinking doesn't solve anything, but I think it does. Sometimes. In the least, it should quiet my nerves and slow down the nattering in my brain.

I topped off a wineglass and took a long sip.

Was I really considering that the dream I had was something more than that? Like what—a vision or a premonition? *That* was crazy, hocus-pocus nonsense. And if it wasn't, I didn't really want to know where that left me. My aunt Judy and uncle Harold—rest his soul—had taken me and my brother in after our parents' crash. Judy was a devout Catholic, though she accepted I wasn't so much a practicing one but the kind that showed up at church on special occasions and for holiday mass. Regardless, the faith had become engrained in me, and to entertain visions, clairvoyance, and their ilk simply felt as if I were committing the unforgiveable sin.

My best friend, Trish, would have a ball with all of this, but she was into the supernatural and the mystery of the universe. Why couldn't she have had the dream—or whatever it was—about the crash?

First thing tomorrow, I'd be calling Catherine's office— Dr. Jacobs to most people—the psychiatrist I'd been seeing since I was fifteen. From my initial visit after Mom and Dad's crash, she'd invited me to call her by her first name. It was probably why I was comfortable speaking with her, but I had a doozy to unload this time. *"Yeah, I had a…"* Had what exactly? I kept circling back to that, refusing to say it was a vision, holding out for a logical explanation.

Harvey sauntered into the kitchen and rubbed against my leg, purring and meowing. I picked him up and snuggled my face into his furry neck, soaking up his unconditional love for a few minutes. I placed him back on the floor. "You hungry, baby?" I dished up some food for him. As for myself, my stomach was a hard knot.

I looked at my wineglass and figured tonight was a liquid dinner. Retreating to the living room with my glass, the bottle, and my laptop, I dropped onto the sofa. I put my legs up on the coffee table and logged onto the internet. Maybe if I took a good hard look at the Texas crash, I'd be able to convince myself I was just blowing my nightmare out of proportion and getting all worked up for no reason.

It wasn't hard to find reports on the crash. The plane had been on its way to Toronto Pearson International Airport in Mississauga, Ontario, from Bush Intercontinental Airport in Houston, Texas, and experienced problems about a half hour into its journey. It went down at 4:03 AM…around the same time as my dream.

I went cold, took a gulp of wine, braced myself, and kept reading.

The cause of the crash was being investigated by the National Transportation Safety Board, which I knew from personal experience could take months. It had taken nine *very* long months to find out why Mom and Dad's flight had crashed. Eyewitnesses at the time had commented that the plane just seemed to drop out of the sky.

What made the timing of their deaths all the more tragic was they'd been returning from a once-in-a-lifetime trip to Europe for their second honeymoon. It had taken my parents years to save for the trip, and their plane went down in Michigan. So close to home. Some might say "at least they got the trip in." Those were the silver-lining people who tried to grasp something good even in the darkest of situations. There were times I wasn't sure there was a bright side to find.

When the "closure" finally came, it didn't make it any easier to let them go. The answer to why—the God question, as Aunt Judy called it—was never satisfying. Some had sought restitution in a payout. Since the pilot was found at fault, there was a suit filed by the families and friends of the crash victims against his personal estate and the airline. It had taken several years but resulted in a twenty-five-million-dollar settlement. Jason and I saw about seventy-six thousand each. A big sum to teens but not touching anywhere close to compensating for what we'd lost.

I took another slug of merlot to drown out my grief and to fortify myself for what I might uncover. In a lot of ways, I was being catapulted to the past—to an incredibly painful time in my life. Did I even want to wallow in those emotions by feeding my mind on other people's tragedies? Or in their grief did I feel a sense of companionship and understanding? After all, I knew firsthand what the loved ones from the recent crash were going through. I took a deep breath and enlarged a photo of the wreckage.

Debris spread out, fire and smoke…and burning wheat. Just like my dream.

"This can't be." The hairs on my arms stood, and the skin at the back of my neck tightened like pulled leather over a drum.

Everything looked just as I saw it in my dream. Even the way the cockpit had torn from the cabin, the angle at which it had come to rest, the positioning of the wings—one here, another there.

"What the hell is happening?" I cried out, though not really expecting an answer.

I should leave a message at Catherine's office, have her receptionist get back to me first thing when the office opened. There were obviously things I needed to discuss with her about my parents' deaths, more emotions to process. If I could deal with them, I could get back to my life as it was before I briefly entertained that I'd had a vision. Wow, even the word. Again, it sent goosebumps spilling over my flesh. But all this was surely my imagination running amok. I had to be projecting my parents' crash on the one from Texas.

I opened another internet tab and brought up an article on my parents' crash. The intention was to look at the associated images objectively, but grief rooted into my chest. This was where my parents had died. I'd avoided these pictures for years; I wasn't sure if I ever really saw them.

I lifted my gaze and looked across the room to a framed photograph of my parents on the mantel. All that talk today about Lauren's daughter, how she hated her mother. I couldn't imagine even if my mom had lived longer that I'd ever have said that I hated her. Mom had been a friend to me, much in the same way I was to Jenna. But maybe if time and circumstance had been different, I'd have rebelled and spewed horrible things her way. There was no way to know for sure, and in this moment, I found a part of me missed the fights we never got to have.

"I will always love you, and I will never forget you," I whispered to them, my chest compressed and heavy.

Harvey jumped onto the couch, making himself comfortable on the cushion behind my back and resting his little chin on my shoulder. I rubbed his head. It was just like Harvey to be there for me when I needed him. He'd been by side through the divorce—his soft fur working wonders to wick my sadness away. Maybe I didn't need to talk out my feelings, I just needed to *be* with them. By morning, all of the nonsense about the dream meaning something could have vanished, and I could be feeling right as rain.

# Chapter Five

I woke up more rested than I'd felt in weeks. No alarm was set, but I beat it anyway. Why was it when sleeping in was an option, I was always up before the sun? I couldn't recall having a single dream from last night, and that made me happy. But it didn't take long for the nightmare of the plane crash to come sweeping in on me. One day later, and it still had a strong visceral hold on me.

"Just your grief," I told myself. But I ended up calling Catherine's office for an appointment. They fit me in for five o'clock.

I went about running errands and busied myself. The hours might have been easier to pass if I were working today. As it was, there were moments when it seemed the clock stood still.

Eventually, I found myself sitting in one of the plush chairs in Catherine's waiting room. But just being there, waiting, made my anxiety worse. As each minute ticked by, it sunk in further why I was there. She'd pull the dream out of me. I'd have to face the memory of it, the vivid imagery and how it felt so real.

"Ms. Stone, Dr. Jacobs is ready for you." It was Catherine's receptionist, Sadie, who had addressed me.

"Thanks." I dipped my head and slowly rose to my feet.

I found Catherine perched in her chair, opposite the couch where I'd been sharing my feelings for nearly three decades. "Good day, Erin. Please make yourself at home." A woman in her mid-sixties, Catherine had a pleasant, round face with soft blue eyes. Her energy was warm and inviting, which encouraged her patients to bare their souls.

I closed the door, then tossed a throw pillow to the other end of the couch and took a seat. I wished for the pillow back the second I'd let it go. It was ridiculous how uncomfortable I felt in here today, but I was afraid my shrink was going to tell me I'd lost my mind. Even after all the years and reasons I had to trust her to be openminded and a confidante. She'd been there for me through my parents' deaths and as I went on through life: facing the pressures of college, meeting Chris, falling in love, marriage, the birth of our daughter… my divorce. This woman probably knew me better than I knew myself.

Catherine held a silver pen over her notebook as she waited for me to get situated. There wasn't any judgment coming from her, but there could have been. It had been months since I'd talked with her last. "How have you been since our last visit?" she asked.

Loaded question—and where to begin? Up until the last twenty-four hours, I'd been fine, normal, like everyone else, just going about my life. "Pretty good." The words blurted out.

Catherine smiled this knowing smile, but let my brief response go. "What brings you in today?" She spoke in a gentle voice and tilted her head in a motherly fashion.

I took a deep breath and reminded myself this was a safe space. "As you know, it was twenty-eight years ago this Friday that Mom and Dad's plane went down." I still often found it easier to blame the plane for their demise, and it was certainly easier to refer to the crash than their actual deaths—even after all this time.

Catherine nodded, but something about her gaze and relaxed facial expression prompted me to continue speaking.

"I had a dream the other night about a plane crash." I let that statement hang, hoping that she'd jump in and run with an assumption, rescue me from continuing, but her job was to listen. "Anyway, it's really stuck with me. I figure since it's the anniversary of my parents' crash, it probably has something to do with that."

Catherine crossed her legs and leaned forward. "Tell me about the dream."

I gave her the gist, watering down the potency and omitting the eerie similarities between the nightmare and yesterday's news headline.

"Erin, I sense there's more you're not telling me. Let's start with how this dream made you feel. How was that?"

*Like I was there! Like I died with those people!* "Sad, incredibly sad. Also real, like I was on the plane. Not that this makes any sense."

"It doesn't need to make sense." She offered a warm smile. "Continue."

"I don't know… It was like, ah, maybe I was in my mother's head at the time of her crash and experiencing it through her eyes." But the woman in my dream had another woman holding her hand. If I was seeing things through my mother's eyes, why wouldn't I have imagined my father's hand?

Catherine wrote something in her journal and asked, "Why do you think you were in your mother's head and not your father's?" She was watching me—soft, kind eyes—willing me to answer.

"I felt that I was female."

Catherine set her pen in the fold of her notebook, looked at me with a serious expression. "You are probably aware that dreams about plane crashes can relate to our waking life. They often come on when life feels out of control or overwhelming. Like we're going to crash and burn, not be able to overcome our challenges. It could, of course, have something to do with you processing more feelings about your parents' deaths."

I latched on to the lifeline that Catherine had extended. "Well, there's the memorial event for my parents' plane crash." Every year, Karen Snyder, who had lost her husband of twenty years in the crash, rented the basement of a bar called Ryan's over in Cabbagetown. It was a central neighborhood in Toronto and also the area I called home.

Catherine picked up her pen again. "Certainly that could be stirring up grief, but I also believe it's possible there's more meaning to this dream. Is something in your personal life causing you stress lately? How is work these days? Are you happy? Are you feeling fulfilled or burnt out? Your job certainly isn't an easy one."

"It's fine. Nothing especially upsetting that I've dealt with recently." *Except I'm losing my mind.* My heartbeat kicked up a bit.

Catherine sat back in her chair, studying me in that unobtrusive manner of hers. "I suspect there's something weighing on your mind beyond your parents' deaths."

If I believed it was possible for people to read minds, then Catherine might have that ability.

"Is there anything more you'd like to tell me about your dream?"

I chewed on my bottom lip almost hard enough to draw blood. "The dream…it was so vivid, like it was real. It was just as clear as me looking at you now. And I had thoughts within the dream." Now that it was out there, I felt foolish.

Catherine's blue eyes lit. "What were these thoughts about?"

I grabbed the pillow and squeezed it tight enough that I'd have strangled the life out of it if it were alive. "I recall thinking about the other passengers, who they might be, and why I was on the flight in the first place."

Catherine scrawled in her notebook.

She was probably writing down that I needed medication or a brain scan. If someone had told me just the amount I'd already laid out to Catherine, I'd have rolled my eyes and corkscrewed a finger next to my ear, like they were a complete cuckoo. But sharing even the small amount I had with another person felt somewhat empowering, though at the same time, it was like standing naked in the city streets waiting for ridicule and judgment. I cleared my throat and pressed on. "You might have heard about it on the news, but there was a crash yesterday…"

"I did, yes." She looked up from her notes. "Do you think that means something?"

*Did I?* "I don't know. I do know that around the same time that it was going down, I would have been having this dream." I was going to be sick. I'd come here to have Catherine tell me that the grief was resurfacing, but the conversation seemed to have taken another direction—one I, for some reason, had steered us toward. I probably just wanted to put it all out there so when she told me the dream was nothing to worry about, I'd believe her.

"That's interesting."

*Interesting or terrifying? Was I nuts or psychic—one and the same?* I wrung my hands. "Uh-huh, and the crash, as shown on the TV, looked quite a bit like the one in my dream."

She regarded me seriously. "Why do you think you had this dream?"

I wasn't liking the sound of this. Where was my reassurance it was nothing but my grief wreaking havoc again? "I don't know," I rushed out, frustration setting in.

"Do you really believe you were somehow on the plane that crashed?"

"I know that's not possible." I squirmed on the couch.

"You know it's not possible?" Catherine volleyed back. "To know something is to be absolutely certain."

I could feel sweat beading on my brow, and I wasn't a person who perspired much. "I don't know, but it is impossible, right?"

Catherine pinched each end of her pen with her fingers, angling it left, right, left like a representation of the scales of justice. But in this case, I imagined my sanity was being measured. "The truth is there's much about our universe and the world around us that we don't know."

With her words, I remembered how Catherine often urged me to open my mind to "possibilities." Like when

I first started seeing her, she'd alluded that a lot of people found comfort in accepting an afterlife. Despite that being a teaching of the Catholic Church, thinking that my parents existed in heaven while I was here failed to deliver any peace of mind. It was far easier to accept that they were hands down gone.

Catherine continued. "You told me the real-life crash from yesterday looked like the one in your dream—"

"If you're trying to tell me I had a premonition…" I was feeling terrified and not ready to hear anything of this nature. I hugged myself and rubbed my arms. Why couldn't she just say it was my grief? End of session.

"I'm not saying that. But who knows?" She offered a gentle smile.

Shivers tremored through me.

"Do you think it's possible that you projected the images from your dream onto the recent crash? Do you think *that's* possible?"

Now we were getting somewhere. I was starting to feel lighter, and breathing was becoming easier. Relief. I *had* blown the dream out of proportion. "Yes, completely possible. I probably just imagined the two crashes were the same."

Catherine regarded me deeply, evidence of concentration cutting lines in her brow. "The way you say that—*probably*—it almost sounds like you want this dream to be something more."

*What?* "That couldn't be further from the truth."

She tilted her head slightly to the right and continued. "I know that you're not a fan—or even a believer—in the supernatural, including life after death, so maybe ask yourself why you want to promote the dream to something of far more importance? Is it to ease the grief you still carry for your parents or for some other reason?"

It felt like my throat had stitched together, and any words I conjured in my mind failed to merge coherently. I had nothing.

"Another thing you might want to ask is: what does this dream represent, or mean, to you?" Catherine's eyes drifted to the clock on her wall, and mine followed.

Time was up.

"Thank you, Catherine." I stood, relieved beyond measure in one way, but burdened in another. She hadn't just given me a pass. She gave me homework.

"No problem at all, dear." She closed her notebook. "I'd like to see you again, say the end of the week, and see how you are then and what answers you've come up with to the questions I posed."

"I'll make an appointment with Sadie." That was what I said as I left her office, but I bypassed Sadie's desk on the way out. I'd take away what I wanted from today's session. It had been a dream representative of something in my life and not necessarily grief for my parents. The only person making it into something bigger was me, and that was going to stop right now.

# Chapter Six

After seeing Catherine, I dashed home, fed Harvey, grabbed a quick dinner for myself, and a change of clothes. Currently, I was headed to Everclear Mind, Body & Spirit for the seven-thirty yoga class. The place was owned by Trish and was her pride and joy. She'd set the place up only a few years after college, to the dismay of her parents who would have preferred she'd put her college education to better use. Why they thought her degree in business and finance wasn't being fully realized as a business owner was beyond me. But people knew what they knew. Those of her parents' generation grew up working for other people. They seemed to fail to realize someone had to own the companies, and it could have been them. It was interesting—and sad—how we could limit ourselves.

Trish and I had been friends from the second our eyes met, and we grinned at each other in college. Kind of like a meet-cute in a romance movie, but it was the beginning of an amazing friendship that would last a lifetime. Trish liked to call our relationship a God appointment, in other words "meant to be." Really, Trish and I were quite different. She'd never married or had kids. Honestly, she never told me much about her love life; I could only assume she had one. It seemed it was the only topic off the table. Her business was her world.

I was an A-type personality and hemmed myself in sometimes doing what others expected of me. Trish was more of a free spirit. But despite our disparities, Trish was the sister I'd never had. She was chosen family.

I popped into the locker room and changed into my yoga pants, workout bra, and T-shirt. I found Trish at the front of the studio dressed in her usual attire of white, white, white. No one would win a debate with Trish about avoiding white after Labor Day.

Trish had always been petite, all of five foot four, and lean—the latter something a lot of girls in school hated her for. Their loss.

She lit up when she saw me, and my heart swelled at the sight of her. It didn't matter that we hung out two to three times a week; we hugged every time we got together.

She wrapped me in her arms, brushed a kiss to my cheek. "How are you doing?"

"Doing good." I said it, and I meant it. *Yep. Mentally stable*—the thought slipped in. "You're looking good as always," I added.

We pulled out of the embrace, and she dismissed my compliment with a wave of her hand. "Although, I should say thank you," she amended with a smile.

Trish read a lot of nonfiction on new-age spirituality and self-empowerment. She was currently working on accepting compliments without deflecting. According to these books, women tended to downplay praise that came their way while men often easily *and* eagerly accepted it. Huge surprise there!

"But really? I look good?" She let her eyelids fall shut. "I feel so tired tonight."

Trish rarely complained of being tired, but if our lives were reversed, I'd have just enough energy for the couch every night. "Are you coming down with something?"

"Never." Trish shook her head adamantly.

She was one of those people who believed she could avoid getting sick by holding tight to the intention of remaining healthy. She'd sometimes get into shielding herself with "divine white light," but that conversation tended to go over my head.

She went on. "I did, however, spend all day reviewing the books for the accountant…" She crossed her eyes, ever the comic. I did find it interesting how she went to school for business, accounting being a big portion of the degree, but she delegated tasks associated with it to employees. That still didn't get her out of the monthly and yearly reviews, which she viewed as due diligence and good business practice.

"Oh." Trish's gaze flicked to the studio door, and she was grinning. "A few new faces. How lovely. Please excuse me." She touched my arm, and off she went to greet them. I imagined her spirit floating toward them—that was how she seemed energetically, anyhow. My heart quickened at my observation. *Her spirit…?* There was no doubt Trish had rubbed off on me over the years.

"Namaste." Trish took each of her new customers' hands in turn. "Welcome."

The women lit up in response to the warm welcome. The one even giggled, but that was Trish—magnetic and charming with her larger-than-life personality. She might not have the flu, but she was contagious, and no one was immune.

I glanced at the clock. Class was set to start in five minutes. I claimed my mat—one Trish kept at the studio for me—front and center. Everyone else had to reserve their spot online and show up ten minutes early if they wanted to ensure they kept the position.

We all got down to it—downward facing dog, etcetera. The hour passed quickly, but during class, time had a way of slowing down. Apparently, that's how it should be with yoga though. Mind, body, and spirit ever in the present moment—Trish's motto and the inspiration for her studio's name.

I showered and met up with Trish in a private living area she had set up at the back of the premises. She could have called the place home if she'd wanted to. Essentially, it was a modest-size apartment.

Trish's love of the lake showed in the soothing palette of whites, creams, grays, and blues that she used to decorate the space. She had wanted to bring a bit of her Muskoka lakefront cottage to her studio—though it wasn't so much a cottage as a small mansion with five bedrooms. She rented it out during the summer months and got away with charging five figures per week. After all, northern Ontario was a vacation hotspot.

And if the colors weren't enough to say "lake," she brought actual water into the room. A large fountain was in the corner with a four-foot-tall Buddha perched atop it. Incense candles rimmed the well and were burning now, smoke rising in tendrils. I inhaled deeply and appreciated the subtle scent of lavender.

This was the space where Trish's spirit resided, as she'd put it before. If it had been anyone else speaking to me like that, I would have been uncomfortable. But I suppose you could say I was like a frog put into a pot and slowly warmed up. Otherwise, I probably would have found Trish's ideologies as shocking as if I'd been dropped into a boiling pot. While I had loosened some of my grip on Catholicism, I only dabbled in new-age spirituality. For Trish every belief or practice was as simple as "partake" or "pass."

The kettle clicked off, and Trish jumped from the couch and poured the water over chai teabags in two mugs.

I took one off her hands. "Thanks."

"You're very welcome."

Trish resumed her spot next to me and put her feet up on the long coffee table in front of the couch. I moved so my back was wedged on an angle between the back cushion and the arm, facing Trish.

She bobbed her teabag in the water by its string. "I shouldn't have complained earlier... You know, when I said I was tired from reviewing reports. I am blessed to have finances to review. I'm grateful for that, believe me, but I couldn't imagine playing with numbers every day of my life." She put a finger gun to her forehead and pulled the trigger.

We both laughed. "It's funny how life takes us places we don't plan for," she added.

My eyes snapped to hers, and my stomach flip-flopped—all automatic reactions, which I immediately wished I could take back.

Trish held eye contact with me, squinted, angled her head. She set her mug on a side table without taking a sip, the teabag also forgotten. "There's something going on with you."

"Me? No." Trish never claimed to be psychic, and if she had, I wouldn't believe her, or I'd run. But she had a way of looking at a person and "knowing" something was up. She'd told me before that she could see auras around people, and I'd nodded to be friendly, but I really didn't want to dip too much into the topic. It hadn't stopped Trish from telling me more though. I'd learned that energies were associated with different colors and that our body was separated into seven main chakras—all represented by a color. These were what showed as auras and were present with every living thing. To me, it sounded like she'd done a little more weed in college than she should have or spent too much time watching *Avatar*. Like that line from the movie, "I see you." She'd found the line incredibly impactful. My knee-jerk reaction was, "Of course you see him. He's standing right in front of you." I wasn't shallow enough to miss the point and to mock the sentiment altogether, but Trish was someone who searched for spiritual meaning in everything. I was happy to accept things more at face value.

"No, something's up. You're spacing out on me. What is it?" Trish tucked her feet underneath her.

"I saw Catherine today." I tossed that out with a noncommittal shrug. There was no harm in admitting that much, and Trish knew Catherine was my shrink.

She put her back against the arm on her side of the sofa. She was looking at me—or more in my direction. Her eyes seemed to be dancing around my outline.

I groaned. "Don't tell me. You see something in my aura."

"It's…muddy brown with wisps of soft pink."

"Mud? Wisps? Okay…" I blew on my tea and braved a sip, burnt my tongue for my troubles.

She showed the subtlest of smiles as if my burnt tongue were punishment for not believing. "You make fun, Erin, but you can't dispute science."

"Auras are scientifically based?"

"Depends on who you ask, I suppose."

"Fine, I'll play along. What does brown and wisps of pink mean?"

"Brown is usually associated with sadness, and pink could indicate conflict. Sadness makes sense, given that you're coming up on the anniversary of your parents' deaths." There was such a softness to her voice, a gentleness that endeared her to me.

"It's never an easy time," I admitted.

"What are you conflicted about?"

"Nothing. I was, but I'm not now."

"Hmm. Your aura says otherwise. Come on. Spill." Trish was the only fortysomething I knew who used the word "spill."

"I just had a stupid dream yesterday morning, and it's been hard to shake. That's all."

"A stupid dream? Was that why you went to Catherine?"

"Who says I saw her because of the dream?" I could hear how defensive I was being, but I was ready to move on from giving the dream real thought—including Catherine's questions about it.

"I'd say you pretty much admitted such with that response. So if the dream was really nothing, why not tell me about it?"

"Hmph." She'd presented it as both an inquiry and a challenge. "Fine, you want to know? But it's really no big deal. Catherine wasn't concerned. I'm not." I tried another sip of my tea, doing so cautiously in case I would be "zapped" again. The liquid was slightly cooler but still a little too hot. "It's really nothing, Trish," I added under her persistent gaze.

"And that's what she told you? That she wasn't concerned?"

"In as many words. Why don't we talk about something else?"

She squinted as if she were still studying my aura. "I'm your best friend, and I know you're troubled. Something about this dream compelled you to pay her hourly rate." Trish had voiced her opinion in the past that Catherine was overpriced, though she did admit that the therapy seemed to have helped me. Leave it to a multimillionaire to act like a penny-pincher, but maybe that was why she had money.

"The dream just had me a little unsettled... But you realize that the anniversary of my parents' deaths is coming up on Friday."

"So it was about a plane crash?"

No one could say Trish wasn't intuitive and a good listener. "It was. Catherine said it could represent any number of things going on my life. Could be grief again or stress..."

"Please. Just tell me about the dream."

"Fine." I set my mug on the coffee table in front of us. "You know it was about a plane crash... It was just really vivid, almost like I was there."

Trish smiled but squashed the expression. "There was a crash yesterday morning—a flight from Texas, if I remember right."

"Yeah. Quite a coincidence. Nothing more." I wasn't going to play into her hands and make a deal out of it.

"You sure?" Based on how her voice rose with excitement, she was making something of it.

"Yes, I mean what else would it be?"

"Well, you haven't exactly told me much of what happened in the dream, but you said it was vivid, like you were there. I'd almost say it sounds like you may have had a vision. Did your dream at all resemble the real-life crash?"

I looked up at the ceiling. "My parents died in a plane crash twenty-eight years ago this Friday. It's just my mind still processing that. Really."

"Hmm."

"No, don't *hmm*. That's all it was, all it is. Besides, you know I don't believe in visions and the like."

"Doesn't mean they don't happen or exist."

I steepled my fingers and bowed my head. "Thank you, wise guru."

"Stop being a smart-ass. It just really sounds like you could have had a vision to me. Again, not that you've given me any details. I'm just going by…" She flicked a finger around me to indicate my conflicted aura.

I rolled my eyes. "Does it matter anyway, and do we have to put a label on the dream?"

Trish smiled again, a victory smile. "Look at you using new-age lingo. *Label*."

I groaned.

"Come on, tell me about it," she insisted.

I drew a sharp intake of breath, in part just wanting to get this over with. "I was on a plane as it was going down. After it did, I saw the crash site—"

"As if you were hovering over it?"

"Sure, if you want to put it that way."

"I do." She gestured for me to continue.

"The real-life wreckage looked like what I saw in my dream, but that's purely coincidental."

"Is it?" Trish was chewing on the tip of her thumbnail, obviously enthralled.

"I think it is. Even Catherine thinks the dream was representative of something."

"Yeah, that you had a premonition, a vision. Label it how you like, whatever's most comfortable for you."

"None of this conversation is comfortable for me."

"I know, I know. I'm sorry." She took a breath and continued speaking gently. "You do believe in intuition, a sixth sense?"

"Sure. I can't dismiss that."

"All right, well, to be intuitional is essentially being psychic."

I groaned again. "I don't know, Trish. And sometimes a dream is just a dream. Didn't that, uh…dream guy—what's his name—even say that?"

"Sigmund Freud?"

"Yeah, that sounds right."

"He did, but I don't think that's the case here."

"I'm sorry, Trish, but I have to believe that's all it is." I was tired of the spotlight, tired of rehashing this dream, and tired of discussing the possibility of it being more than it was.

"Why do you *have* to believe that? Is it because considering anything else has you afraid? Has you thinking you might need to reexamine your beliefs?"

"More like terrified. It's just Mom and Dad's deaths playing on my mind," I repeated. Not that the repetition seemed to help me release the stupid dream!

Trish hitched a shoulder. "Could be. Sure. Now I know you don't accept the existence of an afterlife, but what if your parents were trying to communicate with you through the dream?"

I wasn't sure which sounded more ludicrous—that or it being a vision. It was easier to think when a person died, they were simply D-E-A-D. It was certainly less complicated with fewer questions to consider.

"We don't need to know all the answers right now," Trish assured me, plucking me from my thoughts. "Answers always come at the right time. You just need to surrender, keep moving forward, doing you, and if the dream was— *more than a dream*," she said instead of "vision" under my daring eye, "then you'll know soon enough."

I wasn't exactly sure what she meant by knowing "soon enough," and I was afraid to ask. If I was going to get any sleep tonight, I had to shut out everything related to spirits, visions, and premonitions. "Okay, enough about me and this dream. Tell me what's going on with you. You're working on the books…"

"Let's not go there. How about something more fun? I announced a fall special for the studio today on our Facebook page. New clients get their first three classes free. Did you see the post? I'm in love with the graphic I designed. It's pretty clever if you ask me."

I smiled at her, fascinated by how much joy tinkering with Photoshop brought my friend and amused by her lack of modesty. "I'm sure it is."

"But you haven't seen it?"

I shook my head.

"I should know better. You ever go on Facebook?"

"Sometimes." The odd time to check on Jenna, but she didn't seem tethered to social media like others her age, unless she hung out somewhere cooler than Facebook. "It just doesn't hold much appeal to me. You know that." It's not like I had a reason to be active online. I didn't have a business or product to promote, a brand to build awareness for. I wasn't about to start posting photos of my meals and informing the world of my every move anytime soon.

"Well, log in and look, okay? It's on the studio's fan page and on my personal timeline. Like it if you want." Trish flashed this charming grin and batted her eyelashes.

This wasn't the first time that she'd asked me to "like" her posts. Supposedly, the more reactions a post gets, the more people Facebook serves it to. I figured it all depended on which way the algorithm wind blew. "I'll check it out."

"All right. Well, I don't know about you, but I'm ready for a meditation, then bed. You're welcome to stay and meditate with me." Trish sounded hopeful, but she knew meditation wasn't my thing. I'd tried to convince her it was because I didn't find meditation fun, but I was quite sure she saw through to my real reason—it made me uncomfortable. Something to do with an idle mind being the Devil's workshop. Yoga was spiritual enough for me. Therefore meditation was a hard pass for me.

"I'm going to head out." I stood and glanced at my tea that I'd hardly touched. "Thanks for the tea."

"You're very welcome." Trish got up, and we hugged goodbye.

Seeing Catherine had made things better, but my earlier anxiety was back in full force after speaking with Trish. Did I have a vision? My hands were shaking on the wheel as I drove home.

# Chapter Seven

I had stared at the ceiling for hours before falling asleep and had contemplated leaving the light on all night. The thoughts of the afterlife and spirits trying to communicate with me was so outside of my comfort zone, it was outside my comfort zone's comfort zone. I imagined shadows darting across the room, just a shimmer, just a flicker, just out of focus. By midnight, I'd finally turned the lamp off and closed my eyes, telling myself I was acting like a child. It's just when you were raised to believe in good angels versus demons, I feared it was the latter reaching out to me, and I wanted nothing to do with them.

My alarm clock went off, but I'd been watching it count down the last few minutes and got to it quickly. The questions that Catherine had raised were lingering, along with the concerns I had when trying to go to sleep. And if I started to believe the dream had been a vision, would I start seeing ghosts, talking with the dead?

Harvey let out a loud *meow* that sounded like a child's shriek, and it had me jumping and my heart jackhammering. I took a few moments to slow my breathing.

"Bad timing, buddy, but good morning." I patted my chest, and he curled on top so I could give him a good rub. They say pets are therapeutic, and that was something I could believe. They still couldn't answer the existential questions about life, however. Nor did they care. Only humans were tasked with that journey. At least we didn't need to lick our nether regions like our feline friends. A fair trade off?

"Time to get up." I shuffled Harvey off me and slid my legs over the side of the bed. I rubbed my face, not feeling like I'd slept at all. Like it or not, it was off to work I go.

I brewed a K-cup, selecting Strong on the machine's settings and the largest cup size, and took it to the living room. I liked to ease awake, sip a coffee, read a nonfiction book, stare into space. I hated TV or music in the morning and usually stayed away from my laptop too. But today, I grabbed it, cracked the lid, and logged in. Mike Dooley's book, *Infinite Possibilities: The Art of Living Your Dreams*, a reading recommendation from Trish, remained untouched on my side table.

It was a new day, and after all the deep contemplation I'd been forced into the last couple of days, something mindless was most welcoming. I logged onto Facebook, figuring I'd check out Trish's ad and click Like. Before I got there, a little red flag told me I had forty notifications and five friend requests. I clicked to see the former, which were mostly invitations to play games. Who had time for that? Though they, along with the friend requests, had probably been kicking around a good month or more.

Harvey jumped onto the couch next to me. I sipped coffee and stroked his back. He purred loudly as my reward, and I turned my attention back to Facebook. "Let's see who wants to be my friend."

One request was from Chris Pittman. My ex. Really? Sure, we managed to keep the divorce and following years amicable enough, but I dropped Pittman and changed back to Stone, my maiden name, the first chance I got. It was a little confusing for Jenna's friends sometimes, as she still had her father's name, but I needed to get my life back. Jenna seemed to understand.

I didn't exactly want to be Chris's friend—on or off Facebook. Still, I found myself clicking on his profile picture to get a better look. I was hoping that he'd let himself go—grown a belly at least. His slide would be a credit to my self-esteem. But again, life kicked me in the pants. He was far more fit than he had been when we were together, and while he'd gone gray around his temples, it gave him a look of sophistication and worldliness. It really wasn't fair how men aged gracefully, and we women…well, we just got older.

I did glean some satisfaction from the fact he never ended up with the man he'd left me for. That's right, a man. I was the new statistic. And I know we're supposed to be supportive of people's choices in life if it brings them happiness—who are we to judge and that sort of thing—but this man had wasted nineteen years of my life, including the year we dated, by living a lie. The good to come out of our union was Jenna. She had just turned sixteen when the marriage blew up, and I was so grateful she was an old soul who handled the divorce with grace and maturity. In an effort to find more good that came from the situation, the hardship of divorce had taught me my own strength. The process to self-discovery hadn't been easy though—and I didn't think that journey ended until the day we died. That's if the last couple of days had taught me anything. As long as we drew breath, change was inevitable.

That didn't mean the divorce hadn't been devastating. It came from out of nowhere. I hadn't seen any signs—not at the time, only looking back. It had been Trish and her new-age thinking that helped me through. Well, her, my brother, Aunt Judy, and Catherine. Come to think of it, religion hadn't helped me at all. My true breakthrough came at my lowest point. I'd drunk heavily and sunk to my knees on the floor, wailing. I was really battling with the mind game that if Chris didn't want me, no other man would either. I even considered suicide, for which I still felt moments of guilt. After all, life is a gift, and Jenna deserved her mother. But there I was on that floor when I heard a loud voice tell me that no one had the right to hurt me this badly. It was almost like the voice had come from outside of myself; it was just so clear. Well, I picked myself up, and nothing had been the same since. I realized that I'd deceived myself into thinking booze was a friend because it numbed my emotions. Instead,

I started journaling and writing down a list of things I was grateful for every morning. These practices helped. As did the books Trish recommended. So, in a way, I owed my ex a lot. It was because of him that I looked at the world and myself differently.

And now life had thrown me another curveball that had me questioning my viewpoints and beliefs yet again.

*So much for not thinking deep this morning...*

I hovered the mouse over the screen, deciding Chris and my fate as Facebook friends. We shared a child together, and while I had forgiven him, there was still far too much history there, too much heartbreak. I declined his friend request and took a sip of my coffee.

The next request was from Lauren, which I accepted without thought, and the other three were from men I'd never seen before. I deleted those requests without looking at their profile pages.

Next, I went to Trish's business page, saw her ad, clicked Like and commented, *"What a great promotion!"* What I wouldn't do for my best friend...

I left her page and waded through the timeline. I stopped scrolling when I caught an image of Monday's crash, linking to a newspaper article: "Crash Victims from Downed Texas Flight Identified." Lauren had shared the post, and I wasn't sure if I wanted to read what it had to say or not. After all, I'd decided to let the dream go and move forward, but maybe by looking at it face-on would make it even easier. Noting the differences between the real-life crash and the one in my dream could be reassuring.

I clicked the link and— My phone rang.

"Holy crap!" I flinched enough that Harvey took off down the hall. It was only five thirty in the morning. Who could be calling so early? I picked up the cordless phone on the table next to me. Caller ID told me it was Jason. I answered. "Why are you calling so early?"

"Nice way to greet your only brother."

"It's early." But it was more than that; my heart was pounding from just the thought the article might propel me down a rabbit hole. I closed the lid on my laptop; I didn't want to be distracted with Jason on the phone.

"Hasn't bothered you in the past. You okay?"

"I'm fine." It came out a little tart. For a tough city cop, my brother could be sensitive—a strength in my opinion, and something that made him good at his job. At least he wasn't like some cops who operated like unemotional cyborgs with frowns on their faces and an alcohol problem from trying to bury their emotions. "Sorry, but yes, I'm fine. Just tired." At least half of that was the truth.

"You sound it. You work today?"

"I do."

"Going to make for a long one, then. Well, I'm calling because I assume you're aware of what this Friday is…"

I didn't need to reply to that; Jason would know fair well I did.

"Are you going?" he asked, referring to the memorial.

"Suppose I should." I hadn't anticipated giving that response, but it was just the one that came out.

"What's that supposed to mean?"

"I know it means a lot to—"

"It should mean a lot to you too. We both lost our parents."

I pinched the bridge of my nose and shut my eyes. "A long time ago—not that it hurts any less," I rushed out. "I'm just not sure how healthy it is to keep up this morbid reunion of sorts." It did make me extremely uncomfortable reminiscing about our parents with people we barely knew and only saw once a year.

Jason's end of the line fell silent, and I was only left to guess that he disagreed.

"I'll go. For you," I offered.

Jason didn't respond.

"Jay, you can't tell me that a day goes by that you forget them. They'll always be a part of us, in our hearts." Somehow, just saying that struck as such a cliche, something that was said to ease pain while not coming close to doing so.

"I know." He didn't say anything more, and the silence over the line held an energetic charge.

*Energetic?* I shook it aside. "Is Natalie going?" She was Jason's wife of fifteen years and normally went with him.

"She's bowing out this year, and that's fair."

"As I told you, I'll go."

"That means a lot to me."

"I know it does."

"You don't have to stay long. Just have a drink or two and leave."

"I already said yes." I found myself smiling. Jay had a way of continuing to push his pitch when he already had the sale.

"Thank you."

"You're welcome. Don't make me regret it," I teased.

He laughed. "I won't. Hey, well, I should get going. My shift starts at eight. See you Friday night." With that, he hung up, not even waiting for me to say goodbye—and he had the nerve to criticize how I'd answered his call? But that was my brother, always clipping off quickly. Whenever I did get a word out before he was gone, it was usually "good" with "bye" lost to the void.

I put the phone on the cushion beside me and opened my laptop. I keyed in my password to unlock it, and the article on Monday's crash was staring back at me. More to the point, the image was. Again, this bitter sensation of déjà vu, like I'd gone down with the plane and survived. Pain and sadness tightened around my heart, squeezing with the subtlety of boa constrictor. I touched a fingertip to the screen. All that death… But I drew my hand back. While I could feel for the people who'd lost their lives and those left behind, this really wasn't about me.

I scrolled the article. The reason for the crash was still being determined with no hint as to which direction the findings were leading investigators. Beneath the basics of the crash, the victims were listed in alphabetical order. Some had bios and photographs but most remained faceless without any profile.

My eyes stung with tears, and my chest heaved as if I were grieving someone I'd personally lost. I continued to read through the names but came to a stop on a man's face.

*This can't be!*

I gasped, slammed the lid closed, and tossed my computer to the cushion beside me. My arms turned to ice, and shivers laced down my spine, my skin exploding with a million goosebumps.

I stood and shook my head. "No, this can't be. This can't be happening. No. Nope." I stared at my laptop, seemingly harmless, sitting haphazardly on top of the couch.

The man, the picture…

He was in my dream. He'd been the one that I'd guessed to be a wealthy businessman or leader of organized crime. He was the one reading from a book, his lips moving in a reverent undertone as the plane went down. He'd been with three men, all watchful of him like bodyguards.

There was no doubt in my mind, the man from the article was the one in my dream. But how?

I squeezed my eyes shut and paced.

Then in a flash, I saw his face in front of my eyes, as if he were looking straight at me. A small scar over his right eyebrow was narrow and wriggly like a worm. Intense green eyes that could cut through the night. A Roman nose and thick lips. A head full of black hair.

"What the—" I dropped onto the couch and rubbed my forehead. "This is *not* happening." But it had and it was. I had to be losing my mind. I'd never seen that man before my dream—not that I remembered anyhow. And I certainly wasn't physically on that flight; I had been in bed. It couldn't have been a vision. There was no such thing.

But what if there was?

I whimpered as I reached for my laptop. My fingers grazed the lid, and it was like I had been bitten by a snake. I recoiled and wasn't sure if I wanted to proceed.

I closed my eyes again, trying to summon strength from somewhere deep within. *Here goes!*

I logged in. There on the screen was the man's face I'd just seen and the one in my dream.

"No. This is my overactive imagination, that's all. It was just a dream. Just a dream." I'd repeat it like a mantra a million times if it helped bring some logic and semblance of normalcy back to my life.

My gaze returned to his photo and then to his miniature bio. My fingers froze, wrapped around the sides of the laptop like they were in rigor.

Howard Hayes. He had been a wealthy oil mogul heading to Toronto on business.

*Oil mogul...* Okay. That was something I could work with. I had probably seen his face in the news before. Easy enough explained.

But that didn't explain the flash I'd just seen—here in my living room. It was easier to excuse images and events that played out during a sleep cycle, harder when wide awake.

I let out a lungful of air and tried to process. Had I experienced a vision, a premonition? And if I had, why? That was almost the better question. But it still didn't sit well for me. I gripped my head with both hands. There had to be something wrong with my mind. I needed to see my doctor and get him to order a brain scan.

There was no way I could go to work with this hanging over me, but I'd never called in sick a day in my life. Though if there was a time for it, now would be it.

My hands shook when I called work and rang through to Loughlin. My voice quivered when I told her I wouldn't be in. "I'm sorry to do this to you," I added.

"We'll get by. You sure you'll be fine? You don't sound well at all."

"Why I called." Sometimes Loughlin wasn't that bad. I summed up my illness as "feeling under the weather," and she seemed to accept that. Then again, why wouldn't she? She didn't know I was cuckoo.

"Fair enough. Take care," she said.

"Thanks." I hung up as fast as possible but held onto the phone and made another call. Trish answered on the second ring. "I need to talk to you right now."

"Erin, are you—"

"I'm fine. You still at home?"

"No, I'm already at the studio. What's up?"

"Stay put. I'm coming right over." With that, I "pulled a Jason" and ended the call, giving her no opportunity to probe me with questions. Besides, she'd be doing that soon enough in person. All I knew was if there was anyone on this planet who could help me make sense of all this, it was Trish.

# Chapter Eight

"How is this even possible?" I paced around Trish's room, raking a hand through my hair. I'd already filled her in about playing hooky and one of the crash victims being the man I saw in my dream. I hadn't been able to bring myself to tell her that his face popped into my vision clear as day in my living room an hour ago.

I stopped in front of my laptop that was open to Hayes's picture on her coffee table and gestured emphatically toward the screen. "How could I dream about a man I never even knew existed? On the same night he died!" As much as I'd been trying to talk myself down from considering the dream was more than just a dream, I was having a hard time convincing myself now. But could I accept it was a vision? I wasn't quite there either. It left one thing. "I really am losing my mind."

Trish was on her couch, watching me wear a path in her bamboo flooring, and smiling.

"I'm happy you find all this amusing."

A slight shrug. "I'm just observing you through all this."

"Gah!" I flailed both arms in the air and sat next to her. "Please, what is all this exactly? I could really use some guidance here. I'm one step away from getting myself admitted to a mental hospital." That was probably the only logical and reasonable next step.

Trish put a hand on my forearm, her touch soothing. "Just take a few deep breaths."

There was flicker in her eyes that told me she had something to say that wasn't going to please me. "Go ahead," I said with resignation. I had come here because I wanted her help, so I should at least hear her out.

"Have you given any more consideration to someone reaching out to you from beyond the grave?"

"What?" I spat. "That guy?"

Trish's brows pressed down, and she angled her head. It seemed she was being serious.

"Doesn't matter. You know I don't believe in that sort of thing." I was hiding behind my beliefs again like they were an impenetrable wall. But if they were busted, I'd be left with loss and confusion.

"As I've said before, whether you believe in it or not doesn't matter," Trish stated firmly. "And really, why do you so stubbornly resist the possibility of life after death? Your aunt is a staunch Catholic and believes in heaven and hell, angels. You were raised that way."

"Sure, and the Church also believes in demons."

Trish winced. "I don't think any angel would like to be called that, and really, isn't 'demon' a label that humans have put on spirits they don't understand?"

"I believe in the existence of good and evil."

"All right." She bobbed her head. "But who makes that determination?"

I huffed and shook my head, flailed my arms some more. "No idea."

Trish leaned back and propped her elbow on the arm of the couch. "Do you believe in God?"

"Sure, but—"

"A living spirit being, a life force, source, the universe… Whatever you want to call it. An eternal entity, right? No beginning, no end?"

"Yeah."

"So, why is it a stretch to believe that in a vast, mysterious universe, we might live on after physical death? You ever notice when attending a wake that the body is like a shell that's been left behind? Ever wonder why?"

I didn't honestly want to think about it too much. I shook my head. "It just is. But let's say, for shits and giggles, people live on and become angels or spirit beings—whatever. Why would any of them be talking to me?"

Trish grinned. "That's something we need to find out."

I rubbed my arms and hugged myself. "And if I don't want to? This is all so outside my—"

"Your comfort zone, I know. But what if we threw those two words away while we're at it? Even pretend that you, we, have no boundaries."

"Sure," I said slowly. Here I was questioning my sanity, but maybe Trish's was on the line as well.

"Tell me about the dream again."

I acquiesced, then added, "I told you I'd pegged this man as a wealthy businessman or the leader of some criminal organization. Turns out the former was true. He's an oil baron." As I spoke about Howard Hayes, I felt I needed to come clean with Trish. "There's probably something else I should tell you."

Trish leaned toward me, a smile not far from her lips, her eyes glistening with excitement.

Her reaction wasn't making it any easier. I knew the moment I told Trish about the vision-like trance in my living room, she'd never let the dream rest. "I saw him again… before coming here."

"In another dream?"

"No. My eyes were wide open. It was only briefly, but his face appeared in front of me as clearly as I'm seeing you." My heart was racing and my stomach tossing. I was going to be sick.

"Wow. Just wow."

I'd expected a far more exuberant reaction from her, but I could tell Trish was excited. "Why couldn't this—whatever it is—have happened to you instead?" I know I was whining, but it couldn't be helped. I'd stomp a foot too if I'd get away with it.

"Because it was supposed to happen to you. It came to you for a reason."

I pressed a finger to my temple where my racing pulse was kicking up a migraine. "There has to be a logical explanation for all this. Right off, I can think of one. Insanity."

"You promise to listen to me all the way through and not interrupt?" She sounded a bit like a mother about to lecture her child, but I nodded. "You have a responsibility to do what you can to find out what that reason is. Now obtaining the answer in cases like this takes effort."

"'Cases like this'?"

"When it comes to the spiritual world, a lot of it can present itself as a riddle to unravel."

"Now, you've lost me."

"I've told you about my personal experiences interacting with my guardian angel." She paused like she'd posed a question, but she'd remember having told me. I'd reacted rather, uh… strongly as she relayed connecting with her guardian angel through a medium and being in physical contact with the spirit. It had been too much for me to handle at the time. Still was.

"You did." I shifted on the couch, suddenly very uncomfortable.

"Well, I received a message from him, she, *it*… Though I felt a male energy attached to my guardian angel. Anyway, it took me months to figure out the meaning of what was said. We're talking about grand beings who have been around for millennia."

"Trish," I beseeched her. "How does this apply here?"

"He told me, 'Life isn't brick and mortar.' In other words, it's more than flesh and blood, more than what we can see. But he didn't just come out and say it in those words. Rather, I had to ponder its meaning. Just like to find a treasure, there's not a map that says, 'Go here to find the gold.'"

"Yeah there is. It's called a treasure map." I chuckled, and so did she.

"Okay, bad example." She paused, seeming to collect her thoughts. "Here's a better way of putting it: even if you had a treasure map, there would be surprises along the way, and depending on what routes you took, time could be added to your journey. But you'd also learn things."

"So, no shortcuts?"

"Right. Seeking answers to our spiritual questions takes time and sometimes requires different experiences to take place in order for us to see things from another perspective."

"Okay..." I was following somewhat, but there was a big part of me that was starting to freak out about my mental health more than anything.

"Did the article say what caused the plane to crash?"

I shook my head. "Just that it's under investigation."

"This might be a long shot and not the reason you had the vision, but—"

I groaned.

"What is it?" she asked.

"I can't get on board with the idea of it being a vision—not yet—despite all the coincidences."

"You mean the ones stacking up?"

I stared her down. "Yes, even with them."

"You saw the crash clearly. The event actually took place. One of the people you saw in your dream—Howard Hayes— was a real victim. I absolutely believe you were given a vision and possibly through the eyes of one of the deceased, though they wouldn't have necessarily been deceased when you had the vision. But I'm not going to get into time, space, realities."

"Good." I loved Trish, but she could get carried away. Life was much simpler when sticking to a more traditional belief system. But even that called for faith in invisible beings— God, angels, demons, the Devil... Why was I finding it so hard to accept that we went on after death? I asked the question so directly, my brain fired back the answer: it meant my parents were watching over me, just out of reach. Tears sprang to my eyes, and I sniffled.

Trish frowned, her eyes glistening in immediate empathy. "Oh, sweetheart, I can only imagine how very overwhelming all this is for you. And you might not appreciate it right now, but this vision is really a gift."

Yet, so far, this "vision" had managed to flip my life upside down and shake the very foundations of my beliefs. It was far more like a curse than a gift—and it terrified me. "Do you think I had this dream to discover the reason for the crash?" I was freaking out under the weight and responsibilities that would entail.

"Could be. Might not be."

"So a victim of the crash might want to reveal the reason for it…to me?" I heard the question but didn't know why I was considering any of this.

"Sure." Trish patted the arm of her chair and bit on her bottom lip, a faraway look in her eyes. These mannerisms usually indicated she was going to say or do something that made her uncomfortable, which was rare. "You're trying to apply flesh-and-blood logic to a spiritual universe. You see how that doesn't make sense?"

I did, but like a petulant child, I didn't want to admit as much to her.

She pointed a finger at me. "Of course you do. And you know there's a lot of phenomena we can't explain with science and textbooks. It's why there's such a thing as faith and the ability to 'see' the unseen."

"Literally, apparently."

"That's the spirit." She smirked at her word choice.

I grimaced. "I don't know…"

"If this was me we were talking about, I'd look more into this Howard Hayes. Plus you have to be curious whose perspective you were in. There's probably a reason you were given that woman's point of view." I had told Trish before I was a woman in my dream. Trish added, "If you saw her picture, would you know her?"

"No, I never saw her face, just her hands."

"Did she have any tattoos, jewelry? Something distinguishing?"

"Not that I recall right now. Oh, I do remember she hated flying and was questioning herself for getting on the plane."

"That sounds like someone I know."

"Can you blame me?" I countered.

"Nope."

I tried to remember more details from the woman's viewpoint. "She kept watching Howard. She observed how unfazed he was as the plane was going down. She thought he seemed to be 'on another plane of existence.'" I did air quotes on the last part as I blinked back tears, my body trembling. "That's not me, Trish. That's not how I think."

Trish shifted down the couch and settled in next to me. "Like I said, the universe, the divine, whatever you wish to call it, often speaks to us in riddles. But it doesn't leave us on our own. You'll understand what you're supposed to when the time is right. The pieces will fall into place—the right ah-ha moments, the right people, at the right time. You just need to do your part, and that's to take the next step."

"Did I really have a vision?" I couldn't even bring myself to look her in the eye.

Trish rubbed my arm. "No doubt in my mind. I'm here for you, and please know that you can handle this. It wouldn't have come to you otherwise."

"What if I have a tumor or some other health issue? I should get some tests done."

"If it puts your mind at ease, by all means, but I think you'll find you're in perfect health."

I sort of wished she was wrong about that. An ailment could provide a sound explanation for what was happening to me.

"So, what are you going to do?" Trish's voice was gentle, but it encouraged action.

"I'm going to make a doctor's appoint—" Images from the dream flashed into my mind. Holding hands with an older woman. Her face grandmotherly with warm blue eyes.

"Erin?"

"I just saw snippets from the dream…and something new."

Trish inched forward on her cushion. "New? Was it right in front of you, the real deal, like before when you saw Howard at your house?"

"Not quite as clear, but the woman was holding hands with the person next to her. An elderly lady. I just now saw her face. I don't remember having seen it before."

"Well, maybe if you find out more about that elderly lady, you'll be able to find out whose perspective you were in. I said it already, but there's a reason you were seeing things through that woman's eyes. At least, I feel there must be."

"Not sure I'll ever sleep again."

"There's nothing to fear. This is a gift, trust me." She squeezed my arm.

"And if it's nothing but a tumor on my brain?"

"Still a gift, because it brought the illness to light."

"Look at Miss Sunny."

"I'm here for you, no matter what." She leaned over and put her forehead to mine. I took comfort in our close friendship. If—and that was a gigantic *if*—I had been given a vision, at least I had a friend like Trish to guide me through it all.

# Chapter Nine

The first thing I did after leaving Trish's yoga studio was make an appointment with my doctor. Thankfully, they were able to squeeze me in that afternoon. I just wanted to put my mind to rest. For some reason, it was almost easier for me to accept there was something mentally or physically wrong with me than the alternative that I was some sort of conduit for the spiritual world.

I stuck a coffee pod in my machine, pressed the button to start it brewing, my mind miles away. Trish considered my dream a vision and a gift. She had said if she were me, she'd try to discover whose point of view she was in during the dream and dig up more on Howard Hayes. What good could possibly come from doing that? Did I really think I'd discover why the plane crashed? I remembered what it was like not to know, to wait around for some sort of closure. If I could help those people… *No.* It wasn't my responsibility.

The machine sputtered out the last bit of java. I grabbed the cup and added two sugars and dash of skim milk, then headed to the living room.

Harvey was nestled up in a ball on a throw pillow in the corner of the couch. I petted him on the way to the other end and set my coffee down. My laptop was on the table in front of me, where I'd put it after returning home. It felt like it was staring at me, as if the crash were screaming out from the ether.

"Oh, Harvey." I glanced over, and he didn't even open an eye at hearing his name. Cats. Loved them, but they were so fiercely independent that sometimes I envied them. And he had nothing to worry about or mull over. He ate, he slept, he played. Simple, simple…and boring.

If I were honest, my life had been much the same way over the last few months. Everything had fallen into a predicable routine. I got up, went to work, came home, did yoga or met up with Trish somewhere, spent time with Jenna—though not as much as I used to, but that was okay. My daughter had grown into a strong, independent woman, just as I'd hoped for her. But, yeah, just like little Harvey, my life had become a foregone conclusion with no surprises. But now it felt as if fate was making up for lost time. Even if the dream had been nothing more than the result of screwed-up wires in my brain.

Besides, if it had been a vision or a spirit or the universe trying to communicate—why me? Sure, I dabbled in new-age philosophies relating to our higher selves and the law of attraction. The Church would frown on that too. By accepting the law of attraction, I knew I drew a lot of experiences to myself. At first I struggled with that concept, but then it became empowering. After all, if I concentrated hard enough on what I wanted… *boom,* there it was! Well, not exactly. Some things are outside of our control, and that meant I wasn't a powerful, all-knowing genie ready to grant my every wish. But I still had to wonder what I had done to attract the dream, vision—whatever it had been.

At least at work I felt in control. I calmed callers, directed uniformed cops, and handled tough situations like a boss. I wielded power equal to the police chief, if it came down to it. With this dream, I'd been stripped of any illusion of control. Maybe that was the most uncomfortable thing about it. I had no idea where to even begin. Then again, I might.

My gaze again went to the laptop. Information about Howard Hayes was probably right at my fingertips, one mere Google search away.

I took a sip of coffee and cradled the mug. What I wouldn't give to have my simple, predictable life back. Then

I remembered Trish's words: that I wouldn't have been given the vision if I couldn't handle it.

I picked up my laptop and was confronted with the oil baron's face the moment I logged in. I must not have closed the browser window before shutting the lid.

My arms rose with a rash of goosebumps, and a coolness blanketed me. There was no doubt this was the man in my dream and the one I'd seen before heading to Trish's studio.

I flashed back to the dream and looking at him from across the aisle. He was calmly sitting there, reading in an undertone from a book in his lap, seemingly oblivious to the fact the plane was going down or that I was watching him.

*He is on another plane of existence.* That was what the woman in my dream had thought of the man.

I, Erin, became more curious about what he had been reading. Was it some ancient religious text or a prayer book? Was he praying for his soul and the rest of those on the plane? Did oil barons do that? Were they even religious? Guess everyone came in all shapes and sizes and of different faiths.

As much as I wanted this dream to be nothing more than my overactive subconscious at work, the "evidence" seemed hard to completely ignore. Maybe that was what truly scared me.

I opened another tab, brought up Google, and typed Howard Hayes's name. In seconds, I was looking at a list of articles. "I just saw him in the news," I said to Harvey, but I wasn't satisfied with the explanation. A knot twisted in my gut, a physical tell I'd come to recognize whenever something didn't resonate as the truth for me.

I spent the next while reading articles on Howard Hayes and on his company. He was presented as a man of integrity, but these news pieces could have been written by people who had been paid off to cast him in a favorable light. I was certain there had to be someone out there who didn't care for the man or his ambitions.

I went to his company's Twitter feed. Pinned to the top was an announcement of his death.

*Howard Hayes passed away in a plane crash early this week. Our prayers are with his friends and family as we too grieve his loss.*

Harvey came across the couch and rubbed against me, meowing.

"Hey, baby." I scooped him up and hugged him to my chest. Stroked his fur. "What happens when we die?"

Deep question for a cat, I realized. Deep question for a human.

My gaze landed on the number of Likes beneath the death announcement. Fifteen thousand. I'd never understood why people hit Like in these cases—acknowledgment or happiness that someone had died? Surely the tally would include some of the latter. That meant Hayes had haters.

I clicked on the number beside the heart icon, hoping I might be able to see a list of who'd clicked it. I was actually less familiar with Twitter than I was Facebook, but my bumbling around seemed to be paying off. The tweet popped into its own little window, and there were profile images in little circles next to the Likes. Seeing the number again drilled home the enormity of the task ahead of me if I wanted to dig into every one of them. That wasn't feasible, and then there was the matter of what I really hoped to find. Did I honestly suspect one of these people had been behind the crash? If so, the authorities would uncover that information well before I would.

I ran a hand down Harvey's back, and he purred his appreciation. "What do you think, Harvey? Huh? Should Mommy continue looking into this stupid dream or just forget it even happened?"

The answer came back to me immediately: forget about it. Nothing good could come from poking my nose into this any further.

# Chapter Ten

"You'd like me to order you an MRI?" Dr. Ashraf was looking at me, his head cocked. He probably wasn't used to his patients requesting a brain scan. But I'd had time to think things over, and I'd say all this nonsense had to be a mental ailment.

"It was more than just a vivid dream," I told him *again*, doing my best to stress how unusual it had been. In hindsight, maybe I had tamped down the clarity. For some reason, being face-to-face with him made me nervous about voicing my concerns. My earlier thought that a health issue might be easier to handle was losing power. I did need him to take me seriously, though, in case there was some problem I needed to take care of. "What I didn't tell you was I saw a real person in my dream."

He backed up and parked on a stool next to the examination table where I was sitting. "That's not unusual."

"Okay, sure, if it's someone in my life, but this person is a stranger to me."

"All it takes is for the mind to latch on to someone." He was shaking his head. "I really wouldn't worry."

"But for me to see his face as if he were standing in front of me... That's normal?"

"You have a stressful job, yes?" Dr. Ashraf consulted my chart.

"Yeah, I work at the call center for the Toronto Police Services."

"Could just be stress."

I rubbed my forehead, wrapped my hand around the back of my neck, pinched myself there for good measure. "I think there's something more to this, could be far more serious. There's no logical explanation why I'd see Howard Hayes unless the dream was a vision or a hallucination." I'd say anything at this point to get him to order the test. "I mean obviously something's not right up here." I tapped the top of my head.

"You could have seen his picture in the media." Ashraf's comment came across offhanded, distant. He sat there watching me quietly, the skin around his eyes pinching ever so slightly. "Here's the thing, Erin," he started. "I need a lot more justification than what I'm hearing and seeing to order the scan. From what I can tell in looking at you today, you're in fine health. An MRI isn't a cheap test—and I hate to say it, but money is always a factor. If you find that your memory is slipping or you have another dream like the one you had, come back and see me. I might be able to help you then."

"While the tumor grows bigger," I blurted out, thinking *so much for our good health-care coverage.* I also realized how dramatic I was being, even if I had a sound reason for being paranoid. If my mind and body were healthy, that could mean I'd had a freaking psychic vision. I swallowed roughly on *psychic.* Did that describe me now? That seemed scarier than the thought of having visions.

"We don't know if there is a tumor," the doctor said in all seriousness.

"And we won't know without the MRI." I jutted out my chin, defiant. "If you're not going to help me, I could always find another doctor." A brave claim, considering most doctors had enormous waiting lists, if they were accepting new patients at all.

"You could, but they'll tell you the same thing I am. There is not enough justification to order an MRI."

"So, if I have more dreams or start forgetting things… Wait a minute. I won't know if I have because I won't remember." I snapped my mouth shut, helplessness cramping in.

"I'm sorry, Erin. I truly am. I can set you up with a shrink to talk to about all this. That might ease your mind." He was looking at me with the genuine concern of a loving father.

"I appreciate the offer, but I've already been to my shrink."

"Great." There was a lightness to his voice. "And what did he say?"

"She," I corrected, realizing I might be a bit of a feminist— but, hey, we women have to stand united. "She wasn't concerned either." I got up to leave. "I'll be back if I have another dream."

"My door is always open."

"Thank you."

"You're welcome. Take care of yourself."

*I'll have to. No one else will,* I thought sarcastically as I let myself out of the office. In all truth, though, the medical community was two-for-two for letting me down. If I were to trudge forward and set aside the dream—one, I had to stop reading about it and Howard Hayes, and two, I needed someone who could set me back on the "straight and narrow." The person I had in mind couldn't know anything about the dream, though, or even that I'd entertained it being a vision—for no matter how brief a moment.

Aunt Judy had a way of calming me simply by being around her, but she was also a devout Catholic with a strong faith in angels and heaven and hell. When Jenna had declared herself an atheist, it nearly broke Aunt Judy's heart, but she'd come to simply accept it. I couldn't imagine her being as understanding about me having visions—assuming I was.

I called Aunt Judy through the Bluetooth system in my car.

"Hello?" Her voice was so sweet—always had been. I hoped she'd never change her caring nature, and at sixty-nine, I doubted there was a risk of that happening.

"It's Erin," I said with a smile.

"Oh, sweetie. I didn't check caller ID." She chuckled. She never did, and she likely never would.

"That's fine. Better surprise that way anyhow. I was wondering if you'd be up for a visit."

"You're not working?"

"Day off." It was best to keep it simple; there was no need to tell her I'd called in sick. She'd come at me with a bunch of questions like a master interrogator. Under her pressure, I'd probably come out about the dream, and next thing I'd know, her priest would be there conducting an exorcism on me.

"How lovely. Come right over."

"I'll see you in about a half an hour?"

"Righty-oh." She hung up.

I was still smiling, and that only confirmed the best medication for me was a dose of Aunt Judy.

# Chapter Eleven

Aunt Judy was set up in a lovely townhouse not far from me and still in Cabbagetown. Monthly fees covered grass-cutting in the summer and snow-clearing in the winter, but she was on her own for whatever small repairs or maintenance might be needed inside the home. But between her, my brother, and me, we had it covered. In part, thanks to Uncle Harold—the love of my aunt Judy's life who died thirteen years ago from a heart attack. He'd shared some of his handyman knowledge before leaving us. He used to own a successful contracting company and was skilled in everything from cabinetry to plumbing to electrical to roofing. "Just don't let him touch your car," my aunt would tease.

I rang Aunt Judy's doorbell, more for etiquette than necessity. I had my own key and security code.

"I'm coming," she said in a singsong voice as she approached the door. She opened it wide and threw her arms around me.

Her hugs were the best, and we stood there for a few seconds. I certainly didn't want to bring it to an end. In this moment, everything felt familiar and safe, and all the questions faded away.

She stepped back. "Oh, what are we doing? Get on in here. There's quite a nip out there today."

"Yes, there is, and the leaves are falling like rain." I never used to like the fall, truth be told, but I was beginning to appreciate the season more with every passing year. There was something cozy about nestling under a blanket on the couch with a good book or *Grace and Frankie* on TV.

"It's going to be a cold winter, I'm telling you." She smiled at me, the expression twinkling in her eyes. Aunt Judy had a way with predicting the weather—her forecasts often more reliable than the meteorologists on TV. "Come, I'll put the kettle on."

"Sounds great." I shucked my coat and boots, relocked the deadbolt, and headed up the stairs to the second level where the kitchen and main living area were. I sat at the kitchen table while Aunt Judy moved around the space with a bounce in her steps. "You're sure you don't want any help?"

"I've got it all under control." She grabbed two teacups from the cabinet because, for her, tea wasn't the same in a mug. She set them on the table.

I had a feeling she'd decline my offer to help. No one could say Aunt Judy wasn't independent. As for having things under control, I found myself rather envious, but that was partially why I was here—to add some equilibrium back into my life. "How are you doing?"

"I'm good, sweetie. Always good." She popped a couple of teabags into a teapot and set out milk and sugar while the kettle bubbled furiously in the background. When it clicked, she poured the water into the pot and brought it and herself to the table. She sat down with an audible sigh. She might have said she was good, but she sounded tired.

"It's such a lovely surprise having you here," she said. "I didn't expect you until Monday for turkey day." She smiled at me. There was more to Aunt Judy's statement than just a comment; she was curious what brought me around today. I'd bite her hook.

"I was just thinking of you and thought I'd pop over. I don't really need a reason to come and see my favorite aunt, do I?" It didn't matter she was my *only* aunt. I poured the tea, and we made up our cups.

"Never need a reason." She smiled and blew on her tea, but she put it back down without taking a sip. "I've got the bird already, by the way. Thirty pounds. That should be enough?"

I laughed. "Plenty." There would be only eight of us and three were children, but Aunt Judy always got a larger bird than we needed. As she liked to point out, it wasn't Thanksgiving without full bellies and leftover turkey for sandwiches.

"Lovely. Turkey sandwiches are the best."

I smiled at knowing my aunt so well.

"Jenna is coming for sure? I know she's got a life. Ah, to be young and on the go all the time."

My twenties felt like a distant memory. "She'd never miss a Thanksgiving."

"I'm so proud of that girl. She reminds me so much of you. Ambitious, mind set on what she wants to accomplish. It seems to come so easily to some people." Aunt Judy left it there, like she was going to say more but decided not to. She lifted her cup, blew again, and this time took a sip. I followed her lead.

"I'm proud of her too."

"You should be. You did an excellent job with her. Even with that goof leaving you, doing what he did."

I wasn't about to come to Chris's defense. He *was* a goof for hiding his desire for men *and* for cheating on me. Actually, I'd use a much stronger word than *goof* to describe him.

"I know you don't like it when I talk down about Chris," she said, as if taking my silence to mean I didn't care for what she'd called him, "but he's an idiot for hurting you the way he did. Marriage vows should mean something. Real men don't cheat. They keep it in their pants."

Aunt Judy respectfully never touched on Chris's lifestyle; it might as well have been a woman he'd left me for. It netted the same result either way—a broken marriage due to secrets and lies. "From your lips to God's ears, Aunt Judy, but most men aren't Uncle Harold." Witnessing their marriage and Mom and Dad's when growing up certainly hadn't prepared me for the real world. I was quite sure they were the anomalies.

"And thank heavens for that." Judy lit up. "You know that man drove me nuts. He was so opinionated and stubborn."

I laughed. Maybe it hadn't been absolutely perfect, but it was as close to it as one could get.

Aunt Judy's eyes met mine and sparkled. "But he was faithful and an excellent provider."

She could say the latter bit again. I still remember when she found out Harold's company was worth almost three million dollars, and they had hundreds of thousands in investments in addition to that. She'd taken a seat, and I'd thought it was because of shock, but she'd been livid. "All that money, and he pinched pennies like nobody's business." I'd laughed at the seriousness of her expression, and she'd joined in too. So had Jason, who was present for the conversation.

"So, tell me what's going on in your life," Aunt Judy said.

"Not a whole lot to tell." Lying was a sin, as it had been put into my head, and a splinter of guilt stabbed me. "I'm looking forward to the long weekend," I pushed out quickly—a truth. It was rare that I was able to secure the entire weekend and the holiday off work.

"I bet you are. You work too hard, but you still love your job?"

"I do."

She and I continued with our visit, talking about what was going on each other's lives. She probably spoke much more openly than I did, but I sensed she might be withholding something. She was more tired than usual—yawns inserted periodically. There was no way I'd be mentioning the dream or my doctors' appointments, so I backed off and afforded her the privacy. We ended up going out for a nice dinner, which she insisted would be her treat. I thanked "Money Bags," an affectionate term she'd assigned herself since the inheritance.

By the time I got back to my townhouse, it was eight thirty and I was exhausted, but the last thing I wanted to do was sleep. The time with my aunt had been so normal, I wanted to hold on to it.

# Chapter Twelve

"Pick up, pick up…" I pleaded with the ringtone but landed in Jenna's voicemail anyway. "It's Mom. Give me a call." That came out sounding far more urgent than necessary. I added, "No need to rush. Just call when you get a chance. Love you." I hung up and palmed my phone. It had felt so incredible to be cradled in a bubble of normalcy, and I just wanted to stay there. I figured talking with Jenna would prolong that feeling. It also put off going to bed, which honestly, I was a little afraid of doing. What if I had another dream or vision?

No one to talk to but Harvey. He was always there for me, but right now he was purring loudly. Maybe if I relaxed with a bit with wine and some *Grace and Frankie* on Netflix, I'd doze off once I went to bed without much effort or thought. I grabbed myself a glass of merlot and took a gulp. Delicious.

I'd just settled on the sofa under a blanket, Harvey beside me, Grace and Frankie facing their latest dilemma, when my phone rang. I paused the show and was pleased to see *Jenna* on my caller ID. "Hey, honey," I answered.

"Mom, is everything okay? You said it wasn't urgent, but I thought I'd call right away."

*Bless her sweet heart.* "It's all good," I said in honesty because hearing Jenna's voice was exactly what I needed. "How are your classes going? And how's Professor Lamb treating you?" She'd complained to me on numerous occasions that Professor Lamb—despite the gentle implication of his name—was a hard-ass and held something against her.

"The professor's still…well, a hard-ass, but I refuse to let him get to me."

I smiled at Jenna's determination. "Some people are just there to push us and make us grow," I said.

"I wish he'd be that for someone else," she complained, and for a moment, I detected the little girl I used to tuck in at night.

"Unfortunately, we can't pick our teachers." I then realized how broadly that could apply—far beyond academics to life in general.

"I'm looking forward to this weekend, Mom."

"Me too. It will be so nice to have you home for a bit." Jenna went to the University of Toronto, but she shared a place with two other girls. This weekend, Jenna was coming to stay with me Sunday night through until Tuesday morning. I'd been counting down to this for weeks. "Are Beth and Brittany going to be spending time with their families?" Those were the girls Jenna lived with—the two Bs as Jenna affectionately referred to them.

"Yeah. So, there's really nothing you needed? You're okay?" There was a strained urgency to her voice; she wanted to go.

"I'm fine, sweetie. You know me. Just love to hear your voice sometimes."

"Mom, you're so sappy." Jenna giggled, a song to my ears from the first time I'd heard it. "So dinner on Sunday… You're making my favorite right?"

"Chicken parmesan? You got it, sweetheart."

"You spoil me."

"Remember that. Okay, later. Get some rest. You still have class tomorrow and Friday."

"Don't remind me." Jenna typically loved school, but there was something about the time surrounding the holidays, a certain buzz, a laziness that permeated the air that was infectious.

"Love you," I said.

"Love you." With that, Jenna clicked off.

I stared at the TV where Grace was frozen on the screen, martini in hand. It would have been a rarity if I'd paused it when she wasn't drinking one. I lifted my wineglass, said, "Cheers," and took a sip of my wine.

I proceeded to watch another two episodes, enjoying the antics of two vastly different women as they cohabited and tried to rebuild their lives after their husbands had taken up with each other. Really, no wonder why this was my favorite show. On a level, I could completely relate. I couldn't pick a favorite between Grace and Frankie, with both having admirable qualities that seemed to bring out the best in the other one. Sort of like I'd mentioned to Jenna, about how people help us grow; that's what Grace and Frankie did for each other.

My eyes became heavy, and the next thing I knew, my eyes were cracking open to see midnight on the cable-box clock. I must have drifted off. I stopped the show and turned everything off.

"Well, Harvey—" I yawned "—time for bed."

I went through my nightly routine and crawled under the covers. My head hit the pillow and… I lay there staring at the ceiling. Images from the dream danced in my mind. Howard Hayes and his bodyguards… *His bodyguards.*

Surely that's who those three men traveling with him were. That would be even more proof that Hayes had enemies. Had one of them targeted his flight?

"Gah!" I cried out and put my pillow over my head, half tempted to hold it down. Why couldn't this dream just leave me alone?

# Chapter Thirteen

Thursday morning. Last day of work before my holiday, and I'd hardly gotten any sleep. I couldn't put the dream or the people in the crash out of my mind. I kept wanting to go back and look at the list of the victims—*really* look at all of them. Find out who those men were with Hayes and why they were there. All ridiculous and meaningless. It was just a matter of time before I could convince a doctor to order an MRI for me and I'd be cured.

I got into work, puffy eyes and all, and entered the parade room. It was more animated than most days, which told me right off there was an ongoing situation. Everyone seemed tense, and there was palpable stress in the air.

"Great, Erin, you're here." Loughlin made it sound like she was surprised I'd shown up for my shift, as if I called in sick on a regular basis.

"What's going on?"

"Please sit." She gestured to an available chair. "A six-year-old girl was taken from her home one hour ago. Her name is Lily Brooks. The person who took her is believed to be her father, Anthony Brooks, twenty-nine. He was denied custody in court last week. Brooks has a history of drug abuse and alcohol addiction. He is considered armed and dangerous." Loughlin's gaze took in everyone in the room.

I had this piercing ache in my left temple, and it had me wincing out loud. Lauren, who was sitting next to me, looked over as if to ask if I was all right. I nodded. "I assume it's the girl's mother who reported this?" I asked.

"It was. She was fearful for her daughter's welfare and her own. He'd held a gun on the woman. Thankfully no shots were fired, but Anthony assaulted the woman, and she was knocked out for a bit."

The room was silent. The situation was certainly not a good one—a little girl with a man who wasn't in his right mind, who would be desperate and emotional. Domestic cases were the most volatile and dangerous. Another pain gripped my head.

A flash of a little girl danced in front of my vision—brunette with pigtails.

An intense feeling of fear washed over me, raising goosebumps on my arms. I gripped the table in front of me, as if steadying myself. But my head was dizzy and spinning. *What the hell is happening?*

Loughlin was still speaking. "Police have yet to arrive on scene, but the priority is on returning this little girl safely home. Erin—" she nudged her head toward me "—I want you to take point on this."

"The mother's still on the line?" I asked.

"She is. You'll be taking over the call until units arrive on scene," Loughlin said. She gave everyone else their marching orders and led me to the dispatcher who was on the line with the mother. Loughlin gave me more information. "The mother's name is Rachel Brooks. She and Anthony separated eight months ago. There's a history of physical abuse, and he's served time in jail due to his aforementioned substance abuses, as well as beating on Rachel. You got this?"

I nodded, strictly from a standpoint of responsibility. Ever since the flash of a young girl, my head hadn't stopped spinning, and my stomach was clenched. I traded places with the woman who had been speaking to Rachel, and it seemed like a smooth transition.

"You need to bring her back." Rachel was sobbing, and my heart broke for her. What she was going through was the ultimate nightmare for any parent.

I already had the answers to the five questions we'd normally ask our callers: Where? What? When? Who? Weapons?

*Where?* Her house, which I had the address for on the screen in front of me.

*What?* Daughter kidnapped.

*When?* One hour ago.

*Who?* Girl taken by her father. Drug and alcohol addict, prone to violence.

*Weapons?* Suspect armed with a gun.

"Rachel, I'm Erin, and I'll remain on the line with you until police arrive."

The woman was sobbing almost uncontrollably.

"It's important that you take some deep breaths, Rachel. Can you do that for me?"

A break in the crying. A garbled response.

"Help will be there soon." I could hear police sirens coming over the line, and my display told me they had arrived at Rachel's house. "They are actually there now, Rachel. They will help you and—"

"I just need my little girl back!" More heartrending sobs, and there was a click. She'd hung up on me.

I got ahold of one officer on scene, and he confirmed they were in position and with the girl's mother. I sank back in the chair, taking the deep breaths I'd recommended Rachel take, but didn't have much time. The phone was ringing with another call, another emergency. I did my best to shake off the heartbroken mother, missing girl, and broken man who had been so desperate as to take his daughter from her home.

**Lunchtime came, and from what I gathered, the girl still** hadn't been found. Strange in cases like this, because police had arrived rather close to the time she was taken. He really couldn't have gotten far with her. The area around the Brooks house was being searched, along with any locations Anthony was known to haunt.

I looked at the Amber Alert on my phone.

*Child abduction reported by TORONTO Police Service Victim: Lily BROOKS, Female, 6 years old Suspect: Father, Anthony Brooks, 28, last seen 0530 hrs. If observed call 9 1 1*

There was a link provided in the alert, which I bravely clicked. I hadn't had anymore "incidents" with seeing a vision of the girl since this morning, but I couldn't fight the curiosity to know what Lily looked like.

My heart pounded once the link opened. Staring back at me was a young girl with brown hair and pigtails—just like the girl I'd seen. How was this even possible? I laid a hand over my chest. First the dream, the vision of the oil man in my living room, now… What? I was seeing a missing little girl? But unlike how I'd seen her, in this photo she was smiling broadly and showing off one missing front tooth. How devastating for her poor mother—even if Lily was returned safely, Rachel was in hell right now. My heart ached for her and the girl's safe return.

My gaze went to the father, Anthony Brooks.

*A child wails and a fuzzy image begins to clear. The figure of a man… Then I realize he is coming toward me, arms outstretched, and hunkering down. A small fist bats him away, and I am so afraid.*

*"No!" The voice, that of a little girl. "I want Mommy!"*

*"I'm your Dad. I love you."*

*He comes toward me and lifts me up. I feel so tall.*

*"I want ice cream. Can we have ice cream?"*

*He runs his big hand over my head and smiles at me. "Of course we can, kiddo."*

"Erin? *Erin*?" Lauren dropped into a chair across the lunch table from me. "Are you okay?"

I was slowly bringing her into focus. Fat, warm tears hit my cheeks, and I wiped them away.

"You're crying," Lauren whispered. "Is there something I can do?"

I shook my head and showed her the screen on my phone.

"It's sad, isn't it? I hope the girl is found okay."

"Me too." I rubbed my arms. *So cold.*

"Are you okay?"

I slid my bottom lip through my teeth and nodded. "Uh-huh." I grabbed my phone, got up, and headed for the restroom. *What the hell is going on?*

I locked the door and studied my face in the mirror. My eyes were bloodshot, my complexion paler than normal. I looked like crap. No matter what the doctors said, there was something going on with me. My mind was messed up. It had to be. First a strange dream that corresponds to real-life. A vision of a man's face from the dream. Flashbacks to the dream in stark clarity. Seeing images of a girl, then hearing one, and seeing a man coming toward me as if I were the child. *I'm a total nutjob!*

I paced in a circle, and there was a banging on the restroom door.

"Erin?" It was Lauren.

"I'm fine," I called out, expecting her to request to come in, but I heard her footsteps walking away.

Then I was overtaken by a piercing pain in the back of my skull.

*I'm licking ice cream. It's soooo good. Mommy lets me have ice cream when I'm a good girl, usually after she takes me to the park. I wonder if Daddy will take me to the park after. I don't care that it's cold out.*

*Daddy wipes my chin, and I giggle. Mommy says it's a strange tickle spot, but she says it's just another thing that makes me special. Daddy's smiling too, but he's looking around like he's scared. Grown-ups aren't supposed to be afraid of anything. Mommy tells me there's no boogeymen in my closet. Is Daddy afraid of a boogeyman?*

*"We need to hit the road, kiddo."*

*I still have more ice cream, but when he gets this way, I know I need to do as he says. I've seen that look in his eyes before when he hit Mommy…before she told him to go away.*

*Daddy walks over and holds out his hand, and I take it. I just wish we could stay here and eat more ice cream. I've never been here before, but I hope we come back. Daddy takes me outside, holding my hand a little too tight now and he's pulling on my arm. I cry out.*

*"Shh, baby girl." Daddy's words are nice, but he doesn't sound happy.*

*We leave in a car he said he borrowed from a friend. I look at the building as we drive away.*

"The Ice Cream Factory!" I blurted out. "Oh my God…" I'm panting, trying to catch my breath. As quickly as the vision—it had to be that—came over me, it left. It was like everything played through in fast succession. I knew where Lily Brooks had been, but was she still there? I rushed to the door, but what was I going to do? Actually tell someone what I saw?

I stood there, breathing deeply. I had to admit it was becoming pretty obvious that whatever was going on with me was undeniable. Going from a logical standpoint of stress weighing on me, lack of sleep…why would I imagine what I'd just seen and heard? There'd be no reason.

I needed do something, though, even on the off chance this vision was accurate. I pulled my phone from my pocket. I could block my number and place an anonymous call, report a sighting of the girl. Yes, that's what I'd do.

My heart was racing as I listened to each ring, and my breath froze when someone answered. I passed along the tip, and now all there was to do was wait. Well, that and return to work for the afternoon and act like none of this had ever happened.

# Chapter Fourteen

Somehow I got through the rest of the workday. I drove straight home but called Trish on the way and asked her to come over immediately. She was there when I arrived, and she ushered me to the kitchen table.

She sat across from me. "Something's obviously bothering you. Spill."

"What ever would that be?" I blew out a deep breath. "I'm sorry. I don't mean to be lippy or rude or—"

"Erin…" Trish laid a hand over mine. "Just tell me what has you so worked up."

Tears pricked my eyes. "You see the Amber Alert today?"

"I did."

"I saw that little girl."

"You mean you met her or…" Her eyes widened. "You saw her? As in you had a vision?"

I nodded and rubbed my arms. My legs were bouncing under the table, and I was having a hard time sitting still.

"Wow." Trish sat back.

"Yeah, *wow*. What the heck is happening to me, Trish? First the dream, now this?" I popped up and paced.

Harvey was meowing loudly and circling my feet. His eating schedule was a welcome distraction at the moment.

"You hungry, baby?"

*Meeooooooowwwww.*

A clear response. Yet some people claimed cats didn't understand English. Whatever.

I dished up kibble for Harvey. As he crunched away, I said to Trish, "Either I'm mentally ill or chemically imbalanced."

Trish got up and put her hands on my forearms. She was exuding calm, but I was having a hard time letting it wash over me.

"I saw her, Trish. More than that, I actually *was* her."

"Come on, sit down, and let's talk calmly about it. I want to hear everything." There was an unmistakable ring of excitement in her voice.

I eventually nodded. "Wine?" I uncorked a bottle of red. She grabbed two glasses from the cupboard. I filled them, and we headed for the living room. I brought along the bottle.

I dropped onto the couch, and Trish landed in a chair. Harvey was still pecking away in the kitchen. Soon we'd hear him scratching in his litterbox. His schedule was predictable and timing impeccable. Sometimes I swore he could read the clock.

"All right. Don't leave me hanging here." Trish lifted her glass and proceeded to drink some.

I followed her lead. "I kept telling you that I didn't have a vision, that the dream was nothing, but now…well, I'm not so sure." I could hardly believe that I was swayed to the "dark" side of actually accepting the visions—not like I seemed to have much choice. And it didn't mean the concept still didn't scare the bejesus out of me.

Trish tucked her legs under her and cradled her wineglass in two hands. "Keep going."

I shared everything with her, from the first flash of the girl to the end. "The Ice Cream Factory is in London, and I know the place because I'd go there with Chris and Jenna when I lived in the city. Police discovered the girl's father had stolen a friend's car, so they knew the vehicle to look out for. They apprehended him and retrieved the girl as they were about to get onto the 401 Highway at the Wellington Street ramp. The girl was unharmed."

Trish was just staring at me, her mouth agape.

"You going to say something?"

"Wow."

I smiled. "Something else besides that?"

"I told you so."

I was tempted to throw a pillow at her head, but if I upset her wine, it was my chair and mess to clean up. "What should I do?"

"That is up to you, but me, I'd be taking this seriously. You *are* having visions. You do believe that now?"

"I don't think I have a choice."

"Well, that's an improvement, I guess. But if I were you, I wouldn't be ignoring that dream about the crash. As we've talked about before, you were given it for a reason. Just like the one today about the little girl, Lily. There's something you're to uncover."

"I wish I had your faith."

"You were given a reason for some today. You saved that little girl."

I was grateful for a happy ending, but I hardly felt like a hero who'd saved the day. I'd simply passed along what I'd, uh…seen.

"It took courage to come forward," Trish added.

My cheeks heated. "No one at work knows."

Her brow wrinkled. "How did it all come together, then?"

I told her about the blocked and anonymous call.

"You had to do what you had to do. I'm so proud of you!" She squealed and fist bumped the air.

Harvey was slinking into the room about that time and gave her a wide berth, his tail flicking. He wasn't a fan of loud noises or sudden movements.

"So what are you going to do with your newfound powers?" she asked me.

"I guess I have no choice but to explore them." I drained my glass, poured a little more.

She grinned. "Don't sound so enthusiastic. This can be a good thing. Look how the visions helped reunite a girl with her mother."

I considered, bobbed my head. Smiled. "True."

"Who knows what you can accomplish? And that plane crash? I'm curious what you're going to uncover there."

We talked and drank for another couple of hours. It was eleven when Trish put her feet to the floor.

"I don't want to leave, but if I don't get going, I'll have bags under my eyes like you wouldn't believe tomorrow morning." She pulled out her phone, and I listened as she ordered a cab, then ended the call. She said to me, "I just had a feeling we'd be drinking tonight, so I didn't drive. See? I'm psychic."

"Ha-ha. You just know us too well." We got up, and I hugged her. "Thank God I have you. I couldn't imagine going through this without you."

She squeezed my hand. "It will all be good. As the saying goes, 'Everything will be okay in the end. If it's not okay, it's not the end.'"

"I hope you're right."

A car horn honked out front.

"Sounds like my ride is here already. Call me anytime," Trish said as she left.

I locked the door behind her. The night air was freezing, and it was drizzling. I didn't envy her having to go out in that weather. I returned to the living room with a glass of water, burrowed under my blanket, and turned on *Grace and Frankie*, hoping it would work magic in calming my mind. But that would take some voodoo powers right there. The events of the week, ever since the dream, had me questioning so many things. Today was the game changer. I was curious—though a little apprehensive—about what tomorrow might bring.

# Chapter Fifteen

Last day of work before the holiday weekend, and I was ready to get the shift over with. I was assigned to dispatch and so was Lauren, not that we had a sightline to each other with the L-shape of the room. The morning had passed quickly, and I'd fielded several calls but hadn't entertained one vision. I didn't even know the outcomes of the calls—one of the hardest aspects of the job. Our work usually ended when officers showed up on scene.

Today, not knowing how everything played out came as a relief—a little normalcy. I may have accepted that I'd had visions, but there was still an apprehension rooted in my core. Then again, it was hard to entirely dismiss forty-plus years of being affiliated with certain religious beliefs and their judgment against spirit mediums and the like. I might not be channeling dead people, but visions felt like they were in the neighborhood.

At lunch, I was happily munching away on a garden salad with almonds and sliced chicken breast that I'd brought in from home. I'd topped it off with balsamic vinaigrette, which was my favorite dressing. I was in the middle of chewing a mouthful when Lauren entered the room. She sat across from me.

"What a freakin' day." She rolled her eyes and shook her head.

"I'm actually having a pretty good one," I said, then thought maybe I had sounded insensitive. "Sorry you're not."

"Pft. No need to apologize. Just the way the calls fall sometimes." She unwrapped a sandwich and tore off a large chunk.

"From the sounds of it, I hope they keep falling that way." I laughed.

Lauren narrowed her eyes, but she couldn't speak. She'd just popped a mouthful of food into her face. She chewed hastily and swallowed. The lump going down looked like a mouse being swallowed by a snake. "Nice."

"You know I'm kidding with you." Although that might not have been entirely the truth. I just wanted to coast through today, if that wasn't too much to ask.

"I know." She offered a tiny smile. "And speaking of *not* nice, did you hear the latest news on that plane crash from earlier in the week?"

"No…" I wasn't even sure I wanted to hear what she had to say, but then again, I was going to turn a new leaf and try to be more open to embracing my new gift.

"Rumor circling on the internet is it might have been caused on purpose. Guess there was some rich oil guy on the flight who had a lot of enemies."

A piece of lettuce shot down my throat and had me coughing. I dropped my fork and pushed my container away.

"Erin? You—"

I held up a hand and worked to clear my windpipe. "I'm fine," was what I said, but I was screaming in my head that I was anything but *fine*. Howard Hayes that "rich oil guy" had taken up such a prominent place in my dream, uh… vision. Was it because the flight was targeted due to his being onboard? "Why is the—" I cleared my throat "— NTSB saying that?"

"Oh, it's not them. It's coming right from the man's company. The board is blaming some environmental group that's all for clean energy. Fighters for Future America, or something like that. Apparently, they're not beyond violent acts to get their point across. They've staged demonstrations throughout the US."

After Trish and I had spoken about my dream the first time, I started wondering if the crash had been intentional and if it involved this mystery man who I came to learn was Hayes. Could my intuition have been spot-on? My throat was so tight, it was hard to expel words. "What is the NTSB saying?"

"Officially, the crash is still being investigated. Why do you look like you're going to be sick?"

"Do I? I'm fine." I resisted the urge to rub my twisted gut and gathered my stuff. "I'm just going to get some air."

"Okay." Lauren tore off another chunk of her sandwich.

I wanted to see what was going on for myself and stepped outside the building. I was able to work my phone, but my hands were shaking. Had I been correct thinking the crash was linked to Hayes? I guess I shouldn't be surprised about these gut feelings, especially after the outcome with Lily Brooks yesterday.

A cold autumn breeze gusted around me, and I burrowed into my coat and moved to the other side of the building. I pulled up the internet on my phone, and one of my recommended articles to read on the home page was about the crash. I clicked the link. With every sentence I read, my chest became heavier.

*The owner of Guardian Oil Company, Howard Hayes, was one of eighty-three souls who died when a plane from Houston, Texas, en route to Mississauga, Ontario, Canada crashed into the ground not long after takeoff. Ted Vega, CEO of Guardian, alleges that the environmental group Fighters for Future America is behind the crash. "They've made it known they are an enemy of big oil and Howard Hayes in particular."*

*When asked if any threats were made against the man, Vega said there have been many.*

*The spokesperson for Fighters for Future America, Isaiah Peters, says, "Guardian Oil's allegations are hateful and unfounded. Nothing more than an effort to silence our efforts for a country powered by clean energy." He added, "They are afraid of clean energy."*

*Bill Sauder from the NTSB, who is the lead investigator on the crash said when asked about its progress, "Whether it was due to sabotage, an act of terrorism, a malfunction, or pilot error or a combination of things, it's too soon to conclude."*

Oh those poor families not knowing who to believe—the word of a rich corporation or a government agency. A tough, near impossible, choice.

I glanced up to the sky as if someone up there could provide clarity. Was there an afterlife? If so, were Mom and Dad looking down on me right now? What were they thinking? Were they disappointed I was having visions, or did they view it as a gift, like Trish did? I really might be able to help the victims' families find closure. Just like I had brought a little girl back to her mother.

It was still all too clear in my mind what it had been like awaiting word on what caused my parents' crash. Every passing day without answers had been torture. When the investigation finally concluded, it was like some pressure lifted. I was able to look ahead again, although I approached the future tentatively and one day at a time.

But with the conflicting news in the media, the loved ones of the victims from Monday's crash would be living in a heightened state of anxiety. The families would be calling on higher powers—or cursing them—wanting to know why their loved ones had to be on the plane with the oil baron. Making things worse was that Guardian's claims would stir up more turmoil in an already restless world and would impact the NTSB's investigation. Their energies would be distracted. That was already the case, given the investigator had done an interview with the article's reporter. That time could have been spent seeking out real answers.

My phone rang in my hands, and I flinched, dropping it to the ground.

*Shit!*

It was still ringing, so I hadn't wrecked it, but when I picked it up, I noticed the screen was now cracked.

"Did you see the news?" Trish rushed out when I answered.

"I did." I took gulping breaths, gobbling up air. "I was just reading about it."

"You really need to follow your intuition with this, Erin."

"Yeah, I know." I was well aware of the heavy weight of responsibility coming to settle on my shoulders.

Trish fell silent for a few seconds and then proceeded. "I remember when you were waiting on answers all those years ago. Maybe you can bring these people resolution sooner than later."

"Yeah, I was just thinking that."

"Oh…I'm so glad to hear that. I'm here for you."

"As you've said a million times." I smiled.

"You'd miss me if I was gone."

"Don't even talk about that."

"All right, well, I thought I'd check in. Take care, by the way. You have that gathering tonight at the bar for your parents' memorial?"

"Yep."

"Let me know if you want me to tag along. I'm good for a drink and night out."

"Will do." We ended the call. Now I had to go back to work and, for the second time this week, act like everything was normal.

# Chapter Sixteen

Ryan's was a rather trendy bar in Cabbagetown. I was fortunate that the memorial was held so close to home, considering some flew in for the event. I could only imagine how happy they were when their feet touched the ground. I arrived at seven thirty, about a half hour later than it was set to begin. Nothing much was happening at the bar, but that wasn't a surprise. Toronto's nightlife didn't start until the wee hours.

I headed to the basement where the event was taking place and passed a sign at the top of the stairs indicating that it had a two-hundred-person capacity. There were five people in the room, and none of them were Jason. I was just starting my retreat back upstairs when Karen Snyder, ever the thoughtful hostess, waved and headed over to me.

I smiled at her and let it carry for the other four people, who were all looking at the new arrival. I was probably the most excitement they'd seen in the last few minutes. Three of them I knew, but there was one man I didn't recognize. He was handsome, late forties or early fifties, with a square jaw and a reserved grin.

"Hello, sweetheart." Karen hugged me and pecked an air kiss a couple of inches from my left cheek.

"You're looking great as always," I said. For a woman well into her late fifties, Karen kept herself in excellent shape and knew how to show off her figure in a modest, classy way. Tonight she was wearing a teal skirt suit that hugged her curves. I'd met Karen not long after my parents' plane crash—the same one that killed her husband. As far as I knew, she'd never married again. I assumed she was dating, but she never brought anyone to the memorial.

"Thank you, but you're too kind." Karen took my hand briefly, let it go. "I'm glad that you could make it. Will your brother be joining us?" She looked behind me, and I glanced over my shoulder.

"He's supposed to be here." *He better be coming*, I thought, as I came more for him this year than for myself.

"Such a horrible day, isn't it? It's hard to believe it's been twenty-eight years since we lost them." Karen pressed her painted lips together in sorrow, but unlike previous years, she didn't have tears beading in her eyes. "And how eerie that there was another crash earlier this week. I feel for what their friends and family must be going through."

"I hear you there." It was one major reason why I couldn't just turn my back on the dream. Starting tomorrow, I was going to start digging in earnest, and hopefully something would shed light on what caused the tragedy. While my mind kept conjuring assassination plots against the oil baron, I had to wonder if there wasn't more to this—or less, actually. Something simpler. And really, what could the man have done to make killing him in a plane crash worth all the collateral damage? Although motive would be harder to ferret out due to all the chaos.

But tonight I was going to put it out of my mind and focus on why I was here. As Karen had said, it was a horrible day in history. The ache from my parents' deaths was never far away and could be conjured with little effort. Despite my intention to completely set aside the dream, I could feel the immense embodiment of grief, but it felt like it was outside of myself—for those who lost loved ones in Monday's crash.

I needed a drink. I went to excuse myself, but Karen touched my arm.

"Actually, where are my manners? Let me introduce you to someone. He's from the NTSB."

*The NTSB!* I felt myself go cold. Trish had commented—at some point—that people and circumstances always came together as needed. Could this man help me in my quest to find the truth behind the vision? "Come with me—"

A server came over with a lovely, warm smile, and I ordered a Grey Goose martini with two olives. Karen passed on the server's offer for something to eat or drink.

In the server's wake, Karen regarded me with a raised brow. "A vodka martini. That's a pretty serious drink."

"Serious occasion." I wasn't sure why she'd care what I was drinking. I saw this woman once a year and didn't stay in contact with her otherwise. I started toward the group of four, Karen following.

Everyone took turns giving me a quick hug, except for Roger Styles, who wasn't a hugger by any stretch and struck me as a rather emotionally suppressed person. It surprised me that he came to these memorials.

The stranger was even better looking up close. If it wasn't for the fantastic way he smelled—woodsy, musky, and masculine—I'd wonder if he were an apparition. Then again, maybe smell was a new sensory attribute being added to my visions. He was perched against the bar, a glass with amber liquid on the rocks in hand. Everyone walked off but Karen.

"Darling, I'd like you to meet David Bomber—" Karen gestured toward him with her long, lean fingers and manicured nails. "—And, David, this is Erin Stone."

He held out his available hand, and I took it. Strong grip, soft hands… *Sparks!*

I pulled my hand back, resisted the urge to look at my palm as if it had been zapped. There was something else that was shocking though. "David Bomber?" The name was quite familiar.

"Quite the unfortunate name for a man with the NTSB, I know." He smiled, and the expression touched his eyes.

He was a striking man without a smile, but with one… I needed to get a grip.

The server delivered my drink, which I gladly accepted and took a big swallow.

Armed with some liquid courage, I decided to speak again. "True enough…about your name, but I was going to say you were the lead investigator from twenty-eight years ago." Given that he didn't look older than early fifties, he must have just been starting out in his career at the time. Either way, it seemed like he'd discovered the fountain of youth. I wouldn't mind directions to its location.

"I am. I'm surprised we've never met before now."

"Have you been to any of these memorials before?" If he had been, surely I would have noticed.

"I made it to one or two."

I must have missed those ones, otherwise I would have remembered him. He had an air about him that drew me in. Though I could have been in a different mind space, and depending on when he'd attended, I might have still been married. I know I hadn't attended a couple of memorials— one for Jenna's birth and another when she came down with the measles. I wasn't about to hand her off to a babysitter at the time, and Chris had been working late—at least that's what he'd told me.

"Oh. Jason is here…" Karen was off, the greeting committee of one.

I waved at my brother but stayed put. He smiled until his gaze traveled to David. Wired like a cop, always a brother.

"And Jason's…?" David prompted me.

"My younger brother. I must have missed you at previous memorials. I didn't attend a couple. Life sometimes gets in the way of best intentions."

"For sure."

Something about those two words sank as somber confirmation. Life often went off the rails when we least expected it. Just as no one could predict their flight going down or know it was the day they were going to die. "Anyway, life really is better lived forward and on the day to day." I smiled but then realized how insensitive that might have come across. I rushed out, "Of course, I've been deeply affected, but—"

"You don't want to wallow in the tragedy."

"Exactly." His understanding was welcome, but I wasn't sure when I started caring about leaving a good impression on a stranger before. I took another sip of my martini and angled my head. "What brings you here tonight? I'm going to guess you're an American, given your job with the NTSB. I doubt you just hopped on a plane for this."

He pressed his lips to his glass. "I wish I could say I did."

I detected just a touch of guilt with his words, which told me that he cared what I thought of him as well. Yikes. "Okay, so why are you here tonight?"

"I'm in the city with family."

"Family? Hmm, that's rather vague."

"My mother." His eyes lit; he seemed to find my interest in him amusing and, hopefully, flattering.

I took another sip of my drink, telling myself as I swallowed that I needed to slow down. It had just been so long since I'd found myself attracted to a man this strongly, and I wasn't sure how to handle the feeling. Typically, I focused on the daily responsibilities of life with zero efforts made in the dating arena. One, it was too exhausting to think about at my age. Two, most of the single men I bumped into were like dregs at the bottom of a wine bottle—undesirable.

"Erin?" Jason came up behind me and put an arm around my neck. At least he had the self-control not to give me a noogie on the top of my head. "Who's this?"

"Jay, this is David Bomber from the NTSB. David, this is my brother, Jason." Jason was the *older* brother I never had—protective as hell with a strong bullshit meter. He'd seen it before the rest of us that Chris was a cheating scumbag, though he'd never suspected Chris liked men.

David held out his hand to Jason, but my brother left him hanging. "We met years ago at one of these," Jason said drily.

David pulled his hand back but didn't give any indication he was affected by Jason's rudeness.

"He probably meets a lot of people," I interjected. It would seem David didn't remember Jason at all. That would make my brother like him all the more—not. Jason was leveling a piercing gaze at me. If he could read minds, he'd be getting the message to back off. I wasn't involved with David, but even if I were, Jason had no right to interfere. But I'd play nice. "Glad to see you made it." My voice was leaden with the enclosed message to relax.

"I practically made you come, or don't you remember?" Jason hugged me into his side and flagged down a server, but instead of waiting for her to approach, he headed off to meet her. She was grinning, appearing all too eager to take his order. My brother was a good-looking man. Six foot two, broad shoulders, trim waist, gray eyes, blond hair cut to just above the collar.

I looked away from him toward the door, and Karen was still there being a gracious hostess, greeting everyone as they came in and pecking more kisses into the air. At least twenty people were in the room now.

I lifted my glass for another sip and met David's eyes as I lowered my drink. He was just taking a swallow of his. We stood there, staring awkwardly at each other, smiling like goofballs in the absence of knowing what to say. I would have loved to break the silence with something intellectually stimulating, but all that entered my mind had to do with asking about Monday's crash. Was it even appropriate to bring that up here? A shiver ran through me.

"Hey, you all right?" David reached out and put a hand on my upper arm; his touch warm through the sleeve of my shirt.

"Yeah, I'm fine." I attempted to smile, but the expression failed. My words were such a lie. David was watching me with these soul-piercing eyes, and he smiled. I was able to return it, briefly. "Are you involved at all in the investigation of Monday's crash?" The question tumbled out, and I rushed to backpedal. "I probably shouldn't have asked you that. It's none of my bus—"

"No, it's fine." David touched my arm again with his reassurance.

I wanted this man's hands all over my— I could feel my cheeks flush. How embarrassing. If he'd noticed, he gave no indication.

"I'm not on that investigation, but I know who is."

"Right, uh… Bill Sawyer or something like that?" I remembered the lead investigator was quoted in the article I read.

"Bill *Sauder*," he corrected.

"Do you know which way the investigation is leaning? I mean, it's all over the news that some environmental group is behind the crash because they wanted to take out Howard Hayes of Guardian Oil Company." I'd started talking, and now the trick was getting me to shut up.

"Yeah, well, the media says a lot of things." His face took on hard lines. "But you know more than most how long investigations like this can go on. It took us nine months to get a ruling on the cause of your mom and dad's crash."

"How did you know that I lost my parents on that flight?" I was drinking my martini rather quickly, but I didn't remember that coming up.

"I recognized your name. I make it my business to know who's affected." He said it as if his personal investment in the investigation was a given. He didn't realize he was a saint.

There was a downside to a bleeding heart though—one I was familiar with, given my job, given Jason's, given our father's. Getting too close affected one's judgment and personal well-being. "Aren't you taught to keep an emotional distance from your investigations?"

"Sure. And it sounds good in a textbook, but that's not how life works. People are emotional creatures, even if most of us don't want to admit to it."

*Did this guy fall from the sky?* I noticed the bad play on words in my thought, but he seemed too good to be true. Chris's idea of talking about his feelings had been giving me flowers and mumbling that he loved me—on special occasions *and* if I was lucky. Thinking back, armed with my knowledge now, he probably didn't want to open up in fear of spilling his truth.

A woman with a pleasing, if not loud laugh, snagged David's attention. Rachelle Aldred. She'd lost her cousin in the crash and was talking clear across the room with Karen near the doorway. At least fifty people were circulating the room now, but Rachelle was easy to hear above the din.

"Well, I should move on. I don't want to monopolize all your time." I was hoping he'd say something like "nonsense" or "I love speaking with you," but he raised no objections. I lifted my glass and headed toward Jason. This feeling of disappointment and rejection from men was something I was used to, but it had been foolish to think David would have stopped me from leaving. First of all, we'd just met, and second, any interest he had in me was professional. After all, he "makes it his business to know who's affected." I was just one of many in this room who had lost loved ones twenty-eight years ago.

Once a distance away, I discreetly turned to see if David was watching me, but he was cozied up with Rachelle—her hand on his shoulder, like they were a couple. Maybe they were.

"Erin?"

I turned around to find Trish coming toward me with open arms and a huge grin.

"What are you doing here? I told you I'd be fine." *God, I'm so happy she's here!*

"I know what you told me, but I listened to the words you didn't say. Besides, my intuition simply told me I had to be here. And by the looks of it—" she pointed to what was left of my martini "—it's a good thing I am. Hard liquor isn't your friend. Me, on the other hand…" She led the way to the bar and ordered herself a manhattan.

I downed the rest of my martini and signaled for another one. This one I'd sip and drink slowly. Best intentions and all that.

"Yeah, definitely a good thing I came." Trish paid for our drinks, and we moved away so that others could get to the bar.

The gathering might have started off slow, but it was steadily growing in numbers.

"How are you handling everything?" Trish took a sip of her drink.

"Loaded question. You mean here or about my newfound *gift*." I attributed finger quotes to the word, still not fully embracing the idea, but I'd finally accepted that I'd been given a unique ability.

"Ah, whatever you feel like talking about."

"On the whole, I'm good, holding it together. I'm curious about digging into the crash more, figuring out why I had that dream."

"That's my girl." Trish was grinning.

I caught Jason's eye, and he came over, beer in hand.

"Trish…" He hugged her.

"Namaste."

Jason growled softly. I swear Trish just greeted him that way to get under his skin. My brother wasn't a devout Catholic, but he was a believer. He sometimes made it to church on Sundays, and he didn't dabble in anything new age.

"How are you and the family?" Trish asked.

"All good, but I could use a holiday."

"Good thing you've got one coming up, then." Trish, always Miss Positivity.

"I've got to work Saturday and Sunday."

"You have Thanksgiving Day off?"

"Yes."

"See? A holiday." Trish snickered.

"One day. Yeah. Party on. Woohoo." He was being more moody and snide than normal. He drank some of his beer and slid his gaze to me. "So, this David Bomber guy…"

I popped my eyes at my brother to stop him there, but Trish was already grinning like a teenager.

"Who's David?"

"David Bomber is an NTSB investigator who was assigned to Mom and Dad's crash." I stressed his full name to imply unfamiliarity and his occupation to establish relationship.

"Hmm. An NTSB guy. How interesting." Trish looked around the room.

"What's so interesting about it?" Jason kicked out.

I met Trish's gaze; there was no way he could hear even a whisper about my visions. He'd *never* understand.

"Nothing really, I suppose." Trish sipped her manhattan. "Which one is he?"

"That guy." Jason pointed him out, and Trish bit her bottom lip and looked at me.

"Oh, he's yummy. Wow."

"Yeah, I know." I chuckled. *Damn martinis are going straight to my head.*

Jason scowled. "He's not good enough for you. He's—"

"Do you know the guy personally?" I cut in, tiring of the protective-brother act.

"No, but I know his type."

"His type?" I shot back. "And what is that exactly?" I snapped my mouth shut. This conversation was getting out of control far too quickly, but I seemed to be going along for the ride. There was no relationship to defend… *Gah!*

"He's been with a lot of women."

"Looking like that, I don't doubt it," Trish teased and garnered a glare from Jason. "He'd at least know what he's doing in—"

"You sure pass judgment for not even knowing him," I interrupted Trish, feeling my cheeks heat at the mere thought of David, not to mention his prowess…in bed. I cleared my throat. "He's someone I just met and spoke to, Jason. But you do realize that I'm a forty-three-year-old woman, and I don't need you to protect me?"

"I saw the way he was looking at you with his goo-goo eyes."

"Goo-goo eyes?" Trish nudged my elbow, and I shook my head.

"I tried to warn you about Chris, but you didn't lis—"

"Nope. We're not going to do this here." It was one thing that he'd been right; it was another for him to bring it up repeatedly and rub my face in it.

"Fine, have it your way. Not like I can stop you if you want to see the guy, but he's American, and that means he'll be getting back on a plane and flying out of here. At any time. And where will that leave you?"

I could tell him that David's mother lived in Toronto and that he was likely here fairly often, but what would be the point? And why was my imagination getting swept away at any future prospects with the guy? He could be with Rachelle, given how cozy they were, and it's not like he'd stopped me from walking away. "For one thing, we're blowing all this out of proportion. I was merely talking with him, Jay."

"Yeah, well, I don't think conversation is all he wants."

"Oh? What does he want?" Trish cooed.

"Could you both stop?" I pushed out.

"Just don't say I didn't warn you." Jason tossed back the rest of his beer. "I'm off."

"Off where? Home?" I asked, irritated. I was only here tonight because he'd asked me to come. "It's rather early still."

"All good. Natalie will be happy to see me. Besides, I showed up, I saw, now I'm leaving."

"You just drank a beer," I reminded him.

"I came in a taxi, and I'll leave in one. See ya." With that, he was off, and I was facing Trish.

She hooked a brow. "So this David guy…"

# Chapter Seventeen

"Good-looking, attracted to you, and he's from the NTSB?" Trish pressed her shoulder to mine. "Wow, does the universe deliver or what?"

I raked a hand through my hair. "Please don't make too much out of this. You're as bad as Jason."

"You know what I'm getting at." Trish sipped her drink. "He might be able to help you look into the crash—sleuth, clairvoyant style."

Sleuthing sounded like fun. I rather liked it. "I assume that's what we're calling it now? Sleuthing...psychic sleuthing?"

"Oooh, even better. Come on, introduce me to your friend."

"*Friend* might be too strong a term. I just met him." My words were intended seriously, but after a few sips into my second martini, I hadn't exactly pulled it off with a straight face.

"Ah. See?" She pointed at me. "You do like the guy. Let's get to know him better." Trish hooked her arm through mine, and we headed toward David.

"I don't even know if he's single, and even if he is, it doesn't matter. Jason's right. He doesn't live here."

Trish batted a hand. "Let's go find out everything about him before we write him off."

"He's talking with people." Rachelle was nowhere around him now, but Karen was there, along with the Andersons, a husband and wife who'd lost their son on the plane.

"He'll soon be talking to two more." She flashed a mischievous grin.

Trish inserted herself into the group with a bold smile and a flamboyant, "Hello." Karen slowly turned her head toward Trish. Her eyebrow lifted, ever so slightly, from the interruption, but she recovered from her obvious initial irritation and smiled.

"Everyone," I said, "this is Trish Gamble, a good friend of mine."

"Hello, Trish." David held out his hand.

Karen shook Trish's hand too, but my friend reeled her in for a brief hug.

"Namaste." Trish had this quality about her that she didn't seem to notice when she bothered people—or she did and was determined to wear them down.

The Andersons cordially dipped their heads in unison, then excused themselves.

"Trish wanted to come and support me," I added. "She owns a yoga studio here in the city." I had no idea why I'd provided that tidbit, but there was something about David and his silver-blue eyes that unsettled me.

"Oh, yeah? Very nice. Maybe I'll stop in one day," Karen said, but didn't ask the name or location of the studio. And she lived outside of the city, so I suspected her comment was more for etiquette purposes than a genuine intention.

Trish grinned. "That would be lovely. It's Everclear Mind, Body & Spirit."

"All right." Karen's gaze drifted away from us. "If you'll excuse me."

One thing was certain, Trish and I had a way of clearing a room tonight. First Jason, and now Karen and the Andersons. I half-expected David to get up and go, but he didn't. He stayed put, took a small sip of his drink, and gestured to the vacated stools next to him.

"You two going to join me?"

"We'd love to." Trish sounded overeager as far as I was concerned.

I dropped onto the stool that was two away from David and left the one next to him for Trish. She gave me this look like I was being foolish passing up the opportunity to be closer to David. Whatever. I had my heart and sanity to protect.

"So, I hear you're from out of town," Trish began, and I fought the urge to roll my eyes at the banal small talk.

"Yep. From Flint, Michigan."

"Not too far from here," she said. If it wouldn't be so obvious, she probably would have nudged me in the shoulder.

"Which is a good thing, given that my mother's here and I like to visit her," he said.

Trish looked over a shoulder at me, back to David. I imagined her thinking something along the lines of, *You can tell a lot about a guy by the way he treats his mother.* I tucked my chin into my shoulder, and this time, I couldn't resist rolling my eyes, though I hoped David wouldn't notice. The eye-roll certainly wasn't for him.

"Your job must keep you pretty busy," Trish said.

*Please, shoot me now.*

"You know what my job is?" The slight strain to David's voice told me he was looking around Trish and at me—before we'd locked eyes.

"I told her," I confessed, feeling embarrassed like one does when they come to realize they've been walking around all day with food stuck in their front teeth. "Hope it's not a big deal."

"Not at all. You were talking about me…" He flashed a smile, and my cheeks flamed again. He went on. "It's not like what I do is a secret anyway. Most of the people here know who I am and what I do." He was still staring at me, not seeming interested in talking to Trish at all.

I plastered on a smile, even though I wanted to shrink into oblivion. I drank some of my martini and then set the vile drink on the counter. So much for alcohol calming nerves; it wasn't working to soothe mine. "You'll have to excuse my friend. She's fascinated with flying, planes…anything aviation." I was grappling for something to say.

"Flying is the safest way to travel, or so they say." Trish's voice lowered as she spoke. She must have realized why she was in this room, with these people. The specific plane their loved ones had been on hadn't provided safe passage.

"That's true if you look at the statistics. When a plane goes down, it just makes bigger news because so many perish at one time." David was being a champ, and it didn't even seem like it took the guy any effort. He really was Mr. All-around Nice Guy. *And damn sexy.* I needed to stop drinking!

"Okay, here's the thing I'm getting at." Trish took a long draw on her manhattan and set her glass down. "You investigate plane crashes."

I put a hand on my friend's arm, hoping to stop what was inevitably next, but all Trish did was pass me a brief glance.

"I'm pretty sure we covered that…" Leery more than curious.

"Are you investigating the one from Monday, the flight from Texas?" Trish asked.

"No, I told your friend that I— Why are you so interested?" David's face paled, and his eyes widened. "Oh, did you guys know someone on the flight? I'm so sorry if—"

"No, it's not like that," I said quickly, not wanting him to feel bad for no reason.

"Do you know who's investigating it?" Trish asked.

David looked at me.

I sighed. "He said a good friend of his is." Trish turned to me, her eyes scolding that I should have told her before now. If only I had a functioning time machine… Besides, I hadn't really had the chance to tell her more. She'd swept me over here in a hurry.

Trish leaned toward David. "Do you know how the investigation is progressing?"

"I'm sure there are other things David would rather talk about. Besides, we've occupied enough of his time." I nudged Trish and moved to get up. For the second time that night, I would be hustling away from David. "Sorry to bother you," I added.

David held up a hand to stay me and studied Trish. "Erin and I already talked about the crash, and I'm not at liberty to say what's going on with the investigation. Next to the investigators, the family should be the first to know any findings. It's not my place to spread any sort of news." He glanced at his drink but didn't lift the glass. He was probably considering hightailing it out of there, and I wouldn't blame him if he did.

"I can appreciate that," Trish said. "I'm assuming you were involved with investigating the crash that killed Erin's parents, and that's why you're here?"

"It is." David drank his booze. He probably needed it to sustain him through the Trish Inquisition.

"It can't be an easy job, being tasked with finding out what causes such tragedies." Trish was showing sincere empathy, but I had a feeling she was just getting started with an ulterior motive.

"It's rough," he conceded, "especially when the answers don't come quickly. What a lot of people don't understand is there are a lot of moving parts—and I'm not just talking about the aircraft alone. You have different departments you need to work with, and you also need to use diplomacy. As an investigator, you're dealing with people from a lot of backgrounds and cultures."

Trish was bobbing her head. "That sounds challenging. Have you ever employed psychics before?"

I leaned forward and hissed in Trish's ear, "What the hell are you doing?"

"I can't say that we…" David settled his beautiful eyes on me. "What is it with you two and all these questions? Now you want to know if I've enlisted psychics to help me do my job?" He buried the beginning of a smirk behind the edge of his glass.

He found this amusing, and the way *psychics* fell off his lips felt ridiculing, like I was some sort of freak. But he was right. I was a freak, unique, gifted…*special.*

I stood and gulped back the rest of my martini. "This is when I leave. Night." I would have been more than happy to part ways with Trish at this point too, but I feared what she might say to David in my absence. "You coming?" I prompted her.

"Ah, sure."

"Actually, before you go—" David pulled a business card from his shirt pocket and extended it to me. "Give me a call sometime."

My hand took the card on instinct, and I was left staring at it like it had manifested out of thin air.

"Nice meeting you," Trish said, rising from her stool.

We headed for the exit—me as fast as my legs could take me there. "What is up with you?" I asked Trish, but I was too angry to look at her. "He's got to think we're crazy, and if he doesn't, he should."

"Now, that's just the vodka making you bitchy. He didn't say psychics didn't exist or roll his eyes—"

"He didn't exactly say he believed in them either."

"He wants you to call him sometime. And if you don't like him, why do you care what he thinks about you?"

I stopped walking and spun to face her. David's card was still in my hand. We were in the main area of the bar, and the place with thick with people. "I'm not a psychic, just for the record." I had to practically yell so Trish would have a shot at hearing me. I stepped out the front door, relishing the cool night air on my flushed skin. Vodka did make me a bitch, *and* it spiked my temperature.

"You know that you are." A flicker of pain flashed across her eyes, and my stomach sank.

"I'm sorry. Just maybe I don't want to be."

"All this must be stressful for you," she said in a gentle tone.

"That's putting it mildly." I wrapped my arms around myself. The air was damp and seeping through my coat and bones. Just when I thought I'd reconciled myself with having visions, to have others outside of Trish know, it felt so much more real. And I couldn't shake David's reaction—a smirk, on par with ridicule. "I wish you had the dream," I mumbled. "You view it as a blessing."

"Not just a dream, Erin. And you helped reunite a little girl with her mother. Or are you forgetting that?"

I sniffled. There was no way I'd be forgetting that—ever.

She went on. "Remember how I've told before that the universe provides as we need something? Well, now you have a connection inside the NTSB. A connection who invited you to call him."

"Last I checked, it wasn't my job to solve plane crashes." It came out with a lot of heat, but I was feeling rebellious. After all, I never asked for this *gift*. "I just wish my life had stayed the way it was before…" I fished in my coat pocket for my cell phone to call a taxi, finding it strange I didn't see a single one. Usually, they were lined up outside restaurants, bars, and hotels in ample supply.

Trish put a hand on my shoulder. She didn't say a word. I found myself filling in the silence.

"I just need to go home, get some sleep, enjoy the holiday weekend, and forget all about the dream, the visions." The last word rolled off my tongue as bile.

"That would certainly be easier." She said it in a way that was loving, affirming, and understanding, but I also sensed disappointment.

"I need to move on. My life was fine as it was." My head was spinning from the booze, and I hated myself for drinking so much.

"Well, you could always ignore the dream. That is an option."

I narrowed my eyes at her, certain she was employing reverse psychology. "It might be a smart one. It seems to be causing more harm than good. Most of the time, I'm sure I've lost my mind entirely. Other times, I'm taking on a crusade that doesn't necessarily exist, or if it does, it isn't mine to take on."

"Take one day at a time, then. Don't rush things." Trish put her arm around me. "It will all be fine."

"I hope you're right." I shuddered as a chill tore through me. Visions, premonitions, clairvoyancy…being psychic. Sure, none of these things reconciled with my upbringing, but reuniting Lily Brooks with her mother had felt right. Then there were moments like now when I felt adrift and lost again.

A cabbie parked at the curb, and I held up a hand to let him know I was coming.

"You didn't bring your car?"

I shook my head. "I took a page from your book and got a ride here."

"Smart call. Mind if we share the cab?"

"Not at all." I regarded Trish curiously. She was my best friend. Of course I didn't have a problem sharing the cab with her. She had this deep look of concentration, and I wished I could read her mind as good as she could mine.

We told the driver where to take us. I'd be dropped off first, given where we were leaving from.

"Nice night to be out, ladies," the driver said.

"Yep." I hoped that compact response would discourage conversation. I preferred my drivers silent, but ever since driving services popped up, cabbies seemed to make it their mission to initiate and carry out friendly chitchat in hopes of a good review. I gave five stars for friendly, *quiet* service.

I looked over at Trish, who hadn't said a word since we got into the cab. "You tired of talking now?" I smirked at her, and she popped her middle finger at me and smiled. "You did kind of interrogate the guy," I said.

"I might have been a tad zealous." She pinched her fingers close to touching and chuckled.

I laughed.

"I'm just excited about what's going on with you."

"It did feel good to find that little girl," I admitted.

"I bet it did."

Neither of us said anything more until I was getting out of the cab at home. Then Trish said, "You should call David. He's a hottie."

"Night." I closed the door on her, but I could easily get carried away dreaming about Mr. NTSB. Then again, he probably thought Trish and I were both cuckoo. *But* he did tell me to call him *after* the mention of psychics. Maybe I had misread his smirk.

# Chapter Eighteen

The plane's bucking wildly, and its nose is dipped downward.

This is how I'm going to die. There will be no begging for redemption or saving. Everything is about to be over.

My heartbeat pounds in my ears—a reliable rhythm, but it brings no comfort. Rather a sense of chaos. It's so loud, more like music playing in the distance, only the thump-thump-thump of the bass making it to me.

The plane drops altitude again, like it's descending a giant staircase. With each step, my stomach lurches in my throat, and I grip the armrests tighter.

This plane is going down unless a divine being intervenes—and for that, I'm not holding my breath.

The oxygen masks long ago dropped from the ceiling, and I'm sucking back on one for dear life. As if that will save me. I can't help but feel it's only prolonging my agony. Will I feel it? When the plane impacts the ground, will I be aware?

People are screaming.

Babies are crying.

I look across the aisle. That mysterious man is still cool and calm, reading from the book on his lap. It must be full of prayers. I wish I had faith at a time like this, but I have none. No god to believe in. No afterlife to comfort me.

I turn to face the sweet elderly woman to my right, in the window seat. We'd changed spots when she'd asked.

She has the face of an angel. Round, cherubic, soft, and innocent. She's squeezing my hand, her blue eyes staring into mine, begging for answers.

*My heart aches for her. She has everything to lose. I have nothing.*

**My eyes bolted open. It was like I was there again, going** down on the plane with everyone else. The loss sat heavy on my chest, and I was panting for air. When visions brought such intense, visceral reactions, how can that be a good thing? And when my family found out…well, they simply couldn't find out.

But I was curious.

Whose eyes was I seeing this dream through? And even if I knew who she was, why was she coming to me?

This intrusion made me angry, honestly. I'd never asked for this. I didn't even believe in the afterlife, just as the woman in my dream, but I did believe in God. In the sense that he, or she, was out there, but more in the role of an observer than someone who became involved with humankind. My perspective may have changed with the loss of my parents, but I don't remember giving God too much thought before then either. I certainly didn't think God intervened on our behalf. After all, God probably had better things to do that our brains couldn't comprehend. So, really, where did that leave visions? The work of the Devil?

Still, it felt like I was in far too deep already. A person can't have their curiosity sparked and simply turn away without satisfying it. The thought of doing so didn't seem natural.

And maybe I'd had another dream about the crash simply because of last night. I'd engaged with people who had lost loved ones in a crash, surging my personal grief. Combine that with the alcohol, and anything was possible. I had probably just taken on their emotions and jumbled it all up and—

Harvey meowed loudly and jumped onto the bed.

"Why are you so noisy?" I asked him as I petted him.

Harvey was usually quiet unless he was hungry. It was then I realized that light was coming in around my curtains, and I glanced over at the alarm clock. *10:40 AM.*

I vaulted out of bed. "Oh, Harvey, let's get you some breakfast."

I dished him up some food and made all sorts of apologies and promises to be a better cat mom. I brewed myself a coffee and drank it black. If I was going to pursue looking into the crash, I needed to be thinking clearly. Caffeine was always a good place to start.

My phone rang, and I sloshed my coffee. It was definitely going to take a lot more than one cup to wake up today. I looked at the caller ID. *Unknown.* Probably a telemarketer, but … oh, what the hell? I answered.

"Erin?" a man said. There was something familiar about his voice, but I couldn't quite place it. "It's David Bomber," he added. "We met last night."

*David is calling* me? I pinched the collar of my pajama top together modestly, as if he could see through the phone line. "Ah, yes, I remember you. What's up?" I rolled my eyes at my question. *Am I fifteen?*

"I hope you don't mind, but I asked Karen Synder for your number. I wasn't sure if you'd call so I… Oh, listen to me ramble."

I smiled. "It's fine." I was flattered that he went through the effort to reach out, but I still didn't know why. "Is there something I can do for you?"

"You could have coffee with me," he tossed back without missing a beat.

"Coffee? I…I don't know about that."

"Don't say no."

"It's the Thanksgiving weekend, and my daughter's coming home tomorrow and…"

"Are you out of excuses?"

My mouth gaped opened, but then I found myself smiling again. "I guess it would depend on when you wanted to go."

"This afternoon too soon?"

*Yeah, but…* "Not at all."

"All right. I don't know which part of the city you're in. You tell me where you'd like to meet up, and I'll be there."

"So you call me up and ask me out for coffee, then I need to plan the details?" I laughed. I liked this guy. I gave him the location of a Tim Hortons, a few blocks away from my townhouse. "Two o'clock?"

"It's a date." His smile carried over the line.

"You got it." The words came out easily and naturally, and I shook my head at my eagerness.

"See you there."

We said goodbye and ended the call, and I sat on my couch, cupping my phone in my hand. I'd just made a date with Mr. NTSB, and I had no idea why. I didn't understand what he saw in me anyway. Last night wasn't my shining hour. If Trish were here, she'd fill my head with assurances and build-me-ups to remind me I was lovable and deserving.

As I sat there savoring the rest of my coffee and relishing in David's invitation, thoughts of the most recent dream crept in. The emotional, tacky residue was still very much there—the fear, the regrets. The older woman's face.

Before now, I'd just seen her hands. The near translucent skin, blue veins, and age spots.

I grabbed my laptop and clicked on the bookmarked article that listed some of the crash victims, hoping her picture would be there. Though I didn't remember seeing an elderly woman before.

As I went down the page, reading each name in turn, my heart hurt with the realization that each one of these people had left family and friends behind. No matter the cause of the crash, nothing would bring them back to life. But, in a way, my visions resurrected them. I was at least a witness of sorts to their last moments alive.

I stopped scanning when I saw a photograph of a man and woman holding a young baby.

*A baby's cry…*

Tingles laced down my arms. *Can it be?* A baby had wailed in both visions. I recalled turning to look at the woman, but her face hadn't made an impact. Even seeing her now, nothing clicked.

I read the caption and small writeup, culling the details. Nick and Irene Sutton of Newmarket with their daughter, Larisa. She was their only child, and the Suttons considered Larisa a miracle when conceiving a child had seemed to be impossible. They were returning from visiting family in Texas.

I stopped reading to ponder. Death really was so meaningless, so empty. The saying that "time heals all wounds" was of no real comfort when faced with loss of that magnitude—and it's a lie. At best, the wounds scab over, but they continue to fester. The hurt is never completely gone; it's always there, lingering in the background, ready to cripple its prey.

I glanced at Mom and Dad's picture on the mantel, and an ache jabbed my heart. "I miss you both so much," I said to them, wishing they could hear me.

I took another gulp of coffee and returned to the article, this time with the intention of not letting myself get too emotionally invested.

And that was when I saw a small writeup about an elderly woman who'd died on the plane.

Betty Mavis, age seventy-eight, wife of Peter Mavis. Both were residents of Texas, but Betty was flying solo to their daughter's place in Toronto to meet their newborn granddaughter. Peter wasn't with his wife, as the article explained, due to health issues.

The woman in my vision ached for her. *She has everything to lose.*

It would seem the woman in my vision knew what Betty Mavis had at stake. Did she know the woman? I shook my head, dismissing that question as I recalled the older woman was a stranger to her. So *how* did she know what the elderly woman would be leaving behind? And that was assuming that Betty was *the* elderly woman. I needed to find out what Betty Mavis had looked like to see if it matched what I'd seen in this morning's dream. There wasn't a picture of her included in the article.

I typed *Betty Mavis* into Google and several results came back. One was an obituary. I winced and clicked on it. The page opened to a newspaper obit post:

> *"Betty Mavis, 78, died tragically in a plane crash, leaving behind her loving husband of fifty-six years, Peter Mavis, daughter Isabella, newborn granddaughter Darcy, and many friends."*

I'd say this obit belonged to the Betty Mavis I was interested in, but there was no picture. I scrolled down the post and found where they were holding the memorial services. Then I opened a new tab and googled the funeral home. Often they posted photos of the deceased. I entered Betty's name into their search field, and seconds later, a familiar face was staring back at me.

*The face of an angel. Round, cherubic, soft, and innocent.*

First, Howard Hayes. Now, Betty Mavis. Both real-life people had been in my vision. The question that had been circling a lot lately was back again. What did I intend to do with the realization my dream was something so much more?

# Chapter Nineteen

I drove to Tim Hortons to meet David and ran a few yellow-to-red lights, stopped at a green, got honked at. My mind was occupied with Betty's face and those blue eyes of hers that were seeking answers. I'd do what I could to find those answers and unravel this universal riddle I'd been given. The largest question out there, if you asked me, was *why*? That dreaded "God question."

I pulled into the coffee shop's lot and went inside.

As per usual, Tim Hortons was busy. Lines of people waited at the counter, and for a Saturday afternoon, it would seem here was quite the hot spot to hang out. David waved at me from a corner table and stood when I approached. *Stood*…like an old-school gentleman.

"Fancy meeting up like this," he tossed out in a casual manner, and I envied how relaxed he was. On the way over, I'd been so focused on the plane vision I didn't have time to stress about our "date." Now that I was facing him, my heart was beating fast.

"Yes, such a surprise." I smiled, and he flashed that devilish grin of his. *Hold on to your heart, Erin Stone*, I coached myself.

"So, what can I get for you?" he asked.

"Oh no, don't worry about it. You go grab yourself something, then I will. I'll save the table in the meantime."

David tilted his head to the right. "I asked you out for coffee. I fully intend to pay for it. I'd even buy you a donut or croissant. If you'd like, I could splurge for a sandwich." He winked, and my heart melted.

I'd become so accustomed to taking care of myself that I found it hard when someone else offered to do so. *Get over it, Erin.* "I'll take a medium double-double. That's two sugars, double cream, in case you didn't know."

"I'm in Canada enough to know Tims coffee lingo." He smiled again. "Anything to eat? I meant what I said."

I considered his offer but declined. I wasn't sure food would stay down. On the way to the coffee shop, I'd convinced myself that I needed to probe him about Monday's crash—hopefully in a smoother manner than Trish had done.

David left and returned, what seemed like only seconds later, with my coffee. "Here you go."

"Thanks," I said as I took a steaming white mug from him. It was strange getting a Timmys in a mug; I was so accustomed to their coffee in a cardboard takeout cup.

"You're very welcome."

"Rarely do I actually just sit in a Timmys and sip coffee."

"I hear you. Life's hectic at the best of times." He lifted his mug in a toast gesture. "To new friends."

A woman at the table next to us winked at me. I smiled and touched my mug to his. He was just quirky enough that it was attractive and not a turn-off.

I blew on my coffee and took a sip. "Oh, it's better fresh like this. Maybe it's time to slow down and taste the coffee." The minute I'd made the lame joke, I wanted to disappear into the floor, but David laughed.

"You're a little nuts, but the right kind of nut."

"Me? A nut? I was just thinking the same thing about you," I served back.

"So, you've been thinking about me." He flashed his devilish grin again.

"Fine, I admit it."

"I'm glad to hear that. When I called, I was afraid you'd tell me to take a leap." He let out a puff of air, the first chip in his confident demeanor showing.

"Nah, I'd never do that."

"Uh-huh, I'm sure." He paused, looked down at his coffee briefly. "I just wanted to see you again." He admitted it with such raw honesty and vulnerability, the air between us crackled.

"Honestly, I thought you'd want nothing to do with me."

"Nonsense. Just because you have a strange friend…"

"Hey, I'll have you know that Trish is my *best* friend." I wasn't about to dispute the "strange" bit; she was off her game last night.

He smiled, and I could tell he'd just said it to rile me. "I am curious about you, about Trish."

"Ah, so you want to see us both? Have a coffee date with her later today?"

"Dinner plans."

*Ouch.* I winced playfully.

"I'm just kidding." He laughed.

I narrowed my eyes at him again. "Good."

"I am curious, though, and when I get curious, I like to satisfy it."

I could relate to the feeling, more than he knew. "Oh?" Heat flooded my cheeks as brief fantasies of tossing in bed with him took hold. I cleared my throat. "Ah, what are you curious about…specifically?"

"Why are you and your friend so interested in Monday's plane crash? You said you didn't know anyone on the flight. Usually, when people ask me questions like you two did, it's because there is a personal connection."

"Nope. Nothing personal." I pressed my lips to my cup and took a sip. This was likely where any fairytale ideas I'd entertained of David Bomber would go up in a puff of smoke. His reaction to Trish asking him if he'd ever employed psychics in investigations came back with gut-curdling awareness.

"Why the interest, then?" His steel-blue eyes were piercing mine. He wasn't going to take a brush-off response, but if

I answered honestly, I risked turning him away for good. Then again, did I really have anything to lose? He was new to my life: easy in, easy out.

*Here goes…* "I had a dream in the wee hours of Monday morning, around the time of the crash." I stopped there, scanning his face for any signs that I was losing him.

"You had a dream," he prompted. "Go on."

"Ah, yeah. Anyway, the rest of what I'm about to say might sound weird to you."

"I've heard a lot of weird things in my life."

I narrowed my eyes at him, and he laughed.

"All I mean is I'm fine. Continue."

"Okay, but you asked for it. Everything in this dream was crystal clear, like I was there on the plane when it crashed. I could see people, hear people, feel other people's touch. It was just as real as you are here in front of me now." The words kept spilling out, and David was watching me intently. His expression was hard to read, but he hadn't gotten up and left. Bonus.

Seconds passed in silence.

"Say something," I pressed.

"Your friend asked me about psychics, if I've ever used them in an investigation," he started. "Now I know why. But in answer to her question, no, I never have."

"Why am I not surprised? You think I'm nuts."

"I already told you that." He paused to smirk. "But it has nothing to do with your vision."

I sat up straighter, speechless. He didn't sound judgmental in the least. If anything, he was quite open-minded.

"I figured the minute your friend asked about psychics that you were one." His lips twitched like he was going to smile, like he found some sick satisfaction in holding on to this little secret.

"Oh, I'm not a…" I couldn't get my throat to part with the rest of my defense. It was a lie. I was a psychic—at least these days.

"You are. Based on what you just told me."

In a way, I wished I could protest, tell him the dream about the plane crash was all I'd seen, but that would be a lie. "I don't know if I'd go so far as to put the label of *psychic* on me." I was still trying it on. I continued. "The dream was certainly strange, different, supernatural." I stopped talking as the realization sank in again that he'd asked me out *after* pegging me as a psychic. "My being a psychic doesn't scare you." It was intended to be a question but came out as an affirmative statement.

"Nope. Why should it?"

"It's just…well, most people would be more shaken or think I was crazy. My family, all of Catholic background, would flip if they found out—"

David was smiling.

"Am I missing something?"

"Nope." He was outright grinning now and shaking his head. "Just because I haven't employed psychics for investigations doesn't mean that I don't believe they exist or give them merit. And for the record, I'm not Catholic or part of any other organized religion."

"So, you believe in psychics?" I just wanted to make sure I was hearing him correctly.

"I do." He said it as if paying tribute to two words that bonded a man and woman in matrimony.

I glanced down, looking for his ring finger, but his left hand was out of my line of sight. I should have checked during our first meeting, but I hadn't really adapted to being single.

"I'm not married," he said, holding up his left hand for a good view, obviously not missing my endeavor. "Never have been."

"I wish I could say— Actually, I don't mean that. My ex gave me my beautiful daughter, Jenna."

"Nice. How old?"

"She's nineteen, attending the University of Toronto. She's smarter than me, prettier."

"Hard to imagine that."

I tilted out my chin, wanting to say something to the effect that flattery hadn't worked on me for the better part of thirty years. *Thirty years…* Now I felt old. And flattery *did* work coming from David. "You compliment all the ladies, I'm sure."

"Only when it's true."

Alarms pinged in my head, sounding much like my brother's voice telling me David was no different than Chris. A player. I had enough to handle with the visions, let alone getting my heart involved with some guy—

"And not in a very long time, I should add," he said.

Either he was an exceptional liar, or he was telling the truth. "Really?"

He held up his hands. "Really. This is the first date I've had in months. Life is—"

"Hectic," I finished. "And can you really call coffee a date?" The question spilled out, and I wished to reel it back in.

"It passes these days."

"Right, for those not sure they want to commit to an entire meal with an essential stranger." I'd already dipped a toe in, time for full surrender.

"Yeah, something like that." He snickered. "You're nuts, remember. Just wanted to get a feel for how nuts before I jumped right in."

"Huh," I shot back, teasing. I hadn't flirted with a man for far too long and was embarrassingly rusty.

"This must be hard on you."

He'd switched tracks, and I wasn't sure where he was headed. "In what way?"

"You said your family is religious and not understanding?"

"Oh, that. Well, they don't know about this dream I had or that I'm a psychic."

"What they don't know won't kill 'em."

"Won't hurt them anyway. It was enough just for me to assimilate." I stopped there, hesitating to tell him about the shrink and the doctor I'd gone to, but I ended up doing just that.

"Given your religious upbringing, I find that completely understandable. And it's best to be sure."

I smiled and considered telling him more about the plane crash dream and about Lily Brooks. But would that be pushing things? Believing psychics exist and being beaten over the head with the fact that he was sitting with one were two entirely different things.

"So, have you only had the one vision?" David drained the rest of his coffee. His eyes really had a soul-piercing quality. He'd kill it in the confessional booth.

"Ah…" I squirmed, suddenly feeling a little uncomfortable. It was like he'd been reading my mind. And he'd been super understanding up to this point, but how far would that extend? Would he find the situation with Lily Brooks fascinating, or would it scare him off? "I don't know how much I should say. I mean, we don't even really know each other."

"Something I'm trying to change."

His counter made me speechless.

"Come on, talk to me. So it's a yes, you've had more visions?"

I nodded and went on to tell him about Lily Brooks.

"Wow." He sat back and was spinning his empty mug. "That's incredible. And police caught the guy, the girl's father?"

I nodded. "A happy ending."

"I'd say."

Betty Mavis, her obit, her face slammed into my awareness, draping a wet blanket over the enthusiasm I felt about Lily. "Anyway, now you know why I'm interested in Monday's crash. And I don't think the crash was an accident." I spoke barely above a whisper, shocked that I had the courage to say as much to David. If there was a lesson in the past few days, it was to forge ahead despite fear. I was slowly improving in that regard.

His face became shadowed. "Because of your vision?"

I nodded, feeling dread in the pit of my stomach. "You can go if you like. Nothing's keeping you here."

"Are you in a hurry to get rid of me?" His tone communicated irritation.

"No, not at all."

"Good." He ran a fingertip around the top of his mug. "It's just that you've been so open with me, I feel like I should be the same. Though if it gets out that I've talked to you about…well, what I'm about to talk to you about, I could be in a lot of trouble."

"What is it?" I was intrigued, my entire body electric with anticipation.

"Is now a good time to tell you that your instincts line up with my colleague's suspicions? He's leaning toward foul play being behind the crash."

# Chapter Twenty

For the first minute or two, maybe more, after David told me Monday's crash might have been intentional, I couldn't speak. My mouth went dry, and my throat stitched together. My emotions and thoughts were all over the place. I had decided on the way to meet him that I was going to uncover some answers, even tackle the big "why" the crash had to happen. Now my hunch about the crash aligned with the thoughts of an investigator within the NTSB.

"I didn't mean to upset you," David said. "I just thought you'd like to hear that."

I nodded, numb.

"It's all speculation at this point. Nothing's proven. I shouldn't even have told you that. So, please, please, keep this between us."

"I will. I promise. Do you think the crash has anything to do with that Fighters for Future America group mentioned in the news?"

"Too soon to know, as I said. There's a lot to consider besides. Crashes are usually the result of numerous variables—each of which, on its own, wouldn't take a plane down but combined are lethal. And most incidents are caused by human error."

"Like was the case with Mom and Dad's plane," I got out, barely above a whisper.

"Yes," he responded gently.

"What about the pilots of Monday's crash? Have they been investigated? The black box listened to?" I remembered the black box playing a part in the investigation into my parents' crash.

"I'm sorry, but I've probably said too much about the investigation as it is."

"You've said too—" I snapped my mouth shut. He'd hardly shared at all compared to how much I had.

"The pilots are still under investigation," he offered but didn't seem too pleased about doing so.

"And the black box? Come on, it's not like I'm going to tell anyone."

"Found."

Instantly, images seized me.

*A river…no, a stream. My legs are taking me through long grass toward a…big rock. Around me, a farmer's field.*

*"Erin?" I heard his voice, but it was like it was coming to me from miles away.*

*A stream, long grass, a big rock, a farmer's field…*

"Erin," he prompted louder, "are you okay?"

My heart was pounding. I could see the black box clearly. "Where was it found?"

David peered into my eyes. "I can find out."

"Uh-hmm. Please," I squeaked out. It didn't seem to matter how many times elements of my dream-slash-vision were verified, I was still hungry for proof. Even after Lily Brooks.

"Are you all right? You're really pale."

I gulped and went to speak, but my tongue felt like a foreign entity in my mouth. I tried again. "I…I just saw something."

David shifted into a stiff upright position, back straight. "I was wondering if you did."

He seemed eager to accept that I'd had another vision; me, not so much. Even though I was starting to accept the fact I was seeing things that others did not, it didn't make it any less unsettling. And it was one thing to see images in a dream and quite another to zone out and see these images while I was awake. I ran a hand over my mouth.

David reached out and touched my arm. "It's okay. You're safe."

I blinked rapidly, willing away the tears. "I don't know if I'll ever get used to seeing the things I do."

He peered into my eyes, like he was prying into my skull. "I take it this is all new for you?"

I nodded. "Pretty much spankin' new."

"Okay, so you've had a vision or two. You're all right. Safe," he said, reassuring me again.

I put my elbow on the table and rested my head in my hand, massaged my temple. "I'm not sure I'll ever get used to this happening while I'm wide awake. It's disconcerting."

"No doubt. Do you want to tell me what you saw?"

I shook my head. "Maybe after you find out where the black box was found." *After I had more proof…* Oh me of little faith. If I did have guardian angels, as Trish believed, they were probably frustrated as hell with me.

"Okay," he said slowly.

"Thanks."

A bit of time passed, and then David said, "You also seemed to blank out on me a bit when I told you my coworker's suspicion that the crash wasn't an accident. You have a vision then too?"

"No. It was just hearing that someone else was of the same opinion as me."

David leaned across the table. "And you feel the crash was intentional because of your vision for the simple reason that you had it? Or did you see something to push your suspicions that way?"

"Not exactly, but I like to think that I had the vision for a purpose. You know, maybe to expose something or someone." As I said all this, I realized how comfortable I was talking about it with him. In fact, the more I spoke about the visions and my psychic ability, the less scary it all was. In the place of fear, a sense of overwhelm moved in at times. It was tethered to feeling responsibility toward what I had been granted to see.

David smiled and drew his hand back. "It's understandable you're searching for a reason."

"Yeah. It would have been better for this to happen to Trish. She's really into new-age spirituality and elements, belief in the afterlife, the magic of the universe—all that. She even believes in fairies."

"Do you?"

"Fairies?" I snickered and shook my head.

"Huh, too bad. I mean they sound like cute little things. What about everything else...the magic of the universe? That sounds pretty heady."

"I believe more in that every day."

He gestured as if to say, *of course.*

"I've accepted LOA for a while now actually."

He angled his head. "LOA?"

"Law of attraction."

His brow pinched.

"You've never heard of law of attraction?" Suddenly I had an irresistible urge to educate him on the matter. "The basic idea is everything is energy and carries a vibration. Like attracts like." I paused to gauge his comprehension, and he still looked confused. I continued. "Basically, we're masters of our own lives and have the power to draw things and experiences to us."

"So, on some level, you wanted to have a vision."

I tilted my head to the right. "Now you sound like Trish." He smirked.

"The visions came on their own, I assure you. I believe some things still remain outside our control, but there's a lot we determine. A simple one: whether we're going to have a good day or a bad one."

"It's all in our attitude."

"Exactly. LOA is rather simple in concept, complex in execution. Our minds can get in the way. If you want to know more about LOA, you should watch *The Secret*. It makes it easy to understand."

"I'll check it out. I assume it's a movie."

"More documentary, but yeah."

"LOA sounds fascinating."

"I know I was excited when I first found out about it."

"It's completely believable."

I narrowed my eyes. "You tease."

He held up his hands. "No, I'm being quite serious. Life is so abundant and complex, how can we even comprehend all that is? Then sometimes there is proof of something that isn't visible or even tangible. It's more a…feeling."

"You're a deep guy."

"Thank you."

I just nodded. "And you sound like Trish."

"I must say the more I hear about her, she sounds awesome." David smiled.

A small span of silence passed between us, and the woman and her friend from the next table left. Vultures swept in before their chairs would have cooled.

"So what are you going to do about your visions?" David asked.

"I think I just need to hand myself over to them—not like I can really control them anyhow. As for the crash, I feel quite strongly that I should look into it, but I don't know the first thing about doing that." I met his gaze, curious if he'd pick up on my silent plea for assistance.

"Well, it's a good thing you know someone who might have a clue about such things."

I bit the urge to tell him about Trish's confidence that the universe had put him in my path for that very reason.

"Why don't we work together?" he asked.

"Really? You told me you weren't assigned to Monday's crash."

"I'm not, but my colleague respects my input."

"Sure, but does he respect psychics?" This time the admission as to what I was came out easily…even, dare I say, naturally. Talking with him had helped.

"Honestly? The subject's never come up before. I can't imagine him being as open to working with one as I am, but he doesn't need to know about you. Actually, it's far better for me if he doesn't."

"And he won't be curious when I start sending you on little intel-gathering missions?"

"Meh." David shrugged. "He's used to me by now, and curiosity never killed anyone."

"Tell that to the cat." I laughed, and so did he. "Sorry. Blame my father for my warped sense of humor."

"I'd thank him."

This guy must have fallen from heaven. He *got* me—my humor, my weird quirks, my ability. That was the big sale. He gave my visions credibility and didn't ridicule me for them. He was sitting across from me, smiling, even appearing eager to start investigating the crash as a team. I felt I should tell him about the fairly big role Howard Hayes had played in the initial vision. So I did. Even told him about Hayes's three companions whom I'd pegged as the man's bodyguards. When I was finished, he was staring at me, as if wanting me to stitch it all together.

"What do you make of that?" he ended up asking.

"I can't help but think a man of his wealth and stature would have enemies."

"Like the Fighters for Future America."

"Them for one."

"You think the plane was targeted by them because he was on it?"

"I am curious. Not sure if that group was behind it. Maybe if we did some poking around there—or with Hayes's business, Guardian Oil Company, we might find something."

David's face took on hard lines, and he got to his feet. "I'm going to grab another coffee. Want one?"

I shook my head, and he walked off, surprisingly to the counter and not out the front door. David placed his order and didn't look back at me while he waited for its fulfillment.

"You're going to tell me to leave it alone now," I accused when he returned to the table.

He took a sip, and time seemed to crawl before he responded. "Not at all."

"What is it, then?"

"I think we need to get more details in order before we reach out to anyone."

I considered his words and recalled how I'd felt for the victims' families being thrust into confusion by the allegation hurled at the Fighters for Future America. "You're right."

"Yeah, no sense stirring things up unless we have facts to back us." David took another sip of his coffee. His eyes were a storm, testifying both to discomfort and conflict. "I think we need to consider every move we take before we make it."

Slow, methodical, like a cop planning a sting. "I can do that." Sudden emotion whelmed up in my throat, and my eyes beaded with tears. I sniffled. "I know the pain of waiting for closure and explanation. I just want to help the friends and family of the people who died."

He put his hand on the back of mine, his palm warm. "I understand, believe me."

I held eye contact with him. "I believe you do." After all, his connection to the victims' loved ones was what had dragged him out last night. "So, what do we do now?" With the question out, I realized how fast I'd accepted him as a partner.

"We can dig more into Howard Hayes on the q.t. You mentioned he was traveling with a few men?"

"Yeah."

"We'll identify everyone in your vision with who they were in real life. Also, you said you were in a woman's perspective. If we find out who she was, there might be some answers in that."

"Could be. Doesn't hurt. Only thing is I don't know where to start. I don't even know what she looks like." A memory jogged loose. "Oh, I know that she traded seats with Betty Mavis." I told him how I had ID'd her.

"I may know someone who could get their hands on the flight manifest."

"You can? Right, of course you can." I smiled at him. Having a partner in this endeavor was going to be incredible.

"And I will under one condition."

"What's that?"

"We are in this together. You have any more revelations or visions, any impulses to do something, we talk it out first."

"I can agree to that."

"All right." He held out his hand to shake on it. I took his and swore that sparks crackled between our palms when we touched. He reacted like he'd felt it too.

# Chapter Twenty-One

I had a partner in all this, whatever *this* was. There were times I was tempted to call the visions a divine assignment—divine being the closest I came to getting God involved with this—and other times, I felt like a real fraud. After all, I was a communications officer for the living in the here and now, not some big-shot psychic who channeled spirit beings. The worlds were far apart in my mind—not that I hadn't heard of psychics being consulted to help solve crimes.

David and I left Tim Hortons with a plan of action. We'd meet in a couple of hours at my house. In the meantime, he was going to contact his friend at the NTSB for a flight manifest and ask where the black box had been recovered. While he did that, I worked to bring my place to a shine. Harvey had just finished eating his dinner when there was a knock at the door.

David was on my step with a laptop satchel over a shoulder, holding a takeout bag from Tim Hortons and a tray with two coffees.

"You didn't have to do that." I pointed at his offerings.

"I know I didn't *have* to, but I wanted to. Besides, maybe I'm not planning to share."

"Uh-huh." I took the bag and tray from him and led him into the house. He shucked his shoes and coat and hung the latter on a hook by the door.

We went upstairs to where the kitchen and main living areas were.

David looked around. "Nice place."

"Thanks." It wasn't until then that I realized I had invited a man I barely knew into my home. But there was something so natural and comfortable about being around David, I didn't fear anything about him.

Harvey paraded across the kitchen, strutting, as if letting David know who was boss of this domain.

David moaned. "Oh. You're a cat person."

"Hey, cats are the best."

"Dog man myself."

"Well, I'll forgive you." I smiled at him, and it faded as I realized why most people had a problem with my feline friend. "Are you allergic to cats?"

"I am actually, but only mildly. I'll be fine." He pointed to the kitchen table. "Did you want to work here?"

"Sure." I'd had my mind on the softer pillows of the couch, but it was probably wiser to stay in the kitchen—not get too comfortable. It would keep me alert and focused on why he was here in the first place, and I'd be less likely to get caught up in his good looks. "I just need to grab my laptop from the other room."

Harvey was rubbing against David's leg, and I scooped him up. "Sorry about that."

"Don't worry about it."

He was pulling his laptop from his bag when I was leaving the room, and it was already fired up by the time I returned a few seconds later. I snatched the coffees and the takeout bag from the counter and put them on the table.

"I got the flight manifest from Bill," David said. "It was no big deal. He didn't even ask any questions."

"Wow."

"Well, he knows me. I can be sort of…" He stopped talking and met my gaze. "How do I say this without you thinking I'm nuts?"

"Too late for that, so we can move forward." I chuckled.

"Ha. Comedian of the year."

"Let me guess—" I tapped my chin with a finger "—you can be obsessive." It wasn't really a clairvoyant revelation though. His comment at Tim Hortons about Bill knowing how he could be led me to that conclusion.

"Obsessive? That could be one word for it. It's just that I like my job so much, it doesn't feel like a job to me. I go over-the-top all the time, get too involved—that much you know."

She nodded. "That's why you go to memorials for friends and families of crash victims."

"Something like that." A flicker of vulnerability danced across his eyes. What some might consider a weakness, I saw as a strength.

Being together like this—our little rogue investigation aside—probably crossed some sort of line, but neither of us seemed likely to point that out.

"I asked Bill about the black box," David began.

I'd been dying to know about the black box and where it was found since that flash of imagery at Tim Hortons, but I wanted him to bring it up. My heart nearly stopped beating as I waited for him to continue.

"It was found by a stream, in a farmer's field close to where the plane went down."

My eyes were brimming with tears. More confirmation.

"That's what you saw?"

"Uh-hmm. Yep."

"Guess I'm psychic too."

I smiled at him. "Trish says we all are to some degree or another. But I think my reaction is giving me away."

He held his fingers pinched close together and smiled.

"I saw a stream, like a trickle of water, long grass, a big rock, a farmer's field."

"Yep. You've got the gift." David leaned back in his chair. "It seems you keep longing for proof of your ability."

"I do. It's just so different for me." I held up my cup of coffee. "Too bad there isn't something-something in here. I could use some."

"Some something-something? Which is?"

"Booze."

"Nah, it's not the answer to everything. Though drinking can be fun." He winked. "So you want to work on getting some answers?"

"Absolutely."

David brought up a list on his computer. "This is the passenger manifest."

"Can you show me what seat Howard Hayes was assigned?" It was another test—for me and my confidence.

He went to his name and brought up a picture of the plane's interior with the seating chart. He pointed to the aisle seat in the left exit row.

More validation—in black and white. "Exactly where I saw him. Can you tell me who was assigned the window seat in the row across from him? In my vision, the mystery woman had changed seats with Betty Mavis, and there was mention of the elderly woman being next to the window."

"Okay. The right exit row…" He dragged a finger down the screen as he scrolled. "Mavis was assigned the aisle seat, but… Oh." He stopped scrolling.

"What is it?" I leaned in to get a better look at the screen.

"No one was assigned the window seat."

"What? How is that possible?"

"There could be many reasons there wasn't a seat assignment. The mystery woman changed seats with Betty; she could have changed seats with someone else."

"So, she moved from somewhere else on the plane entirely? But why?"

"Maybe she'd gotten up to use the bathroom, and the plane hit turbulence on her way back to her assigned seat, so she just sat in the closest one to her."

"That wouldn't explain their switching seats," I countered.

"That still could have happened." He paused for a few seconds. "Either way, her name has to be on the manifest somewhere."

"How would we even go about finding it?"

David appeared stumped, but it didn't last long. "One sec…" He clicked on his keyboard. "The plane wasn't full.

There were empty seats, including the window seat in the right exit row."

"I'm not sure where you're headed with this."

"Well, she obviously came from another part of the plane. All we have to do is go through the list of passengers, find out who they were, get pictures, etcetera."

"But I don't know what she looks like." The feat of finding the mystery woman seemed to be getting larger by the second.

"Huh."

"Yeah, *huh*. All I would say about her is she's probably somewhere in her twenties."

"Based on?"

"Her hands."

"Her hands?" he asked, amused.

"Her skin is young, no age spots or wrinkles. Smooth, fair complexion."

"Was she wearing any rings, or did she have any tattoos?"

I shook my head, wishing that I had some identifiers to provide. Then a color flashed in my vision. "Oh, she was wearing fun nail polish. Orange."

"Not sure that will help us."

"I know, eh? Women change their nail color more than their hair."

"*Eh*?" David laughed. "You Canadians like your *eh*."

I punched him in the shoulder. "Cut it out. You can take it or leave it." I attempted to eyeball him sternly, but my lips were twitching.

"I'll take it." He held up his cup in a toast gesture. "To finding the mystery woman and the truth behind the crash."

I touched my cup to his. "You got it."

We sipped our coffees. Normally, I'd avoid caffeine at this hour—a glance at the time told me it was almost five o'clock—because I'd be awake all night. But I had a feeling there'd be a lot of tossing and turning regardless.

"Cookie?" David held the bag toward me.

"I can't say no. Well, I could, but… Thanks." I withdrew a sugar cookie and happily bit off a chunk.

"Don't mention it." He put his gaze back on the screen and, several seconds later, said, "Okay, it looks like there were fourteen females between the ages of twenty and thirty-five on the flight. Next age would be forty-five."

My eyes landed briefly on the few age spots showing on my hands. "Yeah, I say we should look in the twenty- to thirty-five-year age range."

"All right, let's divvy them up. You work on one half; I'll work on the other half."

"Sure, but what are we looking for?"

"Orange nails." He smirked.

"Smart-ass." But it was the truth; it was the only identifiable marker I had to go by. "Thing is, if someone's going to paint their nails with that bold of a color, it might be something they typically do. Not necessarily orange, but something high-bright."

"Okay, so we'll rule out women with pastel-colored nails."

"It's a place to start."

We discussed the plan was to google the women's names and find pictures of them that also showcased their nails. The odds were in our favor as the age range we were looking at excelled at posting selfies holding a cocktail of the hour. Though it would still take some digging. We didn't have the ability to pull backgrounds like the police, so we did what we could. He probably could have asked for these reports from his colleague, but it might take longer to get them that way. Besides, those reports didn't exactly note preferred nail polish color.

As we each dug into our separate online searches, I looked over at David occasionally. It had been a while since I'd worked with someone like this. I was strapped to remember a time when Chris and I functioned as a team toward a common goal—not counting running a business together.

Every time I googled a woman's name from the list, I wondered if she would be the mystery woman I was looking for. It was strange as I had no idea what the mystery woman's face looked like, but a part of me sensed I'd just know when I saw her. Of course, little good that would do if she were in David's stack.

The next time I looked at the clock it was eight, and my stomach grumbled loudly. I clamped a hand over it.

"Someone's hungry." David raised his brows, comically bobbed them.

"What can I say?"

"You don't have to say anything. Your stomach said it all." He laughed.

I loved the sound of his laugh, the curve of his smile, the spark in his eyes. I was utterly hopeless. It was best to remind myself that we were friends the universe brought together for a purpose—to resolve my vision. But he was so easy to be around. Trish was always telling me how efficient the universe was. Maybe he and I would become more than friends.

"We could always go out, grab something to eat, blow the stink off us," he suggested.

"Are you telling me I stink?" Though we had been noses down into our work for a while, collecting everything we could on the women—cataloging photos, links to their social media, copying and pasting obits as we found them— all in the search for brightly colored nails.

"I'm smarter than that." He cracked a smile.

"Do you like Chinese food? I know of a fantastic place. If we order in, then we can keep at it."

"Ah, but taking a break is part of the appeal of going out."

"Fine," I agreed with a smile. "Just let me get freshened up a bit."

As I got ready, I told my mind to have a talk with my heart. It really needed to get a grip.

# Chapter Twenty-Two

It was going on ten by the time David and I returned to my place. Sadly, the caffeine I'd had during the day was letting me down. I should have suggested putting off the search for the mystery woman until tomorrow, but I didn't want him to leave, and with Jenna coming tomorrow night and Thanksgiving on Monday, there wouldn't be much time for looking into things.

We got settled back at my kitchen table, this time with glasses of water, and started digging into our lists again.

It wasn't until about midnight that we were finishing up. I'd already googled the last woman on my list, and defeat rolled in when seeing her picture didn't trigger any sort of reaction.

"Nothing?" he asked, and I shook my head. He'd finished up his list just moments before.

"Nope. We've spent hours working on this with nothing to show for our troubles."

"Maybe someone will spark your memory from my list, though I must say I didn't notice any brightly polished nails."

How he could remain optimistic was beyond me. "Doesn't hurt to—" A yawn ate my face without warning, and I slapped a hand over my mouth.

"I should probably go. I can send you the file I've compiled on the women, and you can look through the pictures after I leave, or tomorrow, or whenever. You never know. One of them might trigger something for you."

Again with the optimism. Exhaustion had run off with mine. But it only stood to reason that one of these women was the one we were looking for. It's not like she could have manifested out of thin air. "That works." I gave him my email address.

He clicked some keys. "You should have the file now," he said, then packed up and stood. I saw him out and was sad to see him go. It wasn't until he was out of sight that I realized we hadn't made any plans to get together again. We'd spoken of a partnership, though, so he'd probably be in touch tomorrow.

Technically, tomorrow was already here. I should have just walked myself down the hall and gone to bed, but the file he'd sent was taunting me. One peek couldn't hurt. And it wasn't like any work would be involved. I'd just be looking at pictures David had already gathered.

I clicked on David's message, opened the attachment, and started working my way through the document.

It was almost two in the morning by the time I turned off my laptop, and I was no closer to identifying the mystery woman. But what did I really expect? It had been a leap. All I had seen were her fingers and painted nails wrapped around Betty's hand.

I went through my nightly regimen and crawled into bed. It really was time to call it a night. My eyes were burning, and a headache was moving in.

Still, I wound up staring at the ceiling for another couple of hours. *Why even bother trying to sleep at this rate?*

I refused to stop trying though. I plumped my pillow and turned onto my side. My mind replayed everything that had transpired today. No progress in finding the mystery woman, but I'd received more proof that the dream about the crash had been a vision. There'd be no explaining away the fact that I'd seen the location where the black box had been found in real life. Also, the manifest showed Howard Hayes sitting right where I'd seen him. And Betty Mavis.

*Argh.*

I flipped to my other side.

And David was so handsome it was ridiculous. I should know better than to start letting my heart get carried away. But he was great to have around, not just because he made me feel alive, but also because he was on the inside at the NTSB. He had access to information I didn't.

I moved onto my back again. The ceiling still offered no solutions, and the kinks between my shoulders were worsening from all the tossing and turning and *thinking, thinking, thinking.*

I could dig more into the people I did know about—Howard Hayes and his bodyguards. I never did get those three men's names, come to think of it. Regardless, there had to be something about them I needed to uncover, or else why did they keep coming into my awareness? Then again, the plane going down might not have had anything to do with Howard Hayes at all, and I'd be wedged in a rabbit hole with no escape. *Gah*, it was so frustrating, but there was a deepening sense of responsibility to find out the reason for the crash. If not just for Betty's loved ones, for everyone who'd lost someone in that crash.

Tears fell in compassion for what they were going through, but I'm quite sure my own grief was mingled in there as well.

I could still conjure the sound of Mom's laugh, the twinkle in her eyes and how the skin around them would crinkle with the expression. She was the happiest person I knew. Open and accepting of everyone. I only hoped I'd turned out half as amazing as Mom.

And Dad had been a terrific father. The best. When other kids' dads were busy building their careers, Dad had put me and Jay first. We were his pride and joy. Not to say he wasn't a hard worker, but his family was his priority. Second to us was the community he served.

I sat up and let out all the bottled-up grief in a good, solid cry. I replayed family outings to the zoo. How Dad hated all the walking in the heat, and Mom couldn't get enough of the animals and the sun. Adventures at the theme park. Dad loved the roller coasters, but Mom was terrified. She'd scream—I'd swear, at the time as a young girl, just to embarrass me—on kiddie rides.

Yeah, life had been good. I smiled at the memories while pain rooted in my chest. I wished the hurt would just go away, but their loss was a dull ache that I carried around with me and probably always would. A shadow that lurked, ready to jump up at any time, like now. Maybe what stung the most was, despite all the things I could remember, even some fine points such as Mom's laugh, I could no longer see their faces with any clarity. They were like a blur, like an out-of-focus apparition. It could just be greedy of me, but I wished I could see them as distinctly as I did the strangers in my visions.

# Chapter Twenty-Three

The next morning I slept in until eleven, despite Harvey's protests for food and the sun seeping into my room. Jenna was coming today, but thanks to the thorough cleaning I'd given the place yesterday, I only had to take care of making Jenna's bed and picking up some groceries.

I let myself into her bedroom, the one she did most of her growing up in. I let it remain her space, even though she lived with the Bs. A woman always needed a place to retreat, and I was determined that Jenna would have that here at her true home.

I picked up Precious—Jenna's coveted teddy bear that was sitting sentinel in a chair in the corner—and dropped onto the edge of the bed. Jenna had loved the bear immediately and said it was "precious," which ended up sticking as its name. It felt like it was only yesterday when I'd bought it for her. Time sure had a way of flying by. Then there were moments when the clock seemed to stand still, like when Jason and I were told Mom and Dad were dead.

I stroked its ears, and a rush of emotions flooded in—gratitude, joy, sadness, grief. Things changed; they always did. And sometimes they came fast and were completely unexpected. Outside of our control.

I pulled out fresh sheets and a comforter and made up her bed. I looked at my work before leaving her room and smiled. It was going to be so nice having her here. My little girl back under my roof.

A second coffee was screaming for me, and I padded toward the kitchen. On the way, I passed the table where I'd left my laptop last night. I ran my fingers over the lid, tempted to sit and look once again at the pictures that David and I had culled from the internet. But to what end? Did I expect to spot something I hadn't last night?

What I really needed was to see the woman's face in a vision, not just her hand and fingernails. It would at least make finding her identity that much easier.

*My heart aches for her. She has everything to lose. I have nothing.* A snippet of thought from my dream yesterday morning. *I have nothing*, the thought repeated.

What did that really mean? Was it that the mystery woman really had nothing or *felt* she had nothing? Sure, Betty was an older woman with many people who loved her and would miss her—a husband, a daughter, a granddaughter. Did that mean my mystery woman didn't have any of that? Should I reexamine all the women for those who were single and without children?

I proceeded to brew a coffee and, once it was ready, stared at it as if it had answers to dispense. Of course…nada. I could press on with looking into this woman or let her go for the next couple of days. Really what would forty-eight hours hurt? After all, it was the holiday weekend, and Jenna was coming home. I could hardly wait to see her.

But setting aside the investigation made me feel like I was letting the victims' friends and families down. I was blessed to have loved ones to celebrate Thanksgiving with, but those people would be down a place setting or more.

My phone beeped with a text. It was Jenna saying she'd be late arriving tonight.

"*What time are you thinking?*" I texted, keeping things low-key and non-smothering, though I desperately wanted to grill her for an explanation.

"*630.*"

Punctuation always got dropped for the sake of ease in texts. I messaged back, "*OK,*" even though I wasn't really *OK*.

I was disappointed, but if I pushed her, she'd push back. One reason we were probably so close was because I respected her space.

I dropped into a kitchen chair and fired up my laptop, planning to reexamine the fourteen women we'd looked at yesterday for those who were unattached without children. An easier quest might be to find out the names of the men with Howard Hayes. My vision had shown me where they were seated on the plane, but the was one hitch with that plan. I'd need the manifest for their identities, and I didn't have it. That was something David had taken with him. And yesterday I'd been so thrown by the mystery woman, I'd never asked about Hayes's companions. Today, David was likely with his mother, gearing up to celebrate the holiday with her, and I'd already monopolized enough of his time.

There was someone I needed to talk to, though, and in-person would be better than on the phone. I called Trish and told her I was coming over.

An hour later, I was knocking on her condo door, armed with chai teas from Tim Hortons.

"What's your big news? You and Mr. Hot NTSB Guy getting it on?" Trish chortled as we headed to her feng-shui living room.

I took a seat on her cream-colored sofa and crossed my legs. "Well, we did spend most of yesterday together."

"Ooh—" Trish leaned forward on the facing chair she was sitting in "—do tell."

"Well, don't get too excited. It's not what you think. I can guarantee you that." I took a sip of tea.

"That's disappointing, but I'm still sensing you had a good day." She turned her head and looked at me out of the corner of her eye.

I grinned. "He's going to help me…you know, look into the crash."

"Really? Ah, so the psychic thing didn't scare him after all?" She waggled a finger at me. "I told you. The universe provides."

"I'm not even going to bother arguing. I had another vision of the crash yesterday morning. It came to me like a dream, as it had the first time around." I told her about finding Betty Mavis and her family.

"How sad."

"Yeah, and she's only one story. I mean, everyone on that plane left someone behind." Except for maybe the mystery woman. But how could she have absolutely no one? "I really want to bring the victims' loved ones closure. I must."

"I'm sure you will." Trish accepted most things on faith. I viewed it as both a weakness and strength. "So spill. Tell me how you roped in Mr. Hot NTSB Guy's help."

I quirked an eyebrow. "David. Let's just use his name."

"Okay, if we must." She chuckled.

I then told her pretty much everything, leaving out the lead investigator's suspicions about the crash being caused on purpose. I also wasn't supposed to share whatever we discovered, but this was Trish. There had to be an exception that applied, just as it did when you told a married friend something. Even if sworn to secrecy, it was a foregone conclusion that they'd tell their spouse. "We uncovered things that only verified my visions about the black box… and other things." I was temporarily hit with guilt.

Trish's mouth gaped open. "Wow."

I laughed. "You say that like you're almost shocked, afraid even. Yet you've been the one telling me what a gift this is."

"It is…it is." She batted a hand in the air. "It's just really starting to hit me as surreal."

"That's hitting you just now?"

Trish's eyes beaded with tears, and she perched on the edge of her cushion. "You said you verified your visions about 'other things' too. Spill. What are they?"

I considered again the promise I'd made to David to keep our sleuthing between ourselves, but again, this was Trish. That felt like justification enough. Besides, she wasn't going to tell anyone else. "What I'm about to tell you is completely between us. Understand?"

"Absolutely."

"Okay. David got ahold of the manifest, and he let me see it."

"He let you— Whoa." Trish kicked her back into the couch. "And?"

"And Betty Mavis was assigned the same seat in real life that she was in my vision. Howard Hayes was assigned the same seat in real life too. All that, and the black box. No doubts in my mind now. For better or worse, I need to keep digging and find out why I was given the vision about the crash and whatever it is I'm supposed to uncover or expose."

"And what about the woman whose point of view you're in? The one next to the older lady, Betty Mavis."

I shook my head slowly. "David and I looked into women between ages twenty and thirty-five from the manifest and came up empty—not that I had a lot for us to go on. Just some bright-orange nail polish."

"But you know where she was sitting. Can't you just see who was assigned the seat?"

"The seat wasn't assigned to anyone. That's why we worked through all the women aged twenty to thirty-five."

Trish remained silent, holding my gaze. "Huh."

"Yeah, that's what I thought."

"I'm sure she'll turn up," Trish said. "Just go with the flow, and don't force anything. Whatever comes to mind to investigate, do it."

I nodded. I'd read enough nonfiction books on the power of intuition and the law of attraction to know I was to ease into life, follow inspired action, and not force things. The principle sounded simple in theory but was much harder in execution.

"What are you going to look into next?" she asked.

"*Who*. The men who were with Howard Hayes." As I'd thought about earlier, surely this would be an easier thing to pursue than the woman at this point. We had, after all, scoured through pictures to look at every woman's nails in the likely age range of the one in my vision.

Trish nodded rapidly. "Terrific idea."

"The way I see it, I was shown certain people on the flight for a reason."

"Can't disagree. Have confidence you have everything you need at this stage of the riddle too."

*The riddle. Such an apt description of the visions.* It was like before when Trish had brought up the spiritual realm talking in ways that needed time and experience to understand.

Trish's face pinched in thought, and her eyes widened. Her finger shot up. "There is something you might want to try. Actually, you know what…" She winced.

"Talk to me." If she feared freaking me out and enlightening me to some tactic outside of my comfort zone…well, she was too late for that. That ship had already sailed and was in the middle of the ocean. I was living well outside my freaking comfort zone, and so far, it wasn't that bad out here.

"Are you familiar with lucid dreaming?"

"I've heard of it." I didn't want to admit the thought of having one terrified me, and I didn't really know much about them. They say we fear what we don't know though. "It's basically being aware while dreaming right?"

"There's more to it than that." Trish shifted on the couch. "Lucid dreaming, while it allows you to be aware in the dream state, lets you communicate with your subconscious, also to your deeper, higher self."

Trish had talked to me many times about Higher Self, Higher Knowing, Deeper Self, Source Energy—all labels she used to quantify infinite divinity and universal knowledge—but I still wasn't sure how lucid dreaming would help my situation. Then again, understanding what it actually was might prove useful.

Trish continued. "Within a lucid dream, you think, make decisions, decide what to do. You meet different aspects of yourself, which often present themselves as characters."

"I don't know how this applies to my situation."

"If nothing more, the practice of lucid dreaming would help get you out of your head." She held up a hand. "The conscious side. It'll let you tap into Source Energy. When you release the ego—the conscious part of your mind, essentially—you are more receptive to hearing intuitive messages. Both from within and without, though really one and the same."

Trish made it clear to me before she believed we were all *one*, not separate entities, but one spiritual awareness having multiple experiences. That thinking was too hard for me to wrap my head around. "Okay, you're getting a little deep for me."

"Just something to consider." Trish smiled.

Just like her to drop a spiritual thought like a bomb and leave me to assemble the pieces in the aftermath.

She added, "Remember, no need to rush into everything, but if you can slip into a lucid dream, you might be able to dig deeper into this vision of the crash. Maybe request to see the mystery woman's face or even get her name. Maybe uncover the reason for the crash."

Trish made it sound so easy. "I'll give it some thought, but right now, I've got to go. Jenna's coming home tonight, and I need to pick up groceries for chicken parmesan."

"Oh, I wish I was invited."

"You can come for dinner if you want."

Trish shook her head. "I'd love to, but I have plans."

"Sounds mysterious."

"Someday I'll tell you all about it."

As close as Trish and I were, there was one aspect of her life she kept from me—she never let me peek into her love life. I'd always found it strange but respected her privacy. My guess was she had some hot date lined up, or she was secretly married… *Nah.*

We hugged goodbye and wished each other a Happy Thanksgiving.

As I made my way home, my steps were strangely light for being tasked with such a potentially monumental thing from the universe.

# Chapter Twenty-Four

Visions. Lucid dreaming. My world had certainly flipped on its head. It was certainly a long way from the safe, comfortable, narrow path I'd walked most of my life. Still, I found myself propelled by curiosity, and this took me to a bookstore.

A clerk greeted me as I entered the front doors. "I'm Amy. Can I help you find anything today?" She was in her thirties and dressed conservatively, professionally. Her hair was pulled back into a neat ponytail.

"Um, I'm looking for…" My heart pounded as if the type of book I wanted was the Devil's work or covered a topic I should be embarrassed to say out loud. But what would this clerk care? "Do you have any books on lucid dreaming?" My heart sped up even more as I put my request into words.

"Lucid dreaming? Absolutely. This way." Amy led me to the New Age Spirituality section, and I shrunk a bit imagining how Aunt Judy would react to my being here, in this particular aisle. Though maybe I was crazy to still be concerned about her opinion at my age.

"You should find what you're looking for in this area." Amy swept her hand to indicate a shelving unit full of books.

"All these are on lucid dreaming?" I gulped, thinking there was a lot more to learn than I could pick up in a CliffsNotes.

"These are." She narrowed her gesturing to two shelves.

I breathed easier. That was a little better.

"Are you new to lucid dreaming?" she asked.

"Oh, I've never had one. I— Yes, I am."

Amy smiled politely. "So, you're just wanting to find out about it?"

"That's right."

"Then I'd start with this one." She hooked the spine of a book and extended it to me. It fell out of her hands in the process, but I caught it.

*Lucid Dreaming Made Easy: A Beginner's Guide to Waking Up in Your Dreams.* Trish told me the universe would give me the tools I needed, and here this book had landed right in my hands.

"Thank you," I told the clerk.

"Don't mention it. Is there anything else I can help you with today?"

"No, that's all." I shook my head and offered a pleasant smile.

"All right. Well, if you change your mind, you know where to find me. Have a great day." Amy grinned and headed to her post by the front door.

I cracked the cover and skimmed the table of contents. I had expected some of the titles to make me uncomfortable, but none of them did. After having visions, maybe I was becoming desensitized to this stuff.

"Erin? Is that you?"

*Aunt Judy!* I hugged the book to my chest and turned, flashed her the largest smile possible. She was standing at the end of the aisle, as if the section had an invisible force field that wouldn't permit her entry. I hustled over to her. "What are you doing here?"

"I'm looking for a new cookbook. You know how I like to try new recipes from time to time. What is that you have there?" Aunt Judy pointed to the book I held.

"Oh, it's nothing. Just something Trish asked me to pick up for her." *Next liar take the stand!* I felt horrible for lying to her about this, but it was for the best—for both of us.

"I see." She pursed her lips as her gaze took in the labels on the shelving. "Well, I better get moving on home. Looking forward to tomorrow." She leaned in and kissed my cheek.

"Me too." I remained standing there for a few minutes. I was a rotten person lying to that sweet lady, and after she'd raised me and cared for me. Although … she *had* accepted Jenna's atheism. She might find some room in her heart not to banish me from her life if she found out I was psychic. I tried to talk myself back from that ledge, but I couldn't stop seeing the way she'd pursed her lips just before she left. There'd be no way she'd be accepting of my gift. But I was an adult. I bought the book and headed to the grocery store.

The lot was packed, but inside it was worse, which I should have expected the day before a holiday. People always seemed to panic and stock up like the end of the world was coming when stores were scheduled to close for a day.

I grabbed everything I needed, and a package of cheese strings for Jenna—a snack from her childhood she still enjoyed—and managed to do so without getting into any altercations. A miracle. Usually there was at least one snippy person along the way that had me pulling on my self-control.

"That will be seventy-five ten," the cashier told the customer at the front of the line, and I got my first good look at the man.

"David?" I said, and he turned around.

He smiled and dipped his head, and it was like time stood still, as cheesy as that sounded.

He settled his bill and waited for me to be rung up. I grabbed my bags, and we headed for the door.

"Fancy meeting you here," he said.

"I don't know. You stalking me?" I teased.

"Well, you were behind me, so if anyone's stalking anyone…" He paused to smile. "Just here for a few last-minute items, not that Mom or I are that into"—he leaned closer to me—"Thanksgiving. I'm still going to make her a nice meal."

I chuckled. "You talk all hush-hush, like you can't admit that out loud."

"In the States, to say you're not into Thanksgiving *is* a big no-no. The holiday's a bigger deal than Christmas."

"For that I'm sorry."

"You love the fat man in the suit?"

"Oh, yeah, he turns me on." I tried to keep a straight face but failed miserably and blurted out a laugh.

We stepped outside and stood there.

"Your family big into Thanksgiving?" he asked.

"They are. Christmas too. Any reason for my aunt Judy to have her family under one roof is a big deal for her. She loves cooking for us."

"She sounds like a wonderful woman."

"She is." A weight of guilt crushed me. Her face in the bookstore, her pursed lips.

"I love to cook myself. What about you?" he asked.

The vision thing didn't have him running, but my next confession might. They say the way to a man's heart is through his stomach—possibly an antiquated viewpoint, but I believed it was still valid. "Cooking isn't my favorite thing in the world. Honestly? I only cook as a means of survival." I bit back the urge to add, *and it's only me, so I don't fuss.*

He laughed. "I know a lot of people like that, but I'd love to make dinner for you sometime."

My heart fluttered, and I imagined myself caught up in one of those Hallmark movies—as if we were destined to be together from our first meeting. Where the analogy missed the mark was David wasn't a *boyfriend* from my past—though, technically, he was from my past. He had investigated my parents' crash… I cleared my throat. "That would be nice."

A woman with a stacked-up cart was coming toward us at the speed of a freight train.

David tugged my jacket and pulled me out of her path.

"Jeez. Thanks. Some people." I glared at her back; she would have hit me if it hadn't been for David.

We started walking, and he accompanied me to my car. It was like he didn't want to part ways any more than I did.

"How did you make out with my half of the list?" he asked. "Did any of those women ring a bell? Though I'm sure if you had any sort of revelation, you would have called to share the news."

"No luck." I considered telling him my thoughts about the mystery woman being unattached, without kids. But all I knew about her from the vision was she had bright nails—not exactly a lot to go on. Going after her identity with just that—again—really felt like a time-wasting endeavor.

"Oh, that's too bad."

"It's okay. I'll find out who she was eventually. When I'm supposed to." *Now I'm sounding like Trish.*

"Let me know if there's anything more I can do… Or if you have any more visions you want help sorting through." There was something in his expression that told me he was hoping I needed him for something.

I considered asking if he would look at the manifest and send me the names of Hayes's companions. After all, he seemed to be stressing that he was eager to help. "There is something…"

"What is it?" He leaned in, and I got a good whiff of his cologne this time. I inhaled deeply and tried not to shut my eyes.

"Ah…I'd like to take a look at the manifest again, if I could." I didn't know why it came out that way, as he could easily do the looking and simply let me know the names. We didn't need to be together for this to happen.

"I can't send you the file. I'm sure you understand."

"Oh, one hundred percent. I should have asked if you could take a look and let me know some names."

"Or I could drop by?"

Just when I thought he hadn't picked up on my enclosed invitation to join me… "Jenna's coming tonight." *Now I was making excuses to back out?*

"Right."

"You should likely get home to your mom anyway," I said. "She's probably waiting on you."

"I probably should." He shifted his bags around in his arms, and it reminded me of the ones I was holding. I popped my trunk and set them inside.

"Tell you what," he began. "I'll drop off the groceries, grab my laptop, and head over."

Apparently, the news of Jenna's arrival wasn't a deterrent. I pulled out my phone and looked at the time. *3:45 PM.* Jenna wasn't going to be to the townhouse until six thirty. "If we make it quick."

"You got it."

David and I stood there facing each other for a few seconds longer, and the magnetic pull to kiss him was tangible. I could only assume that he felt the same way. One thing was fact: he could have easily texted me the names or called with them, but he'd used it as an excuse to spend more time with me. I smiled the entire way home.

# Chapter Twenty-Five

The doorbell rang, and David was standing there with two coffees from Tim Hortons. It felt like a case of déjà vu. Either that or I was stuck in the movie *Groundhog Day*.

I smiled at him. "As long as you keep bringing Timmys, the door's always open."

"Good to know." He handed me the cups while he sloughed off his shoes and hung his coat.

"No cookies this time?" I pouted, though my hips would be happy.

"I can't become predictable."

"Good reply. At least you didn't counter with something about us consuming plenty of calories otherwise this weekend."

"Give me some credit. I'm far too smart to say anything like that."

We went to the kitchen table and settled in. He pulled out his laptop and turned it on. "I can let you write down the names you're interested in, but just like everything we've done so far, it doesn't go further than this room."

"I understand." A spike of guilt at telling Trish what I had ran through me.

"Good." He peered into my eyes, and I feared he'd be able to ferret out my deception. "So, who is it you're looking for?" He brought up an image of the seating chart.

I moved in to get a better view of the screen, and I found myself sniffing his cologne again. Heady in a good way.

He turned to face me, our noses less than an inch apart. His eyes drifted to my lips, mine to his. I cleared my throat and pulled back just a bit, smiling awkwardly. He was too.

"Um, here, here, and here." I pointed out the seats where Hayes's companions had been seated in my vision.

"All right. Vincent Holloway, Mack Gibson, and Shane Fox."

I scribbled their names down on a piece of paper.

He took a sip of his coffee. "What are you going to do now that you have their names?"

"Keep them to myself." I laughed.

He pointed a finger at me and smiled. "Very good."

"Honestly? I don't know. I'm thinking I should probably look deeper into everyone I saw in my vision about the crash. Maybe by doing so, I'll uncover something of actual importance."

"I could ask Bill what backgrounds he's pulled so far. Not sure when he'd get back to me though."

"You could…" I smiled at him, finding it interesting he went straight there today and hadn't yesterday. "Was thinking we could have done that with the women, but most photos attached to backgrounds don't show fingernails."

"No, they don't, and then I'd have lost all that time hanging out with you."

David sure knew how to make me all warm and gushy. "True."

He smiled. "Good old social-media digging work for you?"

"The fact so many people put their entire lives out there for everyone to see certainly helps."

"The way you put that, I take it you're not huge on social media."

"Not even big. Days usually pass before I log on. Honestly, I could probably live without it just fine."

We sipped our coffees, and our eyes met.

"Jenna's coming home, right? What time?"

"Six thirty." I glanced at the clock, and it was five. "You should probably get back to your mother."

"I'm actually fine to stay longer. I dropped off the groceries and grabbed my laptop. I can be gone before Jenna gets here."

"Okay. Sounds good." It was more than okay though; it was wonderful. And it had been so considerate of him to consider when Jenna would be arriving.

"I mean, if you want me to stay."

"Sure." No sense going over the top and swelling his head. I felt my cheeks heat as my thoughts carried me off somewhere perverse.

"So what do you think we'll find out about them?" he asked, breaking through what was becoming a daisy-chain of X-rated fantasies.

I pressed my lips and shook my head. "That's the thing. I have no idea. I'm just following my gut here."

"Well, I'm a believer in following one's gut, so let's get started, shall we? How about you start with Vincent Holloway, and I'll work on Mack Gibson? When we've gathered all we can on them, we'll move on to Shane Fox."

"Works for me." I brought up the internet on my laptop and typed *Vincent Holloway*.

David looked over at me, and I took my eyes from my screen as the search results were loading.

"I just thought of something," he started. "How will I know I'm looking at the right Mack Gibson?"

"Google him, and I'll point out the right picture, assuming it comes up." I scooched my chair over, closer to his.

"All right…" He keyed in Gibson's full name and started scrolling the image results.

No one looked familiar until— "That's him." I pointed at the photo of a middle-aged man with dark skin. He was wearing a sour-faced expression and muscles were visible under the sleeves of his white, collared shirt.

David faced me. "Guy looks intense."

"He was in my vision too. Pretty much just like that."

"Pretty much?"

"Same looks, just he and the other men were dressed all in black—dress shirt and pants."

David nodded and got to work on his intel gathering.

I didn't bother moving my chair back to where it had been. It was rather comfortable this close to David a.k.a., Mr. Hot NTSB Guy. I pulled my laptop over and looked at what came back on Vincent Holloway. I found him quickly, recognizing him from my vision. Dark-skinned and above-average looking. In this particular photo, he was wearing aviator sunglasses and a scooped-neck shirt. He had an intimidating quality to him, just as he had in my vision. I set aside gathering information on him for now, opened another tab, and googled *Shane Fox*.

David looked over. "Thought we were hitting him up after we finished with Mack and Vincent."

"That was the plan…" I was becoming addicted to seeing the real-life faces of those I'd only previously seen in my vision. I scrolled through images of Shane Foxes, but none of them were familiar. "Huh."

"What is it?"

"I'm not finding anything on Shane Fox. At least no one who looks like the man I saw." A thought crept in. People didn't keep a low profile unless it was for a reason. Shane from my vision had a fair complexion, large brown eyes, and a beak-like nose. He also didn't look older than thirty. Millennials were usually always tweeting or Instagramming or whatever social media app was hip at the moment. If Shane wasn't searchable, it had to be because he didn't want to be found. *So what did Shane have to hide?* Sure, he could have made a choice to stay off the grid; some people did that. It didn't mean he'd been behind the crash, and if he had been, was he some sort of martyr? If so, for what cause? Was he, by chance, connected to the Fighters for Future America group?

"Not finding him is troubling you," David said, cutting through my thoughts.

I faced him. "How do you know that?" I was curious if I'd mumbled something out loud.

"It's written all over your expression."

This man was an angel *and* a touch psychic himself. "I am a little stumped." I considered telling him my suspicion about a connection to Fighters for Future America but decided against it. I had brought them up before, and David had wanted more information before pursuing them. Besides, Howard Hayes and his company had a lot of enemies, more than just the group who snatched the accusation and headline for the downed flight. I'd agreed with David to run any steps I took past him, but in this case, I'd rather poke around a bit before roping him into it. There was something he could do though. "You could voice an interest in this Shane Fox guy to your colleague…?"

"To what end?"

"He could already have a background pulled on the guy, or he can get one pulled. We'll wait on this one."

Little lines formed in his brow. "I'm not sure what I'd give him as a reason for my sudden interest in this particular person."

"Maybe just be up-front?"

"That I'm working with a psychic? Yeah, I don't see that going over well. He's more about science and hard proof."

"Right… Oh, I got it." I shifted my body more toward him. "Why not point out the speculation in the news, that the plane was targeted because of Howard Hayes? Tell him you noticed that Shane Fox was seated next to him, and it wouldn't hurt to get more information on him." My heart was tapping furiously as I edged toward my suspicions about Fox's involvement with a group set against the oil company.

David nodded slowly. "Okay, that I believe he'd buy."

"He might even be looking into the man already. You never know," I added nonchalantly, feeling a twinge of guilt for pulling David's strings as if he were my puppet.

"Who knows if he's gotten that far yet. If he hasn't, he will. Bill is very thorough, and we typically examine the black box, the backgrounds of the pilot and copilot, flight crew, passengers—to rule out terrorism and martyrdom—and anyone who touched the plane, such as maintenance crew."

"Sure. And you did tell me his hunch was the plane might have been brought down. Howard Hayes would make a solid target. Play on Bill's leanings."

"I could give that a go."

"The news headlines should help the cause. While you're at it, ask him what he got off the black box. Does what he heard on the box align with his suspicions about the crash being intentional? Or did the recordings tell him something else? If the latter, what?"

A pocket of silence amplified the sound of a key going into the deadbolt of the front door.

"Jenna," I blurted out and looked at the clock. *6:35 PM. Where did the time go?* David shouldn't be here, and I certainly didn't want her to know why he was.

"Oh, your daughter." David didn't move.

"You should probably go." I slapped the lid shut on his laptop. "Sorry, but she has no idea about—" I rolled my hand, testing his mind-reading ability, quite sure he'd pick up that I was referring to the visions and our rogue investigation.

"Mom," Jenna called out and walked into the kitchen. She dropped a stuffed duffle bag on the floor. Her dark hair spilled over her shoulders in the natural waves she'd inherited from my mom. I'd always been blond. Chris was too.

"Hey, sweetheart." I hugged her, wishing David were somehow invisible.

Jenna barely let my arms go around her when she pulled back, grinning and staring at David. Her brown eyes were tracing him from head to toe. "And who are you?" Spoken as if she were fascinated. She probably thought she was seeing a unicorn, given that her mother hadn't entertained a man for so long.

"David Bomber." He came over, extended a hand, which Jenna shook. "Nice to meet you. I'm a friend of your mother's."

"I'm sure you are." Her eyes darted to mine, and she had this mischievous smirk on her face.

"He works for the NTSB," I said, crossing my arms and dropping them the instant I realized how defensive it would look. I was a grown woman; I could have a man over any time I pleased. "He investigated your grandparents' crash."

"Uh-huh." Jenna's response was more than acknowledgment; it contained obvious speculation about the true reason David was in her mother's kitchen. "Did you meet Friday night at the memorial?"

"We did." Two words that I hoped would squash her need to push for more information.

"Very nice." Jenna dragged out the C in *nice* and was grinning like a baboon. When you think of your teenage daughter meeting your male friend, you expect some pushback. The fact there wasn't any made me curious.

David shoved his laptop into his bag. "Well, I should probably get going."

"I think you should stay." Jenna tilted her head, still smiling.

I wrapped an arm around her. "He needs to get back to his mother."

Jenna laughed. "He's a little old to worry about that. No offense."

"None taken," David said. "I don't think…"

"Really, you should stay. Mom's going to make a yummy dinner. Aren't you, Mom?" Jenna was flashing her puppy-dog eyes that I'd always found hard to refuse. "You're making my favorite tonight, aren't you? Chicken parm? You told me you would."

"I have all the ingredients."

"Great, it's settled. You'll stay, David. Mom makes the best chicken parm." Jenna collected her bag from the floor, touched my arm, and brushed past, heading in the direction of her room. "Hey, Harvey, hey." She talked to the cat on her way, and he sauntered along next to her.

David had a big grin on his face. "She's great."

"Don't feel like you have to stay. I know you didn't tell your mother when to expect you, but I'm sure she'd love to spend more time with you."

"I'd like to stay, actually, if you don't mind."

The Devil glinted in his eyes, and in this case, the Devil was damn attractive and hard to resist. "Fine, but not a word about…" I rolled my hand again.

"Lips are sealed." He locked his lips and threw away the key.

"Thank you."

"Of course. So, what can I do to help?"

"How about you clear off the table? I'll open a bottle of wine. You like red?"

"You're one of those people who drink while they cook?"

"You bet. How do you think I make it through?" I smiled at him, but the expression faded as my thoughts went to my daughter in the other room. It might be a challenge to keep the nature of my relationship with David from Jenna. She had an inquisitive mind—something I usually admired— but tonight, I hoped she wouldn't use it against me.

My fears were unnecessary. Through the making of dinner and the eating of the meal, my daughter was nothing but gracious and polite. She didn't grill David, just accepted his presence. Conversation among the three of us came effortlessly. I even found myself daydreaming about what life would be like if David and I were more than partners for a cause. But let's face it; tonight wasn't the first time I'd thought of that. He made it easy to get carried away with wild imaginings of him swooping me off to bed. And I was sure it would be incredible. But I had to be an adult. Forty-three, eyes wide open. A relationship between us wouldn't work. For one, he didn't live in this country, and two, I hardly knew him. *Suppose the latter one could be remedied…*

"That was amazing chicken parmesan," David said as he set down his fork and knife.

"I told you." Jenna grinned at him and took a sip of water, her eyes shimmering. She was blowing my friendship with David into something it wasn't—and here I thought I was doing that enough for both of us.

David had an after-dinner cup of tea with us, then stood from the table. "Ladies, I should probably get going."

It was nine-oh-five. Again, where did the time go? Though, they do say time flies when you're having fun.

"Nice meeting you, David," Jenna said in a singsong voice, for which I shot her a reprimanding look, then proceeded to see David to the door.

He put on his shoes, grabbed his coat from the closet, then slung his satchel over a shoulder. "Thank you for a lovely dinner."

"I'm glad you enjoyed it."

"Your daughter's an amazing girl…well, *woman*," he corrected with a smile.

"I think so too."

"Now, we might have told her we were friends, but I'd like to be much more." His gaze dipped to my lips, and he stepped closer to me. I held my breath, silently panicking.

Before I had a chance to move, his mouth was on mine, his probing tongue parting my lips. I sank into the moment, all rational thought evaporated. When he pulled back, I leaned forward, wanting to continue.

He gingerly brushed my cheek with the back of one of his fingers. "I'll call you tomorrow."

I put my hand over his and nodded, unable to talk. His kiss had made me speechless.

He got the door for himself, but I held it open and stood there until he was in his car. The chilly air blustered around me, but I was toasty warm.

# Chapter Twenty-Six

"I'd really like to know what happened here last night." Jenna was all grins for seven o'clock in the morning on a holiday Monday. It might have to do with her being on her second cup of coffee, but she was still up early, considering she could have slept in.

We were parked on the couch, talking and catching up—David apparently the favored topic of conversation.

"I told you. Nothing." After our kiss, I'd gone upstairs to face Jenna, who was all hands on hips, tilted head, and an avalanche of questions. I'd managed to fend her off, and she eventually gave up and went to bed. This morning I had a feeling I'd have to try harder to ward off her interrogation.

"I'm not buying that you're just *friends.*" She added finger quotes to the last word.

"We are friends." I stiffened, hoping I was convincing her. I wasn't fooling my own heart that was already starting to fall for the man. Ridiculous! Women in their forties didn't suddenly find love like it was a prize in a Cracker Jack box. I certainly didn't believe I had or ever would. But should that stop me from having some fun?

"Yeah, I'm not buying that. He's into you. And whether you want to admit it or not, you're into him. He's old, but he's cute, so I can't blame you."

"He's not old."

"He is to me." Jenna laughed.

"I probably am too."

"He's super nice and so easy to be around." A complete swerve to avoid responding to what I'd said. "But of course you know that he's cute and into you and—"

"Would you just cut it out?" I glanced over at Harvey who was sleeping all curled up across the room on a sofa chair, his tail flicking as his mind paraded in dreamland.

"Nope, no way. I want to hear all you haven't told me." She eyed me over her coffee cup.

"There's nothing to tell." I shifted on the couch, feeling uncomfortable. There was so much to tell.

"Ah." Jenna pointed a finger at me. "If there wasn't, you'd say, 'You know all there is to know,' but you're not saying that, so…"

*Someone should become a detective.*

"Come on, Mom," she prompted.

"It's none of your business."

She grinned. "Yep, you're seeing him."

"Did you hear the part where we just met and are *friends*?"

"Did you hear that I'm not buying it? I can see that you—"

"I'm in the habit of lying to you?"

"You did tell me Santa Claus was real."

"When you were a kid. You need to let things go."

Jenna crossed her arms, her lips curled down in a full-on pout.

"Enough," I said, laughing. "You want to talk about men, let's talk about your dating life." I fully expected to be shot down, but instead she smiled coyly.

"I am seeing someone." She pulled her legs up under her. "I have been for a while."

"You…you have been?" I was stuttering. Maybe this was why she was accepting of David; Jenna was in love. "Okay, tell me about him." Laidback, completely cool, hip mom.

"I'm almost twenty. You can't be surprised that I have a boyfriend."

"It's not that, but… You've been together for a while?" I looped back to her earlier statement, feeling like I'd been kept in the dark.

"Why are you reacting like this?"

"Just a little surprised. I don't remember you mentioning anyone before now." I was a tad stung that I was just hearing about this relationship.

"I wanted to make sure he and I were on the same page first."

My daughter had always been practical. "It must be serious since you're telling me now." I wanted her to be happy, but she was so young. I was twenty-one when I'd married Chris, and there were times, reflecting back, I wished I'd waited.

"I guess." A hitch of her shoulder. "Not sure. You know how important my studies are to me, and they'll always come first."

I didn't have the heart to point out that could easily change if she wasn't careful and let her heart get swept away ahead of her brain. "What's his name?"

"Ryan Holt. You'd like him. He's down-to-earth, and he treats me good."

"He better."

She laughed.

"When do I get to meet him?"

Jenna set down her coffee cup. "I was actually hoping that he could come to Thanksgiving dinner today."

"You want to introduce him to your entire family—in one shot? You said this wasn't serious. It's sounding serious." I might have been rambling, but I was in shock.

"Dad's not going to be there." A simmering heat coated her words.

"You know what I meant," I said, choosing to disregard her potshot. "Isn't it moving too fast, just throwing him into the ring like that?"

"Not really, but I'm starting to think dinner might not be a good idea."

"What's that supposed to mean?" It was how she'd said it more than *what* she'd said.

"You don't have to meet him if you don't want to." Absolute anguish knotted my daughter's face, and I was responsible.

"Of course, I'd love to meet him."

"Okay, then."

"So, your dad hasn't met him yet?" I suspected I knew the answer, given the way she'd phrased things earlier, but asked anyway. I hoped I was right. It was one thing to find out she'd had a serious boyfriend for a while, and another if Chris had known before me. That would feel like a betrayal.

Jenna shook her head, and she avoided eye contact for a few seconds. "I was actually going to ask if you would be all right with me stepping out today, going to Dad's, making the intro, and…"

She kept talking and I listened, but jealousy was making cavernous inroads. Chris might not have found out about Ryan before me, but he'd be the first to meet him. On the upside, I'd have Ryan for Thanksgiving dinner. Still, I'd pay to see Chris's reaction to his baby girl having a man in her life. He could be more protective of Jenna than Jason was of me. And thinking of Jason, Jenna was in for a razzing tonight.

"So…would you be all right with that?" She raised her brows and widened her eyes.

*Wait, what did I miss?*

"Why are you blanking on me, Mom? I'm going to Dad's but will be back for dinner."

I blinked her into focus. "You're going to London right now?"

"Yeah, that's what I just said. It's why I'm up so early."

Here I thought it was to spend more time with me. "It's a couple of hours each way." I was grasping. Today was supposed to be my day with her.

"Right. That's why I'd be leaving now. That is okay with you?"

*Not by a long stretch!* Then again, maybe I was being a wee bit possessive and insensitive to her needs and wishes. "Yeah, honey, I'm sure that will be fine."

"You don't know what this means to me." She shot to her feet, came up behind me, swept my hair back, and kissed my forehead. "You're going to love him, Mom, and don't worry…I'll be at Aunt Judy's in time. Four, right?"

"Three, and don't be late."

"We'll be there."

I nodded absentmindedly. "Okay. Well, have fun." It was hard to make that line sound sincere. I'd really been looking forward to spending time alone with Jenna. "Oh, be sure to ask Aunt Judy if she's good with you bringing someone else."

"I will." She marched along the back of the couch and headed to her room. The next second, she took a dive to the floor.

"Honey!" I sprang to my feet and found her sprawled on the hardwood. My purse was on its side, my wallet halfway out, the book on lucid dreaming right next to Jenna.

"Ouch. What did I trip on?" She picked up the book, beating me to it. "*Lucid Dreaming Made Easy*… Mom, what is this?"

I took it from her. "It's just a book."

"I get that. But lucid dreaming? Isn't that a little out there? Woo-hoo? Since when do you buy into things like that?"

It would have been nice to go on living in a bubble of normalcy with her. I met her eyes, not sure if I should tell her everything, part of it, or none of it. As her mother, it was my job to protect her from things, but was my seeing visions something she needed protection from?

"Why don't you sit down for a minute," I suggested.

"Mom, you're scaring me."

"There's no need to be scared." Easy to say now that I'd had time to adapt to the whole vision thing.

Jenna dropped back onto the couch, and I put a hand on her forearm.

"What I am about to tell you might be a little hard to hear, certainly a little strange," I started. "Are you sure you—"

"Whatever it is, I can handle it."

"Okay, then." I'd always admired Jenna's courage and confidence. "I had a dream earlier in the week. Guess it was actually last week now. Monday, early morning."

"Okay," she dragged out and pointed to the book I still held in my hands. "A lucid dream?"

I shook my head and hugged the book against me to shield the cover. "Not exactly. Before I tell you any more, Jenna, I need you to promise me that this will stay between us. I don't want you saying anything to Aunt Judy or your uncle Jay—no one else. Not even Ryan. Especially not your dad."

"Now you're really scaring me." Her eyes were wide and wet.

I squeezed her arm. "Don't be, please. It was more like a psychic dream I had...or a vision. If this makes you uncomfortable—"

"Of course this makes me uncomfortable," she burst out. "I just found out my mother's a psychic, and I don't believe in psychics, so that makes you—"

"Crazy?"

Her eyes briefly fell downcast, and she sighed. "I'm sorry. I don't mean to hurt you. I just don't believe in them."

"I know, honey, and I wasn't going to tell you—"

"You were going to keep this from me?" she snapped. "Have you seen a doctor? I'm sure there's a medical explanation for what you perceived as a vision."

"I've seen two doctors. Dr. Jacobs and Dr. Ashraf." Jenna was also a patient of both.

"And what? They're not concerned?"

"Dr. Jacobs thinks there might be deeper mental and emotional issues at play. Dr. Ashraf isn't concerned at this time."

"You need to get another opinion, Mom," Jenna huffed. "There could be something seriously wrong with you. A brain tumor?"

I bristled at her honest reaction, unbridled and unfiltered. She came by those characteristics easily enough. But I also remembered now that she'd had a friend in high school who had lost her mother to a malignant brain tumor.

Seconds ticked off before Jenna broke the silence.

"What was it about?"

"A plane crash."

"Grandma and Grandpa's?"

I shook my head but didn't really want to tell her it had to do with last Monday's crash. "I can appreciate that thinking of me having a vision would scare you and make you uncomfortable, and that's fine, but this is now a part of my journey."

Tears beaded in her eyes, and her chin quivered. I put my hand on her head, stroking her long hair.

She looked at me, her eyes full of pain.

"I'm fine, sweetie. I assure you."

She batted me away. "I've got to go."

"Please, Jenn—"

She hurried off to her room, waving a hand over her head. It was one of those times it was best I didn't follow, even if letting her go was breaking my heart.

A few minutes later, she slammed the front door behind her as she left my townhouse. She hadn't bothered to say another word and had even held up a hand to say she wasn't interested in listening when I'd tried to talk to her. That hurt even more than if she'd yelled at me, but it also made me angry. I had reopened the door and shouted at her that she better show up at Aunt Judy's on time. Then I got my own door-slam in.

I pricked with embarrassment. Who was the parent? Who was the child? But I was past the point of rational thought or action.

Life had been so simple before the visions, and a person might argue I could turn my back on them on now—but I really couldn't. I was more driven than ever to find some answers, regardless of how much Jenna resisted.

I brewed myself another coffee and went to the living room with my laptop. It was only nine o'clock, and surely there was something I could do on the investigative front. I did have the names of Hayes's companions, including the elusive Shane Fox. There had also been my earlier thought Fox was associated with Fighters for Future America. There was one way I might be able to find out.

I brought up the website for the environmental group and called the Contact Us number. With each ring, self-doubt entered in, telling me I was crazy for pursuing this line of inquiry. Along with it came some guilt over keeping this course of action from David when I'd basically promised him that we'd discuss our next steps before either of us took them.

"Fighters for Future America." A chipper sounding woman, guessing early twenties, answered the phone.

"Hi…"

"Yes?" A slight ring of impatience.

I'd just gone ahead and punched in the phone number without really thinking about what I was going to say. "My name's, uh…Frankie Bergstein." I hit myself in the forehead. I watched far too much *Grace and Frankie*.

"Yes, Ms. Bergstein. What can I help you with?"

"I'm trying to reach a member of yours. A Shane Fox."

There was clicking on her end of the line. "I can put you through to his voicemail where you could leave a message, but I can't hand over his personal contact information."

"That's fine." The skin was prickling into goosebumps at the back of my neck. Shane Fox was a member of the group—the same one accused of bringing down the plane. But if he was a part of this group, why was he traveling with Howard Hayes? Had he felt so strongly about clean energy and fighting big oil he had been willing to sacrifice his own life to go down with Hayes?

"Actually, ma'am…"

*Ouch.* It never got easier to hear. "Yes?"

"I don't have Shane Fox in our directory. May I ask why you're calling?"

I could just hang up, but I hadn't thought to block my number. I also should have come up with a cover story before getting on the phone.

"Ma'am," she prompted.

"I'm a journalist calling about the plane crash last Monday involving the founder of Guardian Oil Company."

The woman groaned. "No. Comment." She spoke the two words very slowly as if I were hard of understanding.

"If you could just please—"

There was a subtle click. Then the line rang. I'd been transferred to someone.

"Isaiah Peters," a man answered.

The name was familiar, and I knew why. He'd been the one quoted in that article where the group was accused of being behind the downed flight.

"Hello? Is anyone there?"

"Hi? Yes, it's Ms. Bergstein." There was probably a spot in hell reserved for me, given this little shtick. It would have been great if I'd been endowed with acting skills when I was touched with the gift of special sight.

"What can I do for you?"

"I'm calling about Shane Fox. I believe he's a member of your organization." I plowed on ahead, disregarding the fact that the receptionist had said otherwise.

"I can't say as I know that name. You must have the wrong number." He disconnected.

*Huh.* I leaned back against the couch. I'd say Shane Fox wasn't in any way connected to Fighters for Future America if it hadn't been for the strange treatment I'd just received. First the receptionist transfers me to the spokesman for the group, no less. Then he hangs up on me at the mention of Shane's name. I'd almost think the name had spooked him. If so, why?

# Chapter Twenty-Seven

I'd just set down my phone when it rang. It had me jumping—and swearing. "Hello," I answered without checking the caller ID. "Jenna?"

A pinch of silence, then, "It's David. Everything okay?"

I was still preoccupied with trying to sort out the call with Fighters for Future America and whether any of it had to do with the crash. Then there was Jenna weighing on my mind, but hearing his voice had me flushing as memories of our kiss washed over me. "Yeah, I'm fine. Good morning."

"Good morning, beautiful."

*Beautiful?* He was laying it on thick, but I wasn't entirely opposed. It left me a bit speechless though. It had been so long since a man looked at me the way David did, or kissed me the way David had. I fanned myself with my free hand and kicked out a pathetic, "Happy Thanksgiving."

"Happy Thanksgiving to you. It's more your day than mine."

"Right, I keep forgetting you're American." A lie really, as I was too aware of the fact that I was developing feelings for a man who'd be jetting off any day. And maybe *feelings* was too strong a word. It was more like the hormone-driven attraction of a teenager.

"Ouch," he said. "You know how to make a guy feel special."

"Come on, you know that I—" I stopped there. I'd make him feel good; he'd make me feel good. Before we knew it, we'd be naked in bed, the possibility not as far off as it used to be. But I couldn't give it too much serious thought or I'd start hyperventilating. I hadn't been with a man in a very long time, and while I kept myself in decent shape with yoga, I probably wouldn't be leaving the light on.

"Know that you what?" he tossed back casually.

"All right, I'll feed your ego." I was smiling. "I enjoy your company. There, you happy now?"

"Extremely. And you know I feel the same." The admission came from his mouth like it was the easiest thing in the world for him to say.

The sweet-talk, the flattery, the open-mouth kiss… Things were moving far too fast between us, and we were far more comfortable than we should be considering how new we were to each other. We needed to slow down or someone was going to get hurt. I feared that would be me. For some reason, around David, my logic disappeared and my heart took over.

"Well, I won't keep you long," he said, "but I wanted to let you know that I left a message for Bill last night about Shane Fox. I'll be following up with him today."

"It's a— Right, it's *not* a holiday there."

"Are you honestly all right, Erin?"

The depth of concern in his voice had my fight with Jenna slapping me in the face. Tears sprung to my eyes. I sniffled.

"Oh. That's a no. You can talk to me. I don't want to push, so if you're not wanting to—"

"Jenna and I got into a bit of a… I don't want to say a fight, but a disagreement."

"About?"

"I told her about the visions."

"Oh."

One syllable, and a hit to the heart. "Uh-huh. It didn't go over so well, and I never got into any details. Obviously, I never told her we were working together and trying to figure out what happened to the plane."

"You weren't even going to tell her about the visions. What changed your mind?"

"She found this book I bought on lucid dreaming. She tripped over it, actually. Long story." I batted my hand, as if he could see. "Anyway, she didn't understand why I'd have that type of book, and that's what prompted me to tell her about the visions."

David's end of the line went quiet for a few beats. "You're sure it's the visions themselves that prompted your argument?" His voice was cautious, like he was treading where he wasn't entirely comfortable going.

"She  told me I needed to see a doctor and get a brain scan."

"You had the same concerns at first," he pointed out.

"I guess, but I never even got to why I had the book on lucid dreaming. She didn't really want to hear any of it."

"Huh."

I waited out the silence that followed his little guttural response, and it seemed I was missing something. "What?" If I were Trish, I'd be saying "spill."

"Just thinking about the source of your argument. She stumbled over the book. She could have felt that if she hadn't, you never would have told her about the visions. She could be feeling left out and like you don't trust her enough."

"I'd like to think I know my daughter more than you," I shot back, aware he'd hit Jenna's reaction right on the mark. Jenna had essentially come out and accused me of intending to keep the visions from her. Which, of course, had been a thought of mine.

"I never meant to imply that—"

"But that's really what you're suggesting. That I don't know my own daughter. Or that I'm a horrible mother for not opening up to her sooner." My words were getting away from me with a life force of their own. Was I trying to sabotage my friendship with David? Better to end it now then later after I was deeper in?

"I never said either or meant to imply either." His tone was firm and carried an edge. "I should probably let you go. It doesn't seem like a good time."

"Probably." My heart was being chipped away at with a chisel, and I was really the one wielding the tool. He was only reacting the way he was because of how I'd been. But he'd been so insightful into Jenna's reaction that it stung. Then again, how could I fault him for being intuitive when I also liked that about him?

"I'll call you tomorrow," he said.

"Fine." I hung up without so much as a goodbye. Immense emptiness moved in like dusk over day. I wasn't sure what hurt more—Jenna's storming out or David's spot-on allegation. I should have just talked with Jenna before bed last night or even first thing this morning—before she'd tripped on the lucid-dreaming book. I'd convinced myself that she had no reason to know about the visions, and I hadn't wanted to get into a fight with her about them. Yet, here we were anyway.

Tears fell, the coffee going cold beside me.

My phone rang, and I quickly answered. "I'm sorry." Whether it was Jenna or David, I owed both an apology.

There was nothing on the other end of the line.

"Hello?" I prompted, and pulled my phone back to consult caller ID. It was a blocked number.

"Who is this?" I asked. "I'm not interested in buying anything or—"

"You're a fraud, Erin Stone."

It was a man's voice. Deep, rough, husky. My neck tightened with terror.

"Who is—"

"You have a beautiful daughter. It would be a shame if anything were to happen to her."

I went cold but, riding a wave of defiant courage, squeezed out, "Who is this?"

"If you don't stop looking into the crash, I can't be held responsible for what happens to your precious Jenna."

"How do you—" *How does he know Jenna's name? How does he know mine?* My breaths were coming in deep, short, erratic attempts at deriving oxygen. All my years of experience at keeping calm under pressure faded away. "You leave her alone," I seethed, trying desperately to sound as menacing as possible while my body trembled.

"Just back off, and she'll be safe. Good day, Ms. Stone." With that, the caller was gone.

"Oh my God! *Oh my God!*" I brought up Jenna in my favorites list, my fingers fumbling. I couldn't get them to work fast enough. I listened as her phone rang repeatedly. "Pick up!" I shouted to the void. The call clicked over to voicemail.

*"Hey, you've reached Jenna's—"*

"Oh God." My entire body sagged like a deflated balloon at the end of a kid's birthday party. "Jenna." I stopped there, gathered my composure, continued more calmly. "It's Mom. Call me." I ended the call and paced in a circle.

*Why did I get her voicemail? Where is she?*

"She's fine," I muttered. "She just couldn't get to the phone in time. She's with Ryan. She's—" My thoughts dipped into the darkness. *What if she is in danger?* The last time we saw each other, we'd spoken in anger.

I called her again. It went to voicemail again. I hung up.

*Okay, breathe, Erin, breathe.*

I inhaled and exhaled a few times, dropped back onto the sofa, and dialed her one more time.

"Stop playing games," I said to her across the ether. Really, that's all this had to be—a coincidence. She wasn't answering because she was freezing me out; it had nothing to do with the madman who'd just called me. I left another message for Jenna to call. This time going for cool, calm, and collected right from the start.

After all, Jenna had to be safe. *She just has to be.* And who the hell was that man anyway? How did he know I was investigating the plane crash? The answer seemed obvious that he or the "they" he represented had some involvement in causing the crash. Someone at Fighters for Future America? It couldn't be a coincidence that I'd just called them and then this call came.

I gulped. The last thing I needed was a group of extremists after my daughter. I'd never blocked my number. They could have conducted a reverse search on my phone number, got my name and, from there, Jenna's with a little internet sleuthing. But if it was them, they'd reacted to my call quickly. They'd discovered I wasn't a reporter, hence the "You're a fraud, Erin Stone."

Maybe I should bring this up to David, but to do so, I'd first have to admit that I'd broken our agreement to talk about next steps before doing them. He wouldn't take it well—call it a gut feeling.

The thoughts kept circling, but it seemed the smartest thing to do was to stop looking into the crash immediately. He had said Jenna would be safe if I backed off. But how would my caller even know if I halted my efforts? And why wasn't Jenna answering her phone? Too many questions!

I should probably call the police, but then, what would I say? Some man called and threatened my daughter? They'd want to know why and who I suspected might be behind the call—both things I wasn't entirely sure about myself. Though it would seem I might have poked the wrong organization by calling Fighters for Future America. And if I got as far as the part where Jenna and I had been in a fight last we were together, I'd be told to wait things out.

I tapped my phone and looked at the time on my phone. *11:30 AM.* Jenna should be to her father's by now.

I called Chris. He'd just confirm Jenna was there, and I could breathe. I rang to voicemail and left a message. They were probably just visiting, and there was nothing to worry about. End of story. But what if this man had acted on his threat regardless of my response? What if Jenna had gotten into an accident? I really needed to get a grip—and find a distraction. I certainly couldn't sit around here by myself and rehash worst-case scenarios. I'd get ready and head over to Aunt Judy's and offer to help. The threat wouldn't be far from my mind—not until I saw Jenna—but the company and milling about in the kitchen might provide some distraction.

# Chapter Twenty-Eight

Aunt Judy opened the door and cocked her head. "Erin, you're early."

That was part of the reason I'd knocked and hadn't let myself in; I hadn't wanted to scare her by just showing up in her kitchen. "I thought you might like some help." The truth, but not my motivation for being there so early. It had been sixty-seven minutes since the phone call and just under that for my first message to Jenna. My last had been five minutes ago. There was still no answer on her phone, and she hadn't called back. Neither had Chris. I was well on my way to crazy town. Forget "on my way." I'd pitched a tent and was considering investing in real estate.

"I'm not going to turn you away." Aunt Judy opened the door wider, and the smell of slow-roasting turkey was intoxicating. I inhaled appreciatively—and reluctantly. Glorious dinners like today's tortured expectant taste buds for hours.

She unburdened me of the bags I carried full of buns, cranberries, and bottles of wine while I hung up my coat and got out of my shoes.

"How are you doing, sweetie?" she asked.

"Good." A solid lie. It was starting to feel like I was becoming a pro at shading the truth. "Should we get to work?" I took my bags back from Aunt Judy, who relinquished them without argument.

"You bet. I got one large bird," she said, emphasizing the word *large*.

"I remember you telling me the other day. Thirty pounds?"

"Uh-huh. And it's in the oven."

"That I can tell. It's smelling delicious." I headed up.

"Isn't it? Not sure why we don't have turkey dinners more often. For some reason, eating them always requires a special occasion. I do love the holidays, whether it's Thanksgiving, Christmas…"

"I know you do," I said, tossing out a tight smile, recalling how I'd just said as much to David the other day.

"You look so tired."

"That's just life."

"You didn't look quite yourself the other day at the bookstore either. You would tell me if there was something worrying you, wouldn't you?"

"Aunt Judy, I always have." *But not this time.* My visions were off the table, as was the threatening phone call. I didn't want to worry my aunt on either count: my current spiritual state or Jenna's well-being.

Aunt Judy studied me and eventually nodded. I sensed she didn't believe me, but she was choosing not to pry.

The two of us worked in the kitchen for hours, making up the cranberry sauce, peeling and chopping potatoes—in chunks for mashed and sliced for scalloped. We cooked up broccoli and cauliflower for a veggie cheese casserole that was a holiday favorite. Judy had baked a cherry pie, a pumpkin pie, and an apple pie yesterday. No one would leave the dinner table hungry.

But even as I peeled, chopped, and boiled, I was nothing more than a highly functioning robot going about its tasks. I just wanted to hear the front door opening and Jenna calling upstairs for us.

"You're sure you don't want a glass of wine?" Aunt Judy asked for the third time. She wasn't used to me not drinking while cooking.

"No, I…I just want to wait for everyone else to get here." I couldn't tell her I wouldn't be drinking a drop of alcohol until Jenna was in my arms again.

"That should be any minute." Aunt Judy smiled as she poured two glasses of red wine—the preference no matter the meal.

I looked at the clock on the wall. *2:55 PM.*

Judy put the wineglass in my hand and lifted hers before I could refuse. "*Salut.*"

"*Salut.*" I took the smallest sip in the history of mankind.

Everyone had been told to come at three, but my brother and his wife probably wouldn't be here until closer to three thirty or even later—it was just how they worked. But Jenna was usually extremely punctual. Really, she should already be here.

My heart squeezed with terror. What if that man had gotten to her and hurt her? What if—

The doorbell rang, and I ran downstairs. The door was already opening by the time I got there, and it was Jason and his troop.

"You're early," I said, hoping my disappointment that it wasn't Jenna wouldn't come across.

"Aunt Erin!" Cody, the youngest, came over and hugged me. At three years of age, he didn't have any qualms about showing affection.

"Hey, guys," I said to Brent and George, my other nephews, ages eleven and seven. I wouldn't dare hug or kiss either of them. It would be so uncool—if kids today even used that word. They waved at me as they slid out of their boots and coats. Brent did so with his face in his phone.

"What did I tell you?" Natalie went for her son's phone, but Brent turned his back to her. "Put it away, or I'm taking it away."

"Fine," he huffed as he pushed it into a pocket and set off upstairs.

Natalie bugged her eyes at her child's back, then said to me, "I need a freaking huge glass of wine."

"Every mother does." I hugged her quickly to hide any emotion that might be showing on my face.

"Ahem. You're not getting away without hugging your little brother." Jason pulled me in and gave me a big, sloppy kiss on the cheek.

"Really?" I wiped away his slobber. If I were in a better state of mind, I'd pay him back with a wet willy—a wet fingertip in his ear!

Jason laughed. "Brr. It's freezing out there." He rubbed his hands and made a show of squirming like he was shivering.

"If you're cold now, you're not going to survive the winter," Natalie said with seriousness. She glanced at me again. "He's getting older, so he's feeling the chill more in his bones."

"Hey!" Jason slapped his wife's behind. It was intended to be all in good fun, but she cast him a glare that could have frozen lava. She rubbed where he'd hit her and narrowed her eyes. She didn't hold the serious expression for long; it thawed and she started laughing.

These two nutjobs were perfect for each other. I rolled my eyes, used to these little sideshows whenever they were around. It was great to see them both so happy though.

"What should I do with this?" George lifted a plastic shopping bag in the air, to the full extension of his arm, putting it close to his mother's face. Natalie put a hand on his arm to move it out of her way.

"Take it to Aunt Judy."

Cody trailed George. I turned around and glanced at the door, wishing Jenna would appear. *Where is she?* I hugged myself.

Jason hung up his coat in the closet. "What's up with you?"

"Nothing."

"You're staring into space."

I hadn't realized I had been. "Sorry?"

"No, it's just… Do you have something on your mind?"

"She's a woman. We always have a lot on our minds," Natalie chimed in before Erin could respond.

Regardless of his wife's comment, Jason and I held eye contact. If I didn't fill the space between us with some words, I was bound to start blathering on about the visions and the threatening phone call. I took a different route. "Here's something you'll find interesting," I said.

"Uh-huh." He squinted, curious about what I was going to say, but I also sensed hesitation.

"Your niece has a boyfriend, and she's bringing him here today." Thinking positively—exactly what I needed to do.

Jason's mouth gaped open. "Today? For Thanksgiving?"

"Yep." I bobbed my head. "And they should be here any minute." I strained for the sound of closing car doors. For the first time ever, the city was quiet.

Jason rubbed his hands together. "Oh, I'm going to have fun with this."

I shoved his shoulder. "Don't you dare." Though I wouldn't expect anything less of my brother and hoped he had the chance to harass his niece.

"Are you guys going to lurk in the doorway all day?" Aunt Judy called down to us.

"We're coming," Jason replied and bounded up the stairs, taking them two at a time.

Natalie followed him, but I didn't move. I stood there, looking at the door, willing it to open and for Jenna to walk through. Seconds passed. And nothing. I cracked the door and popped my head outside. People were walking to the neighbor's door, but there was no sign of Jenna.

Wind gusted into the house, and I hugged my sweater tighter to myself and slowly, reluctantly, closed the door. I pulled out my phone and called Jenna. It rang to voicemail like before.

"Erin?" Aunt Judy was looking down at me, marked impatience in her tone.

"I'm coming." If only I could get myself to move. *Where the hell are you, Jenna, and are you okay, baby?*

I trudged up the stairs, completely lacking the enthusiasm my brother had. My steps were leaden with apprehension and fear. At least Jason was here. A cop. If, God forbid, some madman had Jenna, he'd know what to do and he'd stop at nothing to save his niece. Of that I was absolutely certain. But I sure hoped it wouldn't come to that. My family would be destroyed for more than one reason. The truth about my visions would come out, laid bare, but I'd go there if I had to—if it meant helping Jenna.

"There you are." Aunt Judy looked at me as if I'd returned from a long journey. She pointed to a pot of boiling potatoes. "They should be done."

That was her way of asking me to deal with them, and I proceeded to do just that, not that my mind was on the task. I heard every car door that closed in the neighborhood and kept imagining the sound of Jenna coming inside.

She still hadn't arrived by the time I'd finished mashing the potatoes, and panic was really starting to brew in my chest. I kept looking at Jason, and thankfully, he didn't seem to notice, but if Jenna didn't arrive soon, I'd have to tell him about the call and the visions that got us to this point.

Then there was a knock on the door, followed by its opening. I bolted for the entry, and Jason quirked an eyebrow at me as I passed him. I shook my head to dismiss his silent inquiry and kept moving.

"Jenna?" I cried out and hurried down the stairs. I got there just as a young man stepped behind my Jenna. She'd never looked so precious and beautiful. *My little girl.* "Hey, sweetheart," I said, scooping her to me and squeezing tight.

"Ah…" Jenna patted my arm. "I…I can't breathe."

"Oh, sorry, sweetie." I pulled back but left my hands on her arms.

"Are you all right? You're acting strange."

"Yeah…I…" Happy tears blurred my vision and paired with a knot in my gut. "Why didn't you call me?"

"I've been busy, Mom." Jenna jabbed her eyes toward the young man.

"Right." I put on a pleasant smile and held out my hand to him, which he took and shook. Good manners. Admirable. I returned my hand to Jenna's arm.

She looked down at it and back up to meet my eyes, as if to say, *What's wrong with you?*

"Ms. Stone, I'm Ryan Holt. Nice to finally meet you."

Make that *very* good manners. "You can call me Erin." Jenna stiffened, and I let go of her. I pressed on another smile for Ryan. "So, Jenna hasn't told me a whole lot about you."

"Maybe that's a good thing?" Ryan winced, as if he had horrible secrets to hide, then quickly grinned. Of course, he was just joking around. He was easily over six feet tall but had an unassuming presence. He had a relaxed, gentle energy about him—not that I got the impression he was a wallflower. He seemed calmer than Jenna though.

Jenna nudged him with her shoulder. "He's a good guy, Mom."

I raised my eyebrows at my daughter. I'd say he'd stolen her heart. "I'm sure he is." I set my gaze on him. "It's nice to meet you, Ryan, and welcome, welcome. Everyone's upstairs, and dinner's almost ready, so good timing, you two." It didn't matter that they were technically late. Jenna was okay!

Jenna slipped her hand into Ryan's, and they headed up. I stayed back, and this time, I was blinking away tears of relief. I swiped a few that had fallen, sniffled, and joined everyone else.

"First comes love, then comes mar—"

"Stop it, Uncle Jay," Jenna chastised, stopping Jason's rendition of "K-i-s-s-i-n-g."

I flicked my brother on the back of the head, and it made a *thwack* on his skull.

"Ouch." He rubbed the point of impact. "I just tease because I care," he mumbled.

"No excuse." I snickered and went to help Aunt Judy dish up everything.

Out of the corner of my eye, I saw Jenna hugging her uncle. I smiled and carried on to the kitchen. Aunt Judy was wielding a large knife.

"Please, don't hurt me," I jested, and she laughed.

She loved to carve the turkey, and I'd happily let her do what she enjoyed. Slicing into the meat and pulling it from the bones certainly wasn't my favorite job.

Aunt Judy and I served up dinner, and everyone set out to devour as much of it as possible amid animated conversation. I was certainly blessed with a close and caring family. Unlike so many families that squabbled over everything and anything, there usually wasn't much tension among us. After dinner, we took turns listing off three things we were thankful for.

Jenna told us she was thankful for Ryan, her good grades, and me. "I saved the best for last," she added, taking my hand.

My chin quivered, and the waterworks started.

"Oh, Mom." She wiped my cheeks. "I love you."

"I love you, sweetie." My God, what would I have ever done if something had happened to her? I never wanted to know.

"So, you said you saved the best for last, huh? And I was first." Ryan frowned and sulked. Jenna rolled her eyes at me and pecked a quick kiss on her boyfriend's lips. My nephews said "ew" and "gross." It was fantastic.

Aunt Judy, Natalie, and I smiled at each other.

"Speaking of *last*, you're up, darling." Aunt Judy gestured to me.

"I'm thankful for all of you. Even you, Jay." I flashed a goofy grin at my brother. "I'm thankful that we all get along so well and are a close family. And, my sweet Jenna, I love the woman you've become and am so happy that you're healthy and happy. I'm also happy that—"

"You're over three things." Jason tapped his wrist as if he were watching the time.

"I'm also happy," I shoved out and carried on, "that I had the day off work to celebrate with all of you today."

"Beautiful." Aunt Judy raised her wineglass and proposed a toast. "To our lovely family."

We all clinked our glasses of wine, except for my nephews who were drinking water.

For starting off with so much uncertainty, the night had gone on to be one of the best I'd had in my life. Everyone I loved all under one roof. It was magical, and my heart was swelled with gratitude.

"So, did Mom tell you she has a boyfriend?" Jenna asked out of the blue during dessert.

Jason faced me with a raised eyebrow. "No, she did not."

"Because I don't have a boyfriend," I said firmly to my daughter.

"Oh, yes, you do." Her eyes were lit up like she was ready to spill a juicy secret. "He had dinner with us last night. His name's David Bomber, and he works for the NTSB. He—"

Jenna kept talking, but Jason had already leveled his gaze at me as if to say, *That guy from the memorial?* I shook my head, trying to discourage him before he started into it.

"He was there for dinner?" Jason kept his eyes on me. "With Jenna over?"

I'd have to be stupid not to pick up on his implication. He knew how possessive I was of my time with her and how I never normally let anything interfere. He was attributing importance to the relationship because I had shared my time with Jenna. "No big deal, Jay," I retorted.

"Oh, it is," Jenna practically squealed. "I'm so happy for you, Mom."

"It has been a while, honey," Aunt Judy said, weighing in on my supposed love life.

I glanced at Natalie, expecting she'd want to contribute something to the scuttlebutt, but she didn't say anything. There was a reason I liked my sister-in-law.

"I'm happy on my own. I lack for nothing." I took a sip of my tea and set the cup back down.

"It can get lonely, though, can't it?" Aunt Judy said. "And you're far too young to sleep alone, so I'm happy you've found someone." She reached over and tapped the back of my hand.

She must have failed to hear or to accept that I'd dismissed any romantic ties to David, but I didn't have the heart to correct her. It felt like yet another lie, but even if I wanted to explore my feelings for David, it couldn't happen. After all, a plane crash—two, technically, with the one from last Monday and my parents'—had brought us together. I wasn't sure building a future on *crashing* was a good omen. Not that it mattered because he'd be returning home. A fact that I constantly reminded myself of but didn't want to accept. Besides, given the way I'd treated him earlier today, I'd be surprised if he ever wanted to talk to me again.

# Chapter Twenty-Nine

"Why were you acting so weird today?" Jenna was perched on the other end of the couch, her back against the arm, watching me. "I listened to your voicemails, Mom. You sounded so panicked on there. You sure something wasn't going on earlier today?"

Jenna and I were nestled in my living room, and the clock was creeping around to ten thirty. We'd left Aunt Judy's just after seven, behind Jason and his family. Ryan was considerate enough to bow out and leave me to be alone with Jenna. Otherwise, it could have gotten ugly. Especially after the scare today, I needed time with my girl more than ever. Score one in Ryan's "pro" column. I was so happy and content in this moment. My daughter was here, safe and sound.

"I'm fine, sweetie." All I had to do was forget about the vision of the plane crash and get on with my life to ensure Jenna's continued safety. Should be easy enough. In truth, though, the fact this strange man had called me continued to gnaw on me. How did he even know I was looking into the crash? I snuggled farther into the couch, hugging my steaming mug of tea, and hoping for it to work its magic.

"I'm worried about you," she said, her voice tender. "Visions? Lucid dreaming? None of that is you."

"It never used to be."

"Mom?" Kicked out almost as a scolding or a wake-up call.

"I'm a grown woman, Jenna," I pushed back. "And I know it's all unsettling to you."

"You can say that again." She crossed her arms.

"I appreciate you not bringing it up at dinner today."

"No way I would. If Aunt Judy found out…" She blew out a whistle. "It just might kill her."

*Might kill her…*

"Though I think it shocked her plenty that you have a boyfriend." Jenna smirked.

I tried to form a smile, but I was still stuck on Jenna's previous words. There was no doubt my visions would upset Judy, even repulse her. She might disown me and cut off communication. But would the knowledge literally kill her? A knot balled in my gut.

"Mom, did you hear me?"

"I did. And you shouldn't have told everyone about David. You made our relationship into something it isn't. Then Aunt Judy gets her hopes up…"

"But you admit it's a relationship?" Her expression took on a hint of smugness, so similar to her father. One I used to even find mysterious and charming. And while on the thought of Mr. Charming, he hadn't bothered calling me back. Good to know I could rely on him in a crisis.

"All friendships are relationships," I said.

"Uh-huh."

"I mean it, Jenna. He's just a friend. And he'll be going home soon." Saying so out loud made me realize I still didn't know when he'd be returning to the States. I didn't really know much about him period.

"Okay. Fine. I'll let it go."

"Thank heavens." I laughed. *And about time!*

Jenna yawned. "I should probably get to bed. School in the morning."

"All right, sweetie."

Jenna came over and kissed my forehead. I rose and hugged her, squeezing tightly. My life had come within a hair's breadth of going topsy-turvy, and I didn't want to take one single moment for granted anymore.

"Mom, I—" She panted like she was suffocating and tapped my back.

I let her go, even though I didn't want to. I could stay in this bubble with her forever. This secure little bubble. "Good night."

"Night." Jenna padded down the hall to bed.

I took our cups to the kitchen, rinsed them, and turned off the lights. Before I did, my gaze drifted to my laptop on the kitchen table. Shane Fox and the mystery woman remained enigmas. Dead ends, the two of them. And Fighters for Future America—why such a reaction to my call? Was it because of dropping Shane's name or because I mentioned my interest in the crash to the receptionist before she transferred me to the spokesperson for the organization? I guess I really didn't need to worry about it anymore. Not my problem.

Chills spread over my shoulders and down my arms. David. He'd left a message for his colleague at the NTSB, and last I knew, he was going to follow-up. Was the person who had threatened Jenna aware of that? Would he view it as actively investigating?

I had to call David. Immediately. His phone rang to voicemail. I couldn't tell him about the threat or my call to Fighters for Future America because of our agreement to run things by each other before acting. I'd broken that promise. It was best to stick to the basics. I hung up and sent him a text message. Clean, clear, and I was in control of the narrative. Also he wouldn't call back and possibly wake up Jenna.

> *"I need to stop looking into crash. Jenna's asleep. Don't call back tonight."*

No doubt he'd have questions, but I'd deal with him—and them—tomorrow.

I headed to bed and mindlessly went through my nightly routine. Once I slipped under the covers, I was wide awake. Someone out there not only knew I was looking into the crash, but they knew about Jenna too. That meant they were watching us. I inched the duvet up a little higher.

# Chapter Thirty

I woke up the next morning at five thirty, and Jenna was already gone. She'd left me a note on the kitchen counter telling me she wanted to stop by her place before going to school. I figured she was probably meeting up with Ryan. Ah, young love. How innocent and beautiful. And exciting. The discovery of another person—not just physically but mentally, emotionally, and spiritually. This made me think of David. Everything new and exciting between us. I pressed my fingertip to my lips, remembering our kiss, but let my hand drop. I needed to leave the crash—and him—alone. Besides, he probably wouldn't want anything to do with me after our phone call yesterday.

My sleep last night had been packed with nightmares about Jenna. She'd been abducted, and I couldn't find her. There was a repetitive image of me looking from overhead on a cornfield maze. I'd spot her location, and the next moment, I'd be on the ground with no idea where to go. But I moved along anyhow, thinking I was heading in the right direction. Then the maze would morph, and open runs became dead ends.

Coffee. That's what I needed to shake the images and icky feeling in my stomach.

Mug full, I went to the living room, leaving my laptop on the kitchen table. I had to leave the crash alone for Jenna's sake. It was surprising to me how often I needed to remind myself of this, but I felt a burden of guilt weighing on my shoulders. Was I letting the victims' families and friends down by not ferreting out the truth?

*Really, Erin?* It had to be my ego deceiving me into believing I was integral to the investigation. And there was no way I could keep Jenna safe *and* unravel what brought that plane out of the sky—not when I didn't even know who was watching me. If only I could figure out who was behind that phone call.

Fighters for Future America could have enough deep pockets to hire some thugs.

*Ridiculous*, I thought. *I watch too many movies.* But there was the call. That was a fact.

What about an associate of Shane Fox? Someone who didn't like us asking questions about him? Still, that circled back to the environmental group. It was hard to ignore that the threat had come immediately after I'd called them. Had that merely been coincidental?

My cell phone rang, and caller ID showed it was David. Now was as good a time as any to get his inevitable interrogation out of the way. I answered with a simple, "Hello."

"Good morning." I could hear his smile. "How was your Thanksgiving?"

Tough question to answer. It could have been better. And the way he sounded, I'd say my snippiness from yesterday was forgiven and forgotten. "It was good. Probably ate too much."

"Ah, calories don't count on holidays."

"I wish." I paused, hesitating to bring up my text but I wanted to make sure he'd received the message. It was crucial that he had. "Did you get my text last night?"

"I did."

*Nothing more?* I'd expected a slew of questions.

He added, "I saw it just after leaving another message with Bill's assistant, Ronnie. You know, in follow-up to my earlier request about the black-box recording and Shane Fox."

My head spun, and my vision pinpricked. "After…"

"Yeah. Is something wrong?"

*You could say that!* "I've gotta go."

"You can't just step back and forget about your vision."

My body stiffened at his directive. He had no idea what was at stake. "I can, and I'm going to." The words came out sharp and blunt and had him going quiet. I added, "It's about time I got back to my regular life."

"I don't know what's changed between Sunday and now, but you were determined to—"

"I've changed my mind. That's all you need to know. I have Jenna and—"

"What about Jenna?"

The way he'd asked had the hairs rising on the back of my neck. I really needed to call her and make sure she was okay. What if the madman had found out about David's call *after* telling me to stop poking my nose into the crash? "I've got to go." I hung up before he could respond and tried Jenna again. Her phone rang repeatedly, and I figured I was bound for voicemail just when she answered. I let out the breath I'd been holding.

"Mom? I left you a note."

"Oh, I got it."

"Okay," she dragged out.

My heart was thumping wildly, but I realized how quiet the line had fallen. Jenna was worried about my health, and calls like this wouldn't help. "I just wanted to check and make sure you're doing okay today. I missed you this morning." *Good save?*

"I'm fine," she said, sounding irritated. "I've got to go now though, okay? Bye."

"Bye, hon—" She'd ended the call.

I held my phone for a while. Maybe Jenna wasn't far off the mark with her concern about my sanity. These visions, the threat… They were making me lose my mind. I caught the time on the wall and realized I had to get moving. It wasn't until I got into the car and was on my way to work that I realized just how horribly I'd treated David. I'd probably never hear from him again for sure this time. Maybe that was all for the best.

# Chapter Thirty-One

"Good morning." Lauren was all smiles when I walked into the parade room. "How was your Thanksgiving?"

"Good." I attempted a smile. After all, there were things to be grateful for. Jenna was safe—at least for now. But it was hard to completely shake the menace of that phone call. Had David's message resurrected the threat? I also had this ache in my chest because of how I'd treated David. If the roles were reversed, I doubted I'd be forgiving. But it was best I just let it all go, live more in the flow—release and surrender—as all my self-discovery books taught me. Sometimes so much easier said than done. "How was yours?"

"Oh." She sighed dramatically. "The turkey was as dry as chalk. Needed wine to wash it down."

"Doesn't sound too bad, then." I smiled.

She laughed, her eyes lighting up. "True enough."

We received our assignments for the day. I was taking calls, and Lauren was on dispatch.

As cruel as this might sound, handling calls would be welcome today. Not because other people would be experiencing some of the worst times in their lives, but it would help get my mind off everything going on in my world. It would be easier to release my fears and personal thoughts if I were busy. And I was. Back-to-back calls, every eight seconds. I'd end one, and the next would be routed right to me.

It was lunchtime before I knew it. I was unpacking the leftover turkey sandwich I'd managed to slap together before leaving home when my phone rang. Caller ID told me it was Brittany, one of Jenna's roommates. The Bs had my number, as I had theirs, for cases of emergency. I answered before it could ring a second time. "Is everything all right?"

"I hope so. Do you know where Jenna is?"

I became rigid and sat up straighter. "She should be at school."

"I'd have thought so, but I haven't seen her, and I can't reach her. That's why I called you."

It felt like an invisible force had its hands around my neck, squeezing. "You couldn't reach her?"

"All I get is voicemail."

"Ryan? You have his number?" A mother fail. I had the numbers for Jenna's roommates but not her boyfriend's. I should have asked for it yesterday. Should have, could have, would have.

"I called him. He hasn't seen or heard from her at all today."

My adrenaline was crystallizing into logic mode. "She could have turned her phone off to focus on her studies."

"Sure, but she's not in the library. She's not at our place. This isn't like her." The more Brittany spoke, panic rose in her voice. "What should I do?"

I wanted to scream an ear-piercing wail but somehow managed not to. "It's okay, Brittany. Just leave this with me. I'll call you once I find out more."

"Ms. Stone?"

"Yes?"

"I hope she's all right."

With that, I ended the call. My hands were shaking, and my eyesight blurred. The madman had acted on his threat: he took my girl!

"Mind if I join— Oh, you look— Are you all right?" Lauren slipped into a chair across from me.

"I've gotta go. Something's come up." I haphazardly rewrapped my sandwich and stuffed it into my lunch bag on the move. My foot caught the bar at the base of my chair, and I lurched forward, sure I was about to faceplant, but somehow I managed to regain my balance and remain upright.

"Whoa," Lauren cried out and moved to help.

I waved her off. "I'm fine."

"Okay." One word, spoken slowly, and it contained all the doubt in the world.

I fumbled out of the lunchroom with one numbing thought: *Someone took my Jenna.*

But maybe I was getting carried away. There could be another explanation for Jenna's absence, but nothing stuck. She wasn't the kind of person to go offline or unplug. And, as Brittany noted, it wasn't like her to miss class.

I stepped outside into the crisp fall air and inhaled deeply. *There has to be a logical explanation for all this.*

This felt different than yesterday when I thought she might have been taken. It was a bone-deep knowing. I needed to get the police on this, but what would I tell them? If I told them about the phone call, I'd need to bare everything—the visions, working with David. He'd probably get into trouble with the NTSB, likely lose his job. But all of this paled in significance next to Jenna's safety. There had to be a way to track down my caller. The number had been blocked, but technology knew very few boundaries these days.

I called Jenna, and it went straight to voicemail. Her phone was off.

She never turned it off.

There was no way around it; I had to call Jason. And I'd have to field questions I wouldn't want to answer.

I picked his number from my Favorites list and, with each ring, willed him to pick up.

He answered on the fourth ring. "Erin?"

"Jay, I…I need your help." My voice cracked, unable to continue talking. My heart was pounding in my ears.

"It's all right. Calm down. What is it?"

I was hyperventilating.

"Erin?" he prompted.

"It's Jenna. She's—" I sniffled.

"What about Jenna? Now you're scaring me. What's wrong with Jenna?"

"Come get me at work, and I'll tell you everything." My baby girl was missing, and I didn't care if Jason judged me for having visions and giving them credence. That time had passed.

"I'll be right there. Stay put."

The next thirty minutes felt more like hours. I'd gone inside and explained to Loughlin that I needed the rest of the day off for personal reasons, simply telling her that it involved my daughter. Somehow, I had managed to keep myself composed. Her words were understanding, but her tone told me she wasn't thrilled that I was leaving mid-shift after having the long weekend off. Still, she consented with a dip of her head. It helped my career to have her approval, but I'd have left without it.

I went back outside, and Jason was pulling up in his cruiser. I slipped into the passenger seat, and he looked over at me.

"What's going on?"

"It's Jenna."

"Yes, you mentioned that on the phone. I told my sarge I had to clock out for a bit. You're going to have to tell me more." His tone was all cop, not brother or uncle.

"Someone took her."

"Someone what? Why would anyone take Jenna?" His face scrunched up.

"There's something I need to tell you." For a brief second, I saw a foregleam of judgment flicker across his eyes. Or was it merely a reflection of my own self-condemnation?

"Talk," he pushed out firmly, stiffening and bracing for what was coming.

"Someone called me yesterday and threatened Jenna."

He shifted his body, so he was facing me more directly. "Why would someone threaten Jenna? I'm still not understanding."

I met his gaze, and a pain stabbed my heart. He wasn't going to understand what else I had to tell him either. He'd probably be disappointed in me—or worse still, cut me out of his life. "Just promise that you'll listen to what I'm about to say."

"I—"

I held up my hand. "Without interrupting." I paused, testing him, and he remained quiet. I went on. "You're not going to understand it, and you're probably not going to like it. But given what's happened to Jenna—"

"Stop rambling."

"It started last week. I had a…a vision." At first I couldn't look at him, but then I braved it. He squinted, his brow wrinkled, and his mouth set into a frown. He remained silent, a deep sorrow rooting in his expression.

"It was about that plane that crashed a week ago Monday, the one from Texas."

"A vision. About a plane crash? Surely you hear what you're saying?"

"Yes. It took me a bit to process it all, but I'm telling you, Jason, I saw that plane go down just as clearly as if I were on board at the time."

Jason shook his head. "It was just a dream. You're making too much out of it."

"Am I? Jenna's missing because of it."

He pulled back. "So, you're telling me that Jenna was taken because you had some sort of dream, vision thing?"

"She was," I stamped home.

"I'm lost. I don't see how…" He was watching me carefully, waiting for me to fill in the blanks. "None of this makes any sense. There's no such thing as visions."

"There are, but that's not the point. Someone out there views me as a threat and doesn't want me looking into the crash anymore. A man called and said as much. Said if I didn't stop, he'd hurt Jenna."

Jason shook his head. "What?" he snapped. "I'm not sure where to start—the visions or… You're looking into the crash?" His eyes widened. "It has to do with that NTSB guy, doesn't it? Did he rope you into this?"

"No. If anything, I…" There was no way I could betray David, but I was starting to feel smashed up against a wall.

He blew out a puff of air. "I don't know what to say. But what the heck were you doing investigating a plane crash, and why would someone want to hurt Jenna because of it?"

"Obviously someone fears I'll get to the truth of what happened."

"Who? How?"

"I don't know. I keep asking myself the same questions. But none of them are getting us any closer to Jenna."

"I knew I didn't like that NTSB guy."

"He has nothing to do with this," I hissed.

"All right, I'll play along. Who all knows you were looking into the crash?"

"I don't know everyone for sure." I realized this now. I didn't know all the people David had talked to, and I wasn't going to bring up Fighters for Future America unless absolutely necessary. There wasn't really enough there to truly point a finger at them. Was there? My mind was a jumble.

"Erin. How can you not—"

"I don't know. Honestly."

"Okay, then do you know why the plane crashed?"

I studied his face, not sure if he was still playing along or starting to accept my newfound gift. More likely the former. "Nope, but this morning…"

"This morning…" Jason rolled his hand impatiently.

To continue, I would bring David in more than he already was, but there wasn't much choice. "*This morning*, David called, and we spoke briefly about the crash."

"You continued to investigate, despite the threat?"

"Of course not," I barked, his accusation cutting deep. "I told him I couldn't look into it anymore. I didn't tell him why." I was still holding back, and I was certain Jason could see it in my eyes, the way his were darting over my face.

"What were you finding in this little covert investigation of yours?"

I gave him a molten glare and shook my head.

"Tell me. You've come this far. Jenna…?"

Hearing her name was all I needed to open my mouth more. "Before I told David I needed to stop looking into the crash, I had him following up on a couple of things. One, a passenger. Two, what had been gleaned from the black-box recording. David had followed up on an earlier message with a contact of his *after* the threatening phone call."

Jason remained speechless for a few beats. "Now maybe we're getting somewhere. You said a passenger? How would you even know— Oh." His face contorted as if he'd been struck.

"It was a person I saw in my vision." Speaking of the vision to my brother didn't get easier with repetition. But there was no way I'd be telling him that David had showed me the flight manifest. I didn't see a need for going there.

"So you really have faith in this…vision?" He swallowed like he'd tasted a mouthful of bile.

"I do."

"You sound like you're crazy."

"I'm *not* crazy," I snapped. "And the reality is, Jenna is missing. Her roommate Brittany hasn't seen her, can't reach her, Ryan can't, and neither can I. Believe in my visions or don't—I don't care—but she's in real danger."

"There could be another explanation for her not answering her phone."

I sighed with frustration. "Her phone's off. She *never* turns it off." I sat there looking into my brother's eyes, pleading with him to set aside his prejudice about visions and likely concerns over my mental health. "No one has seen her today. She can't just disappear into thin air." My voice rose in pitch with each word, and my heartbeat sped up. "Someone took her, Jason. I feel it." I pounded a fist against my chest.

He seemed to hesitate but eventually took my hand. "We'll find her."

Tears beaded in my eyes. "I hope you're right."

He didn't put it into words, but I could tell he did too. "You said her phone's off?"

"Yeah."

"We can try to track it anyway, see if it gets us anywhere. We could also have the number monitored in case it comes back on."

"Do it."

"Let's just make sure she's missing first."

I bit my bottom lip to suppress an outright ugly bawl and nodded.

"We'll start by swinging by the university." Jason put the car into gear, and when he merged into traffic, he touched my forearm. "We'll find her, get her back."

I nodded, sucking whatever mediocre assurance I could from his words. He couldn't promise that—or that she would be okay. If determination and intention counted, sure, but in situations like this, they made no difference.

# Chapter Thirty-Two

"What do we do if she's not at school?" I kneaded the fringe of my coat, staring into my lap.

"Let's just take this one step at a time."

I scowled at him. "I need more than that. I need a plan of action."

"If she's not there, I'll update my sarge and ask for some officers to spread out across campus. That's to start."

"And get on tracking her phone? Also could we have someone in Tech track the blocked number that called me?"

"All those things. Yes. Now, I know how things look, but maybe there's an explanation that isn't all gloom and doom. Let's keep positive for Jenna."

"What are you missing, Jason?" I snapped, but the pain in his eyes struck my heart. "Sorry. I'm just on edge. I told you about the call, the threat. And now she's missing."

"*Seems to be* missing."

"Gah. Listen, I'm her mother, and something's not right." I should have noticed the emptiness sooner, known that something was wrong before Brittany called. I've heard how most of us can sense when our loved ones are in danger, but I went about my morning at work completely oblivious. Me, seer of visions. Where was my gift now? My ability to see what others couldn't? What was the sense in having sight when I couldn't see where my daughter was? "I'm a horrible mother."

"You're a great mother."

"I didn't even have a clue something happened to her."

He looked over at me. "Because visions aren't real, Erin."

I shook my head at my brother's stubbornness. "Not doing this again. Not now."

"Fine, but we don't do any good jumping ahead and assuming the worst. She could be just fine."

"I hope so. Jenna's not the type to do something she doesn't want to do. Bad guys prefer cooperation."

Jason clenched his jaw. "We'll get her back."

That seemed to be his go-to line, and I knew his intentions were good, but with each repetition, it hammered in the fact Jenna was gone in the first place.

He pulled into the University of Toronto campus, parked, and headed for the administrative building. "We'll speak with the dean, tell him we're looking for Jenna, and have her teachers put on notice to look out for her."

How I wished all of this were a misunderstanding, and that she was in class. I pulled out my phone and looked at the time. *1:30 PM.* She'd be in Professor Lamb's class.

Inside the dean's office, we were stonewalled by a stern-looking woman with a brass nameplate on her desk that read *Susan Fowler.*

Her gaze took in my brother's uniform, and her lips pursed. "Can I help you?"

"I'm Jenna Pittman's mother," I said, and her gaze swung to me. "We've been trying to reach Jenna without success."

Susan blinked slowly. "I'm not sure what I can do about that."

"I…I… This isn't about *you*," I spat.

Jason stepped closer to me and took over. "We have reason to believe that Jenna may be in trouble."

Susan's eyes settled on the name badge on my brother's uniform. "And you are?"

"Her unc—"

"What does it matter who he is? Did you hear what he said? Jenna could be in danger. We need to speak to Dean McBride."

Susan slid her jaw side to side, as if considering whether she'd interrupt him or not. Eventually, she picked up the handset on her phone and gave me a pressed-lip smile. I could have smacked it right off her smug face.

"Dean McBride," Susan spoke into the receiver, "I have the mother of a student and a police officer here to speak with you... Yes... Okay, I will." She hung up. "He will be out for you shortly. Have a seat if you wish." She gestured to a couple of chairs.

There was no way I'd be sitting around while some lunatic had my daughter. It was bad enough moving with no clear destination ahead of me. I wished life came with guarantees. And where the heck was a vision when I wanted one? Just a single clue as to Jenna's whereabouts.

"Can I help you?" A handsome man in his sixties approached us.

"Are you Dean McBride?" Jason asked.

"I am," he said sluggishly and drew his eyes from Jason to me.

"We're here about Jenna Pittman," I cut in.

"And you're her mother, Mrs. Pittman?"

"Pittman is my ex's last name. I'm Erin Stone, but, yes, I'm Jenna's mother, and this is my brother, Jason. We can't get ahold of Jenna."

"I'm sorry you can't reach her, but I'm not sure what I can do to help." The dean's gaze again went to Jason, taking in his police uniform.

"We need to know if she's checked in for any of her classes today," I said. "Also, if you could call her teachers for her remaining periods today to let them know to contact us if she shows up for class, that would be helpful."

The dean's face took on dark shadows, and he glanced at his secretary and bobbed his head. "Please do as she just asked. Start with the class she's in now."

"Right away, sir." Susan moved her mouse around and tapped her keyboard.

"She'll find out which class Jenna is assigned right now and call the room. I'm sure—"

"It's Professor Lamb's class," I said.

The dean gestured toward Susan, and she had the phone to her ear in less than a second. A few more after that, she was hanging up and shaking her head.

My legs buckled. I reached for the counter and caught myself, but if I hadn't, Jason and the dean were at my side. Susan had stood but didn't look too alarmed. I imagined if I'd splatted on the floor, she'd wave.

"Come with me," the dean said.

Jason and I followed him into his office, where he sat behind his desk and clasped his hands.

"What do you think is going on here?" The dean directed his question to Jason.

I opened my mouth to speak, but Jason tapped a hand on my arm.

"We have reason to believe that Jenna's disappearance may be the result of foul play." He laid that out there like a policeman talking about someone he didn't know, not his own flesh and blood.

The dean frowned. "I'm at a loss for words."

"As are we," Jason said. "But if you or anyone else sees Jenna or hears from her, I need you to call me immediately." He pulled out a business card and gave it to the dean.

"I certainly will. I just wish there was something else I could do." He glanced at me, apologetic, with sorrowful eyes.

Jason pointed to his card in the dean's hand. "Just call."

The dean nodded, and Jason and I saw ourselves out.

"Now what?" I asked him, keeping pace with his long strides.

"As I said before. I'll talk to my boss, and we'll get some officers out looking for her—here and on the streets. We'll also get someone on tracking her phone and that blocked number that called you."

"And monitoring Jenna's phone."

"That's right. Don't you worry. We're going to get Jenna back and nail this son of a bitch."

All I could do was nod. An intense sadness slammed into me like a wave crashing into shore, and I started to sob.

Jason hugged me. When he pulled back, his gaze had the resolution of steel. "We'll get her back."

This time, his assurance didn't sting, but I realized he never promised her safe return either—just that we'd get her back. I supposed I had to prepare my mind for the possibility that… No. I couldn't. More tears fell.

"Come on, let's get to the car." He pulled out his phone as we walked and asked for Sergeant Tucker. He was from the uniformed division and my brother's superior. We were inside the cruiser when he was connected. Jason put the call on speaker and ran through the scenario, leaving out my vision and watering down the threat as if it came to me out of the seeming blue.

When Jason had finished, Tucker said, "We'll get unies on it immediately. I'll also let the lab know you'll be stopping by. I recommend that you speak to Logan Reese. He's a millennial, and if there's anyone who can unlock a blocked number and trace a phone that's off, it's him." There was a slight pause, then, "I'm sorry you're going through this. Take whatever time you need."

"Thanks, Sarge."

The underlying message wasn't that Jason was taking personal leave but that his responsibilities would be shifted until Jenna was found—alive and unharmed, if there was a god in heaven. But my job had taught that bad things didn't just happen to bad people. More often, they happened to the good ones.

Jason ended the call and looked over at me. He appeared crestfallen, shoulders slumped, and chest ballooning. Sharing the fact Jenna was missing with his boss had obviously made the situation more real, and it was hitting my brother—hard.

"This is all on me," I fumbled out.

He reached over and took my hand without saying a word. He put the car into gear, and we headed for the TPS Forensics Identification Services building that was located on Jane Street in North York, an area in the northwest part of the city, in search of Logan Reese in Tech. I was praying he could work miracles. We needed one.

# Chapter Thirty-Three

My body trembled, my legs wavering, as I was walked with Jason from the cruiser toward the front doors of the forensics building. "I sure hope this Logan kid can help us."

"Makes two of us."

"I'd like to know how my caller knew about me in the first place." I'd been pinballing this thought around since the phone call, and no satisfying answers were hitting. The environmental group wasn't feeling as ominous to me as it had before. I just feared wasting time on them and it taking us further from Jenna.

"If I tell you my hunch," Jason began, "you're going to think I'm judging the guy."

"David wouldn't be behind this. And why would he be?"

Jason met my gaze, and my stomach flip-flopped. "Never said that."

"Your eyes are saying something different."

He stopped walking. So did I. "My eyes are probably full of judgment. Yeah, I don't like the guy. I never made a secret of it. Then there's the whole issue with you having…visions." Again, his lips curled like he had bile on his tongue.

"I'm sorry you don't understand." Neither did I, but for a different reason. Not even one flash to indicate where Jenna was. How was that fair?

"You asked how someone could know… Were you talking to David in person or on the phone?"

"This morning, it was on the phone."

"Okay, so all I can think is maybe someone's listening in—either through your phone or David's."

For the first time since I found out Jenna was missing, I was filled with concern for David. If I was threatened for looking into the crash, surely this person wouldn't appreciate David's poking around. "Could David be in danger?"

"Did he sound off to you this morning, tense or stressed?"

I thought back. "Not at all." He'd seemed more concerned about me, but I didn't share that with Jason. He'd just leap to suspecting David in this mess—which made no sense, but Jason's mind was clouded at the moment.

"I don't know if he's in danger too. I *do* know that you're a mother with something to lose."

"Jenna." I put a hand over my stomach.

"You could have been targeted as the weaker link. Whoever was behind the threat probably suspects you'll do as he says to protect Jenna."

My mind was processing the point Jason had just made. Someone listening in on my conversations with David. "David and I discussed most things in person, not over the phone. How could they possibly know what we'd said?"

"I'm quite sure that people can hack into a phone and record what's going on around it."

I wasn't the techiest person in the world. "That's scary as hell."

"Yep. I don't even think they need physical contact with the phone. It's something that can be set up remotely."

"Jeez. Is technology a blessing or a curse?" Were the people who had Jenna listening in right now? I pulled out my phone and turned it off, assuming that would sever the connection. Hoping it would—if it were indeed tapped.

"Both. But whoever this man is or whoever he represents, must be getting nervous you're going to expose them. I mean, it's gotta be that." Jason kicked the tip of his shoe to the pavement.

I touched his arm. "I know it must be hard to come to grips with all this." I was mainly referring to the vision, which I was quite sure he'd gathered.

"It is." Jason had this blank look in his eyes, and there was a palpable silence between us for a moment. Eventually, he said, "You told me that you last had David looking into a passenger and the contents of the black box? This was before the threatening call?"

"Yes. Probably not long before it." Initially the timing between calling Fighters for Future America and receiving the threat had raised my suspicions against the organization. Now, I was starting to think the tight window might excuse them.

"I say we start with finding out what David found out."

"But Jenna. That would still be investigating the crash."

Jason put a hand on my upper arm. "Not exactly. It might lead us to whoever took Jenna, and if we're going to find her, we need as much intel as we can gather."

I bit my bottom lip. God, I hoped my little girl was okay.

"Call David." Jason handed me his phone. "Get him to meet you someplace near here. Whatever you do, don't tell him where you are now and don't talk much on the phone."

"Okay." After the way I'd treated David, who knew if he'd take my call? But there was another problem. "I need to get his number from my phone." I turned my phone on just long enough to key David's number into Jason's Android.

He held out his hand for my phone. "I'll be inside."

I nodded and placed the call while he entered the building. David's line rang a few times, and just when I was sure I'd be greeted by his voicemail, he picked up.

"It's Erin," I said when he answered, knowing he wouldn't have Jason's number in his phone.

"Are you okay?"

Tears stung my eyes. After the way I'd treated him last we spoke, his first concern was still me. This man was incredible. "I'm okay, but it's—" I sobbed, the emotions bubbling up like a torrent, and I was unable to control them.

"Erin. Talk to me."

"I…I can't talk to you over the phone." For all we knew, someone could be listening in right now. Sickening and such a violation of privacy!

"I'll come to your place."

I imagined him jumping into immediate action, headed for the nearest door. "I need you to meet me somewhere else."

"Name it."

I felt nervous telling him where to meet me, knowing his phone could be tapped. But Jason had said to give David a meeting place near here without revealing my current location. My eyes scanned the lot, then past it. My gaze fell on two golden arches. "Meet me at McDonald's in North York," I said. "It's on Jane Street."

"I'll leave right now."

"Thank you."

He ended the call, and I clutched my brother's phone to my chest. What if my stupid vision had endangered David as well? I also needed to ask how far out that threat might extend—to Jason, his family, Aunt Judy, Trish?

# Chapter Thirty-Four

I bought a small coffee at McDonald's and sat at a table with my back to a wall, where I could watch people come and go. If my stalker was here, I'd be able to see him. But he didn't have to be here. He didn't even need to be anywhere close to here to keep tabs on me. That thought didn't help my imagination.

I had a small notebook and pen in my purse and figured the old-school method would be a private means of communicating the situation to David. After my phone call to him, I'd returned Jason's phone to him inside the building's lobby and told him I was meeting David next door. He reminded me to ask for Logan Reese when I returned.

David walked into the restaurant, and I waved him over. My heart lifted at the sight of him but also contracted at the stress and worry written on his face. He dropped into the seat across from me, and I spun the pad of paper in his direction so he could read what I had written.

> *"Your phone may be tapped. Someone listening in. Don't say anything out loud."*

He narrowed his eyes and cocked his head in confusion. I turned the page.

> *"Received threatening phone call. Told to stop investigating crash. Jenna is now missing!"*

He stared at the last line, looked up at me, then back down at the page. He frowned and reached across the table for my hand and mouthed, *"I'm sorry."*

I took my hand back and pointed to the next message.

*"We need to talk. Come with me next door to the TPS forensics building."*

David nodded, and we both got up and left. Neither of us said anything as we headed toward the building and went inside. The person at the front desk had been made aware of the situation and let us in without saying a word and gave me a note directing us to where we'd find Jason and Logan Reese.

We went down a couple of corridors until we found the room we were after. I could hear Jason's voice filtering into the hall and pointed toward the door. I gestured for David to stay back and let me go in first.

"Jason," I began quietly and took in the space. There was a bank of monitors and computers. A twentysomething guy smiled at me, and Jason waved for me and David to enter.

Once inside, Jason said, "Cell signals and all hacking apps are jammed in this room." He held out his opened hand to David. "Phone."

David put his phone in my brother's palm, and Jason passed it to the twentysomething guy.

"You remember David?" I said to my brother, miffed he couldn't be bothered to say a simple "Hey" or "Hello."

"Yep," was all he said to that, then introduced us to the young man. "This is Logan Reese."

Logan held out his hand to me, then to David.

"Nice to meet you, Logan," I said, and shot my brother a reproachful look as if to say, *That's how greetings are done.* But it sank in what a liar I was. I'd only met Logan because of the predicament Jenna was in. I would have been perfectly fine never meeting him.

"I'm sorry for what's going on," Logan offered.

"Thank you," I said, remorse worming through me at my last thought.

David reached for my hand, and I let him hold it. His touch emboldened me, like I could handle whatever was coming my way. Though I knew it was just a moment of false strength. If Jenna was hurt, it wouldn't matter who was by my side; I'd be destroyed.

"Logan's going to try tracking Jenna's phone. He's also quite confident he can track down the number that called you," Jason said.

"There are many apps out there that help unlock even blocked numbers." Logan held up my phone. "It shouldn't take too long to find that out. It's figuring out the owner of the number that might take more time."

I nodded and glanced at David, trying to draw more courage from him. His eyes were full of loving concern, but there was nothing soft about the set of his jaw that spoke of resolve.

"We find this guy, and I'm having first crack at him," David seethed. Both Logan and Jason looked at him, then each other. "Hey, you can't blame me, can you?" David spat out, aimed at Jason.

"We need to take our emotions out of this. If we don't, we're not doing Jenna any favors." Jason's voice was sharp and pointed.

"But she's your niece."

"I don't need you telling me that," Jason hurled back.

"Enough," I snapped.

Jason's posture softened some. "Tell us what you found out," he said to David.

"What I—" David let go of my hand and stepped back. He was looking at me like I'd betrayed his trust, and I suppose I had.

"You have to understand, David. I needed to tell him. Jenna is my world," I pleaded, certain he'd see my side.

David's face softened, but he said, "What we were doing was to be between us."

"Obviously it wasn't," Jason said coolly.

I held up a hand to my brother and gave him a glare to butt out. "Someone found out. Someone threatened my Jenna, and now no one can reach her. No one has seen her."

David put a hand on my shoulder, and I laid mine over his.

"Please, tell us what you found out," I petitioned, "about the black-box recording and Shane Fox." As I asked him to share his findings, guilt curdled in my gut. I was withholding the information about my call to Fighters for Future America, yet I wanted him to come forward with all he knew.

"The recording on the black box indicates there might have been a mechanical malfunction with the plane."

This was my first time hearing of a malfunction, and I wanted to find out more, but remained quiet.

David went on. "The pilots didn't seem to know what was causing the plane to nosedive."

"Could also be pilot error…inexperience," Jason reasoned.

David shrugged. "Could be. The wreckage from the crash is expansive, and it will take time to conduct a thorough investigation to see if there was a manufacturer defect at play. But a plane, as I probably don't need to point out, has many moving parts."

"So, nothing definitive," I said. "But there was some suspicion of the crash being intentional…"

David met my gaze. "Preliminary speculation. Not proven."

"Why am I just hearing this now?" Jason exclaimed. "Someone sabotaged the flight, you guys poke around, then that person gets spooked they'll be found out." Jason paced the room, raking a hand through his hair. He stopped in front of me. "What have you done?"

The question, barely spoken above the volume of a whisper might as well have been a Samurai sword plunged into my chest. I stumbled to a nearby chair and sat down. It was time for me to come clean, lay everything out. "I called Fighters for Future America."

David's gaze locked with mine.

"I know we said we'd talk before we did anything. I'm sorry."

He kept looking at me but said nothing.

"Fighters for Future America. Why do they sound familiar?" Jason asked, just as the answer dawned on his face. "Oh. They were in the news being accused of taking the plane down."

I nodded, rubbed my arms.

"So, what happened on this call? Why do you think it has something to do with the threat against Jenna?"

I ran through it with Jason, concluding with, "It was a strange reaction, and the threat didn't come long after. That's why I began to think it couldn't be them. They'd have to do some research on me, and would they have had that time?"

"You know how fast and how much you can find online," David said.

"It could have been a coincidence," Jason said. "Though it might not be. Why were you investigating this crash anyway?"

"I told you." My voice was small, but my back was stiff and ramrod straight.

"Because of some dream you had."

"A vision," I corrected.

Jason shook his head. "You put faith in some vision and now look where we're at."

"Her vision was the real deal," David jumped in.

Hearing more blame coming at me from my brother was almost too much to take, but I didn't need someone speaking on my behalf. I looked at David. "I don't need you to defend me," I snapped. "And, Jason, I don't need your judgment."

"There's nothing sane about—" he waved his hands around "—visions. You could have a tumor or a growth pushing on your brain, making you hallucinate."

"My visions have merit in the real world or, yeah, we might not be in this position." The truth sank in my gut. Should I tell him about Lily Brooks? I decided against it; he really wouldn't understand, and I didn't need to stir him up any more than he already was. "We could argue about this all day, but it doesn't get us closer to Jenna."

"This type of thing… It's not even Christian, Erin," Jason said, disappointment in his voice.

David stepped toward Jason. "Who are—"

I held up my hand to silence David and picked up where I guessed he'd been headed. "Who are you to say what is or isn't Christian?"

Jason flinched as if I'd physically struck him. "It's demonic. Clairvoyance, seeing the future. Having an audience with a spirit medium, psychics… It's in the Bible as something that displeases God. You're not to even have company with such people. If you're having visions, Erin, that means you're psychic, and…" He swallowed roughly, and the pain in my brother's eyes shredded my heart.

"You just don't understand," I said. "I didn't at first, either. It scared the shit out of me."

"As it should. None of this makes any sense, Erin. You know that? None at all."

"Jason, I love you, but stop." I was heaving for breath, and my heart was shattering. "Let's just focus on getting Jenna back. That's all that matters right now."

My brother swallowed roughly again, his Adam's apple heaving, tears beading in his eyes. "We need to gather what we can on any aviation companies associated with the plane—"

"Lots of moving parts, as I said. That will be a long list," David pointed out.

"Best to get started, then. We'll also see what we can uncover on this Fighters for Future America group and—" Jason turned to me "—that passenger you told me about. What was his name?"

"Shane Fox," I replied.

"I was going to get around to this," David said, "but my colleague tasked with the lead in the Texas crash accessed the passport the man had provided, and the ID number tied back to a Shane Fox of Newark, New Jersey. Fox was reported missing by his cousin six months ago."

"Missing or…" My throat constricted. Scenes from action movies played out in my mind, and I had the stark realization I was living one and dragging Jenna along with me.

Then came images I couldn't reconcile. They flew across my vision clearly, and all else around me went black.

*A shadowy form above me. Dirt. Fingers stretching out, yearning, grasping upward. To no avail. My throat was getting tighter. It was becoming harder and harder to breathe…*

Next thing I knew, Jason and David were standing over me, both saying my name. There was another voice I couldn't place at first.

*Where the hell am I?* My head was spinning and fluorescent lights beamed overhead, near blinding. Cool tile was beneath my fingertips. "What—"

"It's okay, just lie still. We're getting help." David swept some of my hair behind one of my ears.

"I'm…" I moved to get up and was painfully aware of every one of my forty-three years.

"Just stay still," Jason directed.

"I saw— Fox is dead," I managed to get out.

"Yes, he was killed in a plane crash," Jason replied.

"No." I shook my head, and pain creeped up the back of my neck and around my skull. "The real Shane Fox was buried alive."

# Chapter Thirty-Five

I struggled to my feet, despite protests from Jason, David, and the tech.

David took my hand and helped me up. "You had another vision, didn't you?"

I glanced past him to Jason, who was watching me with skepticism and disappointment.

"I did," I admitted. "I saw a man's hand reaching up toward the sky as dirt came in on top of him."

"Did you see his face?" David asked.

I shook my head. "No, but I *know* it was the real Shane Fox."

Jason clenched his jaw and hooked his thumbs on the waistband of his pants. "The more time we waste on this—"

"So, whoever used the real Shane Fox's passport was the one who killed him," David said, interrupting Jason.

"Possible. Yes," I said.

"Now the question becomes who was the man who died in the crash."

"And does he have something to do with the plane going down—like some sort of martyr—or Jenna's disappearance?" The minute the last words were out, I realized their foolishness. "Never mind. The man's dead. What could he possibly do from the grave?" Goosebumps raised on my arms, but I chose to ignore them.

"I know what you mean. Not him, per se, but possibly someone this Fox imposter was associated with. They might not want us uncovering something," David suggested.

"And if they took Jenna, they still have something to hide or lose, and they believe we're going to find out what that is," I reasoned.

"Before we get carried away, let's take this one step at a time," Jason said firmly and looked at Logan. "Have you gotten anywhere with unblocking the number?"

"Nope."

"Thought that was to be the easy part."

"Me too. No luck tracking Jenna's phone at this point either." Logan slid his gaze to me, his eyes apologetic.

"What are we going to do?" I exclaimed. "We can't just stand around here while Jenna's…" I gulped. Her being suddenly unreachable would hit me in waves, ebb and flow. It would come in distinct heaviness that this nightmare was reality, and then it would soften as if it were just part of a bad dream, an alternate reality without consequences.

Jason fixed his gaze on David. "Could you get a picture of this guy? The one who actually got on the flight? If so, we could run him through facial recognition software."

"I can ask the lead investigator."

"No," Jason stamped out. "From here on out, whatever we do, it stays among those of us in this room."

"I've worked with Bill for—"

Jason held up a hand to silence David. "It doesn't matter. Assuming someone has tapped your phone, they could also be listening in on his as well. Is there someone you could contact at the airport in Texas where this Shane Fox imposter boarded the plane?"

"I could try," David said.

"But it has to be done without anyone else knowing," I stressed.

"He can use a phone here," Logan interjected. "I'll give him a secure email address to pass along."

I nodded. "It's just if Jenna's kidnapper finds out—" I latched gazes with my brother, and it was there in his eyes. I wasn't going to like what he was about to say.

"As I told you, we need more intel."

"At what risk? They could hurt her, kill her."

Jason's eyes drifted to the floor, and he said quietly, "They could have done that already."

I cried out and shoved him in the shoulder. David rushed over.

I didn't want anyone telling me Jenna would be fine, offering false hope, but I also didn't need anyone pointing out what could have happened to her, that she could be—

I doubled over, sobbing.

David wrapped his arms around me until I calmed down.

"Go," Jason waved at David, "and do what I asked. Please."

David's feet remained planted. "You're sure the phone line and email are safe?"

"Everything here is, including the server." Logan rolled over and gestured at the empty chair next to him. It was in front of a second keyboard and mouse.

David took a seat and brought up a login portal for the NTSB, which I could tell by the logo. I assumed he was going to dig for his contact at the Houston airport.

"While David's working on his to-do list," Jason started, "Logan, will you bring up a background on Shane Fox of Newark, New Jersey?"

"You bet."

Seconds later, we were looking at the information on the real Shane Fox, the one buried alive. Accepting my vision, anyway. Which I did.

"Fox was forty-six, single, owned a house in Newark," Logan said. "He doesn't have a criminal record."

"So why him?" I asked. "When David and I were doing some internet searches, the Shane Fox in my vision didn't have an online presence at all."

"The real Shane Fox could be shady as hell too," Jason suggested.

I nodded, supposing that could be true. "Why can't I just see where she is?" The question tumbled out.

Jason looked up at the ceiling, as if he expected God to grant him both strength and patience.

"I saw the plane crash. It happened. I saw Lily Brooks too."

"Who's Lily Brooks?" Jason asked.

I took a deep breath. Did he not see the Amber Alert? "Maybe another time. But why can't I see where Jenna is, and if she's okay? I can't even *feel* if she's okay anymore." I knotted the fabric of my shirt and pinched my eyes shut. Nothing but darkness. When I opened them, my gaze fell to my phone that was sitting on the desk in front of Logan. "There's no signal in here."

All three men looked at me like I'd hit my head hard when I fell.

"What if the kidnapper is trying to reach me?" I screeched.

No one said a word, and I feared they were thinking what had just marched through my mind—another call wasn't necessary. I'd been warned. Maybe this was the end of the line. I gulped back a sob, and Logan held out my phone to me.

"Just be careful. It could be tapped, remember."

*As if I can forget!* I took my phone and headed for the exit.

# Chapter Thirty-Six

I stepped outside and gulped in the cool air. I was afraid to turn on my phone. A message from the madman would make this all the more real, while silence could indicate I was too late, that I'd already sealed Jenna's fate.

My screen lit up with notifications of messages and missed calls, including one from Trish, and a single voicemail. I assumed that was also from Trish. But chills ran through me when I saw one of the missed calls had come from a blocked number. What if I had been too late?

I ran back inside to let Jason know that the man had called again. My phone rang just as I reached the room. I stopped in the hall, remembering cell signals couldn't penetrate inside the room. I looked at the screen. Caller ID was *Unknown*. My hands were shaking so badly, I thought I might drop my phone.

"Jason," I called out, but it came back to my ears more as a croak. He poked his head in the hall, and I said, "It's him."

"Answer," Jason urged. "We're right here with you."

I accepted the call but didn't say anything.

"You didn't leave well enough alone. I warned you, but you didn't listen." The man's voice sounded tinny, and it echoed as if he were calling from a tunnel. I didn't remember that from the first time.

"What do you want?" I cried.

"I told you what I wanted yesterday."

A long, drawn-out silence, then, "One last chance. You stop looking into the plane crash, or I will have no choice but to kill your daughter."

*Kill!* I clamped a hand over my mouth.

"Did you hear me?"

"Yes." It was barely a whisper.

Jason pushed a piece of paper under my nose. It read, *"Proof of life."*

I blinked back tears, stiffened my shoulders. "How do I know she's still alive?"

A few seconds of silence, then, "Mom!"

At Jenna's shrill voice, I stumbled backward and bumped into David's chest. He steadied me with his hands on my upper arms, and I sank against him. I'd never even seen him approach.

"Jenna, baby, are you okay?" *This isn't happening. This isn't happening.*

"He hasn't hurt me, Mom, but I need you to do what he says. Because he will—"

"Enough," the man cut in. "The family reunion is over. Do as I say, or there won't be another one."

"But I've already stopped looking into the crash," I pleaded. "How do I get her back? Tell me."

"From what I understand, that is not true. Stop, or your dear daughter will be left dead at your doorstep." With that, he was gone.

"Oh my God!" I screamed out. "Oh my God! He's going to kill her, Jason!"

Jason put his hands on my arms. "Try to calm down and tell us what he said."

"I need to stop looking into the crash." I met Jason's eyes. "Somehow, he knows I haven't."

Jason leveled a look at David. "What did you do?"

"I haven't done much of anything."

Jason smacked the back of his one hand into the palm of the other. "Every step."

"You've been right here. I called a contact I have at Bush Intercontinental Airport in Houston, Texas, and requested the photo."

"Someone at the airport is behind the crash and Jenna's disappearance," I said and shook my head. "Guess that wouldn't make sense. Not if you just contacted them."

We filtered back into the room where Logan was still perched behind his monitors. He made eye contact with me, but I hated the pity I saw in his gaze.

David dropped back into the chair he'd been in and clicked the mouse. "It doesn't make sense." He leaned in toward the monitor. "I do have an email from the airport though."

"Oh God. Then you know what this could mean?" I was on the verge of utter hysteria. "Someone within the NTSB…" I heaved for breath, and Jason guided me to another chair. "Maybe they're watching logins into the system."

"Or someone external is," David said. "We like to think our system can't be penetrated by hackers but…" He opened the email and clicked the attachment. A photo opened of a man with large brown eyes, a small beak-like nose. "Is that him?"

I took a close look and nodded. "That's the man who was in my vision."

"He looks nothing like Shane Fox," Jason said. "How could he pose as the man? The real Fox's picture would be in his passport. Security always looks. And why assume Fox's identity in the first place? I know you said that already, Erin."

"He could have changed the photo in the passport," Logan said. "Where there's enough money and a criminal mind, the possibilities are endless."

"Not too reassuring," I replied, hugging myself.

"I'll get the photo you have there, David, and run it through facial rec," Logan began. "Odds are he has a record."

I rocked back and forth on the heels of my feet. "They're going to…" I couldn't bring myself to say it, but a wave of extreme rage fired through me. "You said we'd get Jenna back." I leveled a look at my brother. "And we're going to. We're also going to find out who the hell this guy is and what he's hiding."

All three men were watching me, their eyes assessing, their lips slightly parted.

"I'm serious." I punched out defiantly. "I know how upset I got earlier about us gathering intel, as you put it, Jay. But you were right." What I didn't say was that I also owed it to victims' loved ones to keep my head in the game. I had been given the vision for a reason; I was starting to feel that more than ever.

Jason sighed. "All right. Let's keep going. I'll find out more about the real Shane Fox and see what shakes loose. I'll contact the Newark Police Department where the missing person report was filed. Hopefully, I can get ahold of Fox's cousin too." Jason nudged his head toward Logan. "Let me know how you make out with facial rec."

"I'll keep you posted," Logan said. "I'll also keep working to unblock that number."

"Were you able to track Jenna's phone?" I asked Logan.

"Still no success."

I took a deep breath. "And our phones—mine and David's? Were either of them hacked into?"

"I will let you know." Logan started clicking away on his keyboard.

Jason turned to David. "Do your digging outside NTSB servers because they may be compromised. Compile that list of aviation parts manufacturers, and we'll pick 'em apart one at a time if we have to."

"Jenna probably doesn't have that amount of time," I said.

Jason put a hand on my shoulder, an act to calm me, but it did the opposite.

"What can I do?" I was desperate to do something; all this standing around was torture.

"Right now, there's not much," my brother told me.

I held eye contact with him for a while and consented, though it pained me. "I should call Trish, let her know."

"We should call Aunt Judy too," Jason said. "Also Chris. I hate the bastard, but he is Jenna's dad."

"No. I'm not calling either of them right now, for different reasons." The fact that Chris hadn't returned my call from yesterday really ticked me off. I wasn't getting into everything with Aunt Judy unless it was absolutely necessary. It didn't feel like it was that time yet.

"Erin." Jason angled his head. "What if—"

"No, you keep telling me we're getting Jenna back safe and sound, so Aunt Judy never needs to know."

"You just don't want to tell her about the visions," he accused.

"No, I don't," I admitted. "But I will tell her when the time is right. Just as I told you. But I'm not going to hit Aunt Judy with the visions unless absolutely necessary. And there's no sense worrying her about Jenna. Not yet."

Seconds passed in silence before Jason pushed his phone toward me and gestured for me to leave the room.

"I'll need Trish's number from my phone," I said. After I got it, I headed out, and from down the hall, I could hear David tell my brother he needed some fresh air.

I expected David was probably wanting to catch up with me to lay into me about betraying his trust, but he didn't say a word. He just stood next to me and held my hand while I called Trish. The caring gesture had more warm tears filling my eyes.

The instant Trish answered, I blurted out, "I need to tell you something."

There was silence on her end.

I continued. "Something's happened, and it's going to be a shock to hear."

"Go on."

"Jenna's been kidnapped." Matter-of-fact, no sugar-coating.

"What?" she spat. Her typical cool and calm was gone. "Who? Why? *What?*"

"Someone didn't like me looking into the plane crash, and they've—"

"Erin, please tell me she's okay."

"God, I hope so." I looked up at the sky; the sun was quickly sinking, but I picked up on the white trails left from airplanes that crisscrossed the expanse like strokes of a mad painter. "I heard her, Trish." *Proof of life, like they ask for in the movies*, I thought. "She sounded so scared."

"Thank God she's alive at least. But how does this person know you're looking into the crash?"

"That's something we still need to figure out."

"We? You and David or…?"

"I had to tell Jason everything." I swallowed the urge to cry. It was easy to conjure his disgust, his disappointment.

"Oh. How did he handle that?"

"About as good as expected. So Jason's helping, and David, and some kid in Tech with the police."

There was a slight pause on her end, then, "Well, you're obviously getting close to the truth. That's why this person wants you to stop."

"That's what we think, yes, but we're still blind to what that truth is—and who it is. It looks like my phone and/or David's might have been hacked into somehow so this person could listen in to our conversations."

"Oh my God. This is a nightmare."

"You're telling me," I stated sourly.

"Just let me know if I can do anything. Actually, where are you? I'm coming to you."

"You don't—"

"I know I don't have to, but please…"

Emotion balled in my chest. Trish was like a sister I never had, and if the roles were reversed, I'd insist on being by her side. "I'm at the TPS Forensics Identification Services building."

"In North York? Yes, I've seen it. I'll be right there."

"Okay. Love you."

"Love you. Try to stay positive."

I ended the call and wished to hell I hadn't dropped that bomb on Trish over the phone, but I wanted her to know what was going on.

David stood in front of me, his hand still holding mine. He peered into my eyes but said nothing. He had every right to be upset with me for breaking his trust, but instead he was supporting me with both his actions and his words.

"I can't believe this is happening," I cried, and he held me tight. Tears came in fast succession.

# Chapter Thirty-Seven

I stared into my coffee as if it could provide the answers I needed, as if it could bring Jenna to me. God, I wished caffeine held that kind of power.

I was in what I figured was a meeting-slash-training room. There were rows of chairs facing two six-foot-long tables at the front of the room, along with a desk and phone. A whiteboard took up most of the wall behind the tables. Jason felt this was the best place for me to stay for the time being. At some point, I'd have to get my car from the lot at work, but it just didn't seem that important at the moment. And I had refused to go home, not bearing the thought of being alone. David had offered to join me and take care of his business from there. I knew once Trish got here, she'd happily accompany me back to my townhouse too. But there was something about being here, on standby, that made me feel not quite so powerless. An illusion, surely, but one I wanted to cling to.

David walked in holding up a chocolate bar and a bag of chips. "I didn't know what you'd want. Sugar or salt." He slipped into a chair beside me.

"I can't think of eating right now."

"I can understand that." He set the candy on the table. "I'm so sorry I got you involved in all this."

I looked over at him. "You got me involved? I did this. This is all on me." We still hadn't had a conversation about how I'd broken his confidence. Given that I really hadn't had any other choice but to confess that we'd been looking into the crash, it seemed all was forgiven.

"Nope." He shook his head adamantly. "If I didn't pry my nose into Bill's investigation, then none of this would be happening."

"You don't know that." I fell quiet for a few seconds. "Thank you for understanding why I had to come clean about our collaboration. I hope it doesn't get you into too much trouble at work."

"Makes two of us. But you had a very good reason, and I'd be an ass if I didn't understand given the circumstances."

I smiled. "I suppose you would be. Are you getting anywhere with the list of aviation parts manufacturers?"

"Needle in a haystack mean anything to you? There are a lot. Maybe if I had access to hear the black-box recording myself, I'd pick up on something the pilot or copilot might have said. But as your brother made clear, I'm doing this without involving anyone at the NTSB."

Silence fell between us, and in my head, I shuffled through the slow progress we were making as a group. Jason was still endeavoring to get somewhere with the Newark Police Department. Logan had passed on the photo of the Shane Fox imposter to another tech who specialized in facial-recognition database searches. Still no success tracking Jenna's phone. Hadn't heard any more about my blocked caller. In retrospect, it didn't seem like we were making much progress at all. God, I could only hope for a breakthrough.

"I'm not sure what else I can do." David took my hand.

"You're doing everything you can, and you're here." I gave him a tight smile and swallowed the cry whelming up in my throat.

"I'll always be here for you."

If I let myself get caught up in his blue eyes, I'd believe his sentiment, but reality carried a sober note. "You don't even live in Canada."

"What does that matter? We're not in the dark ages." He smiled, but the expression faded quickly. "There's phone, internet, video calling. And, well, I'm technically a dual citizen."

"You are?"

"I am."

"Oh." Something about knowing David could live in Canada applied more pressure to our relationship. Like it actually stood a chance.

"Yeah… *Oh*."

The way he was looking into my eyes, letting his gaze drift to my mouth… I licked my lips, glanced away, shy, timid. But it also didn't seem like the right time to kiss him. "That's good for me."

"Good for *us*."

I nodded and stared into my coffee. This time trying to distract myself from his gorgeous face, his beautiful lips, and the strong urge to kiss him. My mind was despicable! Jenna was out there somewhere with a madman, and it was all my fault. Even if I'd been more open with her, told her about the threat, she could have been more vigilant, and she might have thwarted her kidnapper.

"Getting any answers from your coffee?" David asked.

I met his gaze and shook my head. "I wish I was, and I wish I'd told Jenna about the threat. If I had, maybe she'd be fine now." It was maddening what empty pockets of time did to the psyche. Thinking was highly overrated.

"I can understand how you might feel that way, but the truth is we could be sitting here anyway."

"I appreciate you saying that…" My words trailed off as chastisement rolled in. "I have visions about this plane crash, strangers even. I saw, or sensed, a man I've never met before being buried alive. It was intense enough. It had knocked me off my feet. But I haven't received any visions about where Jenna is being held. Not one image." I sniffled and pinched the tip of my nose to keep the tears at bay.

"There's no explaining visions."

"I'm so grateful you're here."

He rubbed my back.

"You've been so understanding from the start," I went on. "You saw how Jason reacted to my visions." *Demonic.* The word he'd used wouldn't go away anytime soon. I regarded David. "Why are you so accepting of them?"

David pulled his hand back, tore open the chip bag, and popped chips into his mouth.

"You're just going to leave me hanging here?"

He smiled despite a full mouth. Chewed. Swallowed. "Let's just say I have experience with clairvoyants, or psychics, if you'd prefer."

I drew back, surprised. "You said you never employed them in an investigation."

"I never have." Another chip went into his mouth, disappeared.

"Enlighten me, then."

"My sister used to get visions."

"I had no idea." I picked up on the past tense, but I wasn't going to poke that part so he'd keep talking.

"You'd have no reason to." He tossed out a nonchalant smile. "Anyway, let's just say my parents were set against it. They were like your brother. Thought it was the Devil's work. They ousted my sister from the family. Completely cut her off."

"But you kept in touch with her?" It was just a feeling I was getting.

"I did, as much as possible. She was older than me."

I caught the past tense again but wasn't sure if I should ask about it. If I didn't, though, it might come across as insensitive. "She *was*?"

David slowly nodded. "She died a year ago. Well, fourteen months and sixteen days, but who's counting?"

I reached for his hand. "I'm so sorry."

"It wasn't your fault." He tossed out a brief smile. "The big C got her. Not unlike a lot of people."

"That doesn't make it easier," I said gently.

"Not really. Anyway, I kept up a relationship with her as best as I could over the years. Obviously, it was much easier as an adult than as a kid."

"So, the two of you were close?"

"Yeah, you could say that. She never got married, and I was her brother, friend, and confidante. Sadly, she never recovered from the hurt our parents had caused and the ostracism. She didn't let other people into her life. She shut down her heart. Probably figured that way she couldn't be hurt again. She told me more than once that if her own parents couldn't love her, no one could."

"How sad."

"Very. She had suicidal moments, but thankfully never acted on them. I'd like to think I helped her, and she seemed to be in better spirits not long before her diagnosis, but when it came, she just lost her fight."

"That would have been a rough time."

He nodded, remained silent.

"You said she had visions?" I hoped to turn the conversation around to a happier note.

"She most certainly did, and they were spot-on." He paused and smiled, but he also had this wistful look in his eyes like he was caught up in a memory. "That's why I became a believer in her, in visions, in psychics overall. I know there are some out there who are frauds, but I like giving people the benefit of the doubt."

"One of the things I, uh…like about you." I came far too close to saying *love*.

"It's a strength and a weakness. But I suppose it's better to live with one's heart open to the world than shut off. If anything, watching my sister's shell of a life taught me that."

I wasn't going to say as much out loud, but Trish liked to remind me that there was good even in the perceived bad— the silver lining. The life lesson that David had extracted from his sister's heartbreak was a good takeaway. He'd been forever changed from her impact and made a better man for it.

"Anyway, I liked you from the moment I saw you," he said. "And I wouldn't go so far as to say I'm psychic, but I get feelings."

"Intuition."

"Yup. That fits."

"Some might say that our intuition is a psychic part of ourselves."

"Trish tell you that?"

"Yeah."

"Someone say my name?" Trish swept into the room, holding a couple of grocery bags. She deposited them on the nearest chair and rushed to me as I did to her.

"Oh, honey." She pulled me into a hug.

I squeezed my eyes shut, determined to remain strong, but when we backed out of the embrace, the tears in Trish's eyes had me getting choked up too.

She wiped my cheeks with the pads of her thumbs. "You're staying positive, right?"

I sniffled and nodded. "I'm trying."

"Good." Trish pressed her lips together and blinked slowly.

"Well, what have you got there?" I pointed to the bags she'd brought, trying to fend off the assaulting emotions of guilt, helplessness, and despair. Who knew where my baby was and what she was enduring while I was here?

"You may not feel like eating, but you probably should." She retrieved the bags and brought them to the table where I'd been sitting with David.

"Hi, David," she said with a smile.

"Hi."

"We met last Friday," she added.

"I remember. You're Erin's best friend."

"Sister, more like."

My heart swelled at her response. "You never said what you brought." I peeked inside the bags. Enticing aromas arose, but in response, my stomach clenched tighter.

"I just picked up a family meal deal from Metro. Rotisserie chicken, potato wedges, and a couple containers of macaroni salad. Not exactly the dinner of champions, but—"

"No, it's perfect," I told her.

"Metro?" David queried.

"A grocery store chain," I clarified. "Surely, you've seen them around," I added, poking a little lighthearted fun at him.

He gave me a slight eye roll and a smirk.

"And plates and forks," Trish went on as she pulled them from one of the bags.

"You think of everything," I said.

"I try." Trish went about setting out the food and cutlery. "Where's Jason? I assumed he'd be here."

"He is, but he's working on something," I replied.

"A lead?"

"One can hope."

"Hear any more from the kidnapper?" Trish asked, doing so with a delicate touch only she was capable of.

I shook my head. "Nothing."

"Jason has a tech working to see if they can unblock the number and track it," David volunteered.

"Oh, well, let's hope the tech gets lucky."

I proceeded to fill Trish in on the rest of what we knew, including my vision about the murdered man—presumably the real Shane Fox—that had landed me flat on the floor.

"You saw that man's grave?" Trish responded with surprise. "Just like that, at the mention of his name?" She snapped her fingers.

I jumped at the sudden noise.

"Oh, sorry." Trish rubbed my arm.

"Don't worry about it. I'm a little on edge."

"Understandable. So you saw his grave?"

"Not so much that, but it was like I was him being buried alive."

"Ick, but *huh*."

I angled my head in confusion, hoping she'd elaborate.

Trish looked at David, back to me. "I'd say your psychic ability is getting stronger."

"Not too sure about that," I mumbled. "I haven't seen anything about Jenna's whereabouts or her kidnapper."

"Oh, sweetheart, you're being hard on yourself. Give it time."

"I'd love to, but that's probably one thing that Jenna doesn't have."

Jason burst into the room. His gaze went over the three of us, took in the food, then met my eyes.

"Logan was able to unblock the number," he said, not sounding near as happy as I'd expect at the news.

Then I got it. "He doesn't know who it ties back to," I concluded.

"No, he doesn't."

"Shit," David said on an exhale.

"Did you track the phone?" I hugged myself, praying for some breakthrough.

"Yeah. Got all the legalities in order—leaving out some things." Jason looked away from me.

"The visions. You're embarrassed of me." It hurt incredibly to say this, to realize this.

Jason tugged down on his shirt and looked away, a pink hue splashing over his cheeks. I swallowed the urge to cry as Trish gave me a reassuring glance. My brother still needed time to come to grips with my visions, just as it had taken me a while to adapt. I hoped he'd come around.

David looked from me to Jason. "And…what was the result of the trace?"

"It's getting us nowhere still," Jason said. "Same holds for Jenna's phone."

"How did Logan make out with Erin's phone and mine? Were they both tapped?" David asked.

"Only yours was hacked into, which reminds me." Jason pulled my phone from his pocket and handed it to me without looking me in the eye.

"How did you make out with the Newark Police Department?" I asked.

"Got more information on the circumstances surrounding the missing person report," Jason started. "Fox hadn't shown up for work for several days, and the emergency contact they had was the cousin who reported him missing. She went to his place and thought there was sign of a struggle. It was investigated, but the case went cold. According to Fox's cousin, he was a self-professed Luddite."

"That explains no social media presence," I said.

Everyone nodded except for Trish, who hadn't received the entire scoop on Fox.

"Did you tell the woman why you were asking about her cousin?" I asked, curious.

"I just said I was looking into the missing person report. Not a lie." Jason glanced at David. "How are you making out?"

"Oh, I have a list," David said. "I'm just not sure what to do with it yet."

"Have a bite to eat, Jason," Trish urged, probably doing her best to dial down the tension that crackled in the room.

Jason put a hand to his stomach, and I could relate. His gut was likely a steel ball too. Even if food managed to go down, it might not stay there.

# Chapter Thirty-Eight

I tried to eat, but it was tough to swallow when I didn't know if my sweet Jenna was being cared for. Was she being given food and water and afforded basic human dignities?

Jason excused himself to check in with the tech on where things were sitting with the facial-recognition process.

I hated sitting around waiting, hands tied. It wasn't like we could dig anymore into Shane Fox. The man was a ghost, literally, and if you trusted the fake ID, twice. My mind mulled over the facts, which were in short supply. The one was that David's phone had been tapped, not mine. Yet, I'd been threatened, and my daughter taken. Was it as Jason had put it—I was seen as the vulnerable target because they could use Jenna as leverage? Or was there more to it?

"Why your phone and not mine?" I said, turning to David. "And we think your login with the NTSB is compromised. It would seem all of this is about the Texas crash, but you weren't assigned to investigate it."

David's eyes darkened then sparked. "We don't even know how long someone's been watching and listening."

"Oh, this could be bigger than one crash," I said, the thought now occurring to me. "Did you investigate any crashes that were similar to the Texas one? Or do you have any open investigations that would fall into that category?"

"There are always open cases, but none are identical to the one from last week," David said. "Though I did work an investigation a couple months ago where I'd suspected an engine malfunction as one of the contributing factors in causing the crash. I didn't have enough substantive proof though. Still haven't officially closed the investigation."

"Maybe you were closer to the truth than you thought. Could this company's faulty engine have caused the crash from last week too?"

David's face took on hard lines. "Possible, I guess."

"Were they the same type of plane?" Trish asked.

"No, but they'd have similar components and manufacturers in common."

I leaned toward him. "The same engine?"

"There are a lot of variables to consider and numerous sensors. I'm not comfortable stating it was the engine manufacturer. That's why the case is still open."

"Fair enough," I said.

Trish shrugged. "What are these sensors?"

"Too many to list."

"Could we narrow them down or find some similarities between the Texas crash and the one from a couple months ago?" I asked.

"Yeah, I could."

"Without logging into the NTSB portal?" I pushed.

"I can see what I can piece together by researching the plane models online."

"There's still something I'm having a hard time reconciling," Trish spoke up. "Why would whoever-it-is call attention to themselves by kidnapping Jenna? They'd have to know they couldn't just get away with that. Their faulty product—assuming that's what we're looking at here— would definitely be found out then."

"Huge money types think they can get away with anything." David looked from Trish to me. "And if we're looking at deep pockets, there's no saying where they'll stop. I'm sorry, Erin."

I rubbed my forehead. Still not a single image to help me find my daughter. I glanced up at the ceiling, passing on a silent plea to a greater being or anyone who would listen, that my little girl be returned safely. When I lowered my gaze, it aligned with Trish's.

"What were you doing when you had your vision about that murdered man?" she asked.

"I was just standing there," I replied, irritated. Not so much at my friend, but at the unfairness of how easily I had envisioned a stranger's situation but not my own daughter's.

"Just play along," she prompted.

"Um, well, we were just talking about the real Shane Fox. We'd found out he was reported missing."

"Were you really focused on the conversation, on what was going on?" Trish pried.

"Well, yeah. I figured he was a possible connection between the crash and Jenna's kidnapping."

"So you were focused on Shane Fox," Trish repeated.

"Yes." But I'd also been focused on my daughter from the moment I realized she'd disappeared, and that hadn't made a difference.

Trish's eyes widened. "We need to get the number the tech unblocked, the one from the man who took Jenna." She jumped to her feet and left the room.

"Where are you—"

She waved a hand over her head and disappeared into the hall. Several minutes later, she returned with a yellow sticky note in hand. She set it in front of me. It had a phone number written on it. "Focus on every, single digit. Concentrate."

"Why?" I was more than a little skeptical.

"If we're lucky, it will prompt a vision."

I loved her for her confidence and enthusiasm, but lacked faith. "I don't know…"

"Try it," Trish said. "What do you have to lose?"

I glanced at David, and he nodded.

"Fine," I conceded. "If there's any chance it will get my Jenna back, it's worth a try."

# Chapter Thirty-Nine

I did my best to concentrate on the phone number in front of me, and the digits were blurring together. My thoughts kept filling with images of Jenna's sweet, angelic face, her innocence, and the young love she had with Ryan. My heart was breaking. She had to return to us and live a full—

A sharp pain drilled my left temple.

*"We're all going to die." The woman's voice hits my ears. She is sitting behind me. I look over a shoulder, straining the length of cord attached to my oxygen mask.*

*Her face is one of abject horror, her fate drawn in her eyes.*

*Sweat is dripping down my back, and I grip the arms of my chair and face forward again.*

*The wealthy businessman is chanting, loud enough now that I can hear what he is saying. "Oh, Allah! Let me live as long as life is good for me, and let me die if death is good for me."*

*Something from the Quran? An expression of acceptance of what is to come, something of little comfort in the face of certain death—or I used to think that way. I strangely find surrender comforting right now.*

*I sit back, lean against the headrest, and whisper the words the man had said.*

*Rustling of movement across the aisle gets my attention. One of the man's companions is standing, and he's holding a knife.*

*The older woman beside me gasps.*

*Before anything can be done, he slits the neck of the businessman.*

"Erin. Erin!"

Someone was calling my name, but they sound so far away. I fluttered my eyelids only to find they were already open.

"You okay?" Trish was hunched next to me, David at her side.

"I had another vision." My mouth was dry, and I tapped my throat.

David got up quickly, hopefully to get some water.

"Here." He returned with a bottled water and helped me sit up. I took a large swig.

"Was it about Jenna?" Trish asked.

"No. It was a murder."

"Another murder?" Trish's brow wrinkled.

I wasn't sure how to fully interpret her reaction. Was I becoming a conduit for victims of crime? "Yes, murder. I was back on the plane, and I saw the Shane Fox imposter slit Howard Hayes's neck."

"Whoa." Trish wrapped an arm around me and rubbed my shoulder.

"Yeah. That's not all. I think the oil man is a Muslim. He quoted what I'm pretty sure is from the Quran. Was his death a hate crime? And does his assassination have anything to do with why the plane went down? Or are these two separate things?" The questions were multiplying, but I'd add one more. "Why can I see all this and not where Jenna is?"

"Maybe you're putting too much pressure on yourself," David said. "These things come according to their timing."

Trish looked over at him. "Someone sounds like a smarty."

"Like a candy-covered chocolate?" David smirked.

"You know what I meant."

"Thanks."

Trish smiled at him. "You're welcome."

Jason burst into the room.

"Tell me you have good news," I said.

"Yes and no."

"Has Logan been able to successfully track any phone yet?" I asked.

"No, but he keeps trying. The good news is we got a hit with the facial-recognition database on the Shane Fox imposter. His real name was Michael Webb from Newark, New Jersey, recently moved to Houston, where he was employed by Guardian Oil as security for Howard Hayes."

"From Newark, like Fox. That can't be a coincidence," I said.

Jason shook his head. "I don't think so. Webb lived next door to Fox."

"So did Webb target Fox out of convenience?" David asked.

"Wouldn't know," Jason said coolly. "But there's more. Webb has a record of armed assault, served a few years. Currently, he's wanted under suspicion of multiple counts of murder."

I shared a look with Trish and David. Jason didn't miss it.

"What?" he asked.

I hesitated to tell him about the vision and the assassination. It would just be more alcohol on an open wound. But then again, he'd asked. "I just saw him murder Howard Hayes."

"Another vision." Jason clenched his jaw and wouldn't look at me. "Well, we figured this guy posing as Shane Fox may be a killer."

"We did?" I asked, my heart lighter at the thought my brother was coming around.

Jason shrugged. "It is possible, as the real Shane Fox is unaccounted for."

"Because he was buried alive," David said stiffly.

Jason leveled a glare at David. "I don't believe in all this vision nonsense, about which I'm quite sure I've made myself clear on." His voice carried chastisement, and he still wasn't looking in my direction. "I believe in facts with a basis in reality. One, Jenna has been kidnapped. Two, Webb was a known assassin. Whether or not he slit Howard Hayes's throat, well, I'd need to see an autopsy report."

"The fact you have a hang-up about visions is your problem. Not your sister's." David's voice was gruff and carried a bitter edge. I wasn't sure if he was defending me, his sister's memory, or both of us.

Jason's nostrils flared, and he lunged toward David.

"Stop!" I wedged between them. About as stupid as getting between two snarling dogs with bared teeth, but it was an instinctual reaction.

Both men drew back, chests heaving. Testosterone was a stench in the air.

"Tell him what we speculated about that other crash," I prompted David.

It was a few seconds before David spoke. Then he laid it out for Jason. He added, "There might be a connection between the crash last week and another one I'm still investigating."

"Yet you're standing around." Jason looked at me. "We might have been lucky to get an answer about what caused Mom and Dad's crash."

"Jason," I reprimanded. "Listen to him."

"I hadn't written the previous crash off as a mechanical failure, yet, but I was thinking the engines may have played a role. I just needed proof to back up my theory."

"Faulty engines are responsible for bringing down two planes?" Jason paraphrased. "You have to let someone—the FAA?—know about this."

David shook his head. "Not until I have concrete facts. The FAA doesn't ground planes for the fun of it. Nor is the NTSB in the habit of accusing multibillion-dollar companies of supplying faulty product."

"For the fun of it?" Jason mocked. "People have died."

"This is somewhat personal to you, so I'll excuse your attitude," David said. "But as tragic as it is that people have died, there is a process to getting planes grounded."

"I'm going to be sick." *All the planes in the sky at this very moment...* I thought back to the crisscross pattern in the sky earlier.

"There has to be something we can do," Jason said.

"I agree," Trish chimed in.

David held up his hands. "Sadly, there's nothing instant."

His statement had us all going silent. I was thinking about all those who had lost their lives and who still could if faulty equipment was in planes right now.

My mind went back to the bodyguard—now identified as Michael Webb—who had slit Howard Hayes's throat. No explaining the jump in my thoughts, as they were all sort of merging together, seemingly without purpose. But I remembered Trish telling me that I was given visions for a reason. I also considered the number of books I'd read over the years on the law of attraction and about the efficiency of the universe. I was probably given the one about the plane crash for most than a single purpose. It seemed a big one might be to uncover faulty aviation equipment, another to expose an assassination—though that still left questions. Why assume Shane Fox's identity? Was it just due to convenience? Why had Isaiah from Fighters for Future America hung up after I mentioned Fox's name? A coincidence that meant nothing? Had Michael Webb been working next to Hayes to get close enough to kill him? Why, and did someone pay him to do so? It would seem Webb was a hired gun and not connected to why the plane went down—two separate things. But with the plane falling out of the sky, why go ahead and kill Hayes when he'd likely die from the crash? And how did the mystery woman fit in with any of this—or did she?

"You should probably go home and get some sleep." Jason's voice pried me from my thoughts.

I looked at him, but I didn't want to move. Then again, what good was I doing here? "Okay, I'll go," I said, taking the sticky note with me.

"I'll go with you," Trish and David said in unison.

"Come on." I waved for them to follow. "Trish, as long as you're okay to share my bed. David, you can have the couch." I couldn't let anyone sleep in Jenna's bed; she'd be back.

"Works for now." David winked at me and slipped an arm around my waist, and my brother's gaze met mine.

He still cared about me, about Jenna, the visions aside. I could see it in his eyes. I'd take that as a promising sign he'd come around.

# Chapter Forty

"Here you go." Trish handed me a chamomile tea. When she'd offered to make me one, I was surprised I had any in the cupboard.

"Thank you." I took the steaming mug and blew on it, but I didn't take a sip.

David was on a chair in my living room, while Trish and I each sat on one end of the couch.

We hadn't said much since we got here, but it didn't seem like there was much to say. On the way to my townhouse, I had Trish drive me to work so I could bring my car home. It took a considerable amount of effort to convince her I'd be fine to drive.

I put my feet up on the coffee table in front of me. "I hate not being able to do anything."

"I know, sweetie." Trish leaned over, rubbed my leg.

"Maybe it's like you said, David. I'm putting too much pressure on myself to see something." I lifted my mug. "This should help me relax." I attempted a smile. "It's the most grandma-like tea on the market."

"Peppermint's good, too," Trish said, not even taking offense. "But it can wake you up or relax you. Depends."

"Best we don't take any chances tonight." I blew on my tea and took a tentative sip. The warmth from the beverage snaked through me, soothing me, but the fear over Jenna's well-being was ever-present. "What if that monster's—"

"Don't go there," Trish cut in. "It doesn't do any good. Think positive."

I swallowed her admonition like a jagged pill. I spent most of my life trying to be optimistic, and little good—pun not intended—it did for me. My parents had died tragically, my marriage ended in divorce—and *oh, surprise, he loved men all along*—and now my only child had been kidnapped. "I'm starting to have a hard time buying into all the 'think positive' crap at this moment in time."

Trish's brow knotted, and David adjusted his seated position, as if bracing for an argument.

"I just want her back. Unharmed. Now. And I can't stomach hearing 'it will be all right,' 'we'll get her back,' or 'think positive' one more time." I started into a crying jag.

Both Trish and David were there to offer me moral support, and I still couldn't hold myself together.

I took a minute, sniffled and carried on. "The law of attraction is all about getting what you think about. But I never thought of this. Never in my wildest dreams or nightmares did I think Jenna would be kidnapped. Never in my wildest dreams or nightmares did I think I'd have visions. Hell, I was like Jason. I didn't believe in them or the afterlife. And any time I found myself entertaining the idea of either, well, I kicked it from my mind. So, why is this happening to me?" I sobbed, feeling like a horrible mother. This wasn't really happening to me; it was happening to Jenna. Because of me. "Why won't the visions just leave me alone?"

"There are things in life that are outside of our control," Trish said, stepping carefully. "In the end, we have to believe that everything is for the best."

"*Have to* believe? And Jenna's being kidnapped is for the best? Nah—" I shook my head "—nope." I wished for a silver lining to ease the pain, but one failed to crystalize. "I should probably try to get some sleep," was what I said, but I just needed some time alone. I got up and started down the hall. I stopped outside Jenna's room. My legs buckled, and I grabbed the doorframe for support.

Two sets of footsteps raced toward me.

"Erin?" David called out.

"I'm fine. I just saw Jenna's room." As if that explained it all. It hurt that my baby had just so recently been within my reach, and now I might never— No, I had to stop my thoughts there.

"Come on, I'll help you." David made the offer, arms extended, to walk me to my room.

"In a minute." I was drawn into Jenna's room as much as I felt pushed away.

I sat on the bed and grabbed Precious. I stroked the bear's soft, plush ears, expecting that tears would fall, but none did. It was as if I were watching myself sitting there, not really living it.

Trish and David stood at the door, seeming to debate whether they should come into the room.

"You know where I keep the bedding?" I asked Trish, though it wasn't necessary. She'd spent the night many times and knew where I kept everything in the house.

"Yes, don't worry about us. I'll be in your room shortly, but first I'll help David set up the pullout."

"Thank you."

"No problem." Trish and David disappeared from the doorway and headed down the hall toward the living room. They must have both sensed my need to be alone on Jenna's bed, holding her teddy bear.

I rubbed its ears. Why couldn't I just conjure a single freaking image of my daughter's whereabouts? Anything? Just something that would help narrow down where Jenna was being held.

I got up and brought Jenna's bear with me to my room. I set it down on the bed while I flossed and brushed my teeth. Afterward, I crawled under the covers with Precious, hugging it to my chest as I cried myself to sleep.

# Chapter Forty-One

"Jenna, get back here." I am laughing, and Jenna is running away from me giggling.

She is only a little girl, of six or seven, and she's wearing a red and white dress, its ribbon sash blowing and curling in the wake of her strides.

"Here, baby."

More trills of her laughter hit my ears, and I savor the sound, like the song of an angel. My angel.

We are running down a dirt road, and there are deep ditches on each side. Farmer's fences beyond them and fields for as far as the eye can see.

"Mommy can't catch me," she says in a singsong voice.

"Oh yes, I can." I pick up speed, pouring intent into each stride. Before now, I was giving her an advantage, letting her think she was beating me.

She hurries faster, her torso leaning forward, but her legs can't keep up. She stumbles and falls, starts to cry.

"Jenna," I say and reach out to where I saw her go down, only she's gone now.

I look around. Not a sign of her. She's disappeared without a trace.

"Jenna!" Desperate. I hear nothing except for the breeze blowing through tall grass, sounding like gentle waves breaking against a shore.

*Then I make out something new: a red mailbox. And its flag is up to indicate there is mail inside. I race to it and open the box. Inside there's a folded piece of paper. I open it and read the message.* "Mommy can't catch me."

I shot to a seated position. My heart was racing like mad, and my body was drenched with sweat.

"Erin?" Trish shuffled next to me in the bed. It was obvious that I'd startled her.

"I'm sorry. I…I just had a…" I laid a hand over my chest as if it could slow my pounding heart.

"A vision?"

"An interesting dream anyway." And troubling, but I didn't add that part.

"Did you want to talk about it?"

I shook my head and looked at the alarm clock. *4:44* AM.

"That's a good number," Trish mumbled, barely coherent.

"Good. I need all the *good* I can get."

"It means the angels are with you, helping you." Trish fell back against her pillow and was snoring before 4:45. And I knew because I was staring at the clock.

I lay back down, gripping Precious to my chest.

*The angels are with you, helping you.* Trish's words offered comfort, and I drifted back to sleep.

The knock sounded like it was coming from far away, at the end of a long, resonating corridor.

"Erin?" A man's voice. David's?

*Where am*— I opened my eyes to see it was David, and he had his head pushed through my bedroom doorway.

"Jason's on the phone for you," he said.

I glanced at the handset on my nightstand. I hadn't heard it ring. Just as I was trying to make sense of it, I realized David was holding my cell phone.

"You left it in the living room last night," he explained, as if reading my confusion.

"Oh." I shuffled to a seated position, and he came over with my phone. "Thanks," I said to him, then into the receiver, "Tell me you have something we can use."

"We just might."

"What is it?" I blurted out.

Trish stirred in the bed, just clueing in that we had a visitor in the room.

"Logan was able to—"

"Wait, let me put you on speaker." I hit the appropriate button. "Okay, go ahead. It's me, David, and Trish."

"Logan was able to track the user of the app that hacked into David's phone."

"We know where Jenna is?" *Please, God.*

"Not exactly. But he did get an address in Detroit, Michigan," he stressed.

"What's in Detroit?" I asked.

"Techchips," Jason said.

"They program aviation software," David added.

"Software?" I blanched. "How many planes use their software?"

"Probably eighty percent of the planes in the sky," David replied.

"Oh my God," I lamented. "Tell me we can do something. They tapped David's phone, spied on his actions with the NTSB, probably are behind Jenna's abduction."

"Sure, if we can prove all that," Jason said.

"You tracked the app to them."

"Correction. To their address."

"A technicality, Jason. Right now?" Planes being potential deathtraps was horrid, but another urgent, more personal matter was foremost on my mind. "What are we doing about finding Jenna?"

Jason's end of the line fell silent, and neither David nor Trish offered anything.

"Okay, nothing," I groaned as a thought struck. I wished it had occurred to me last night. It was starting to feel like I needed to think of everything—but that was on me, my mind assuming that burden. "Here's something that might be an issue," I said. "The people tapping David's phone have to suspect something's up. It's been inactive all night."

"Yes and no."

I rubbed my forehead. "Jason, what does that mean?"

"Logan worked something up so that it sounded like David was around people."

David cut in. "How did he—"

"He pieced together words from your voicemail greeting and used other people to interact with you."

"My voice—" David cupped his mouth, then dropped his hand. "He got into my voicemail?"

"Without a hitch." There was a barb in my brother's tone. "By the way, who is Josie?"

"None of your business," David shot back, and I shrunk. "So, it's not enough to get into my voicemail for the greeting, but you listened to my messages as well? All of this is illegal, by the way. Did you pull a background check on me while you were at it?"

"Jay did what he had to do," I fired off.

David met my eyes and seemed to deflate. He probably just wanted me to pretend I never heard the name Josie, whoever she was.

"Let's get back on point," Jason said coolly.

"So, it's quite possible this software company were the ones to tap David's phone," Trish said, sounding as if she were finally waking up. "This is a business that would, I assume, pride itself on security measures and the like. Wouldn't they make it a little harder to track them down? Just thinking out loud here."

I nodded. "You have a point, Trish."

"So what? Now we don't think they're the ones behind Jenna's kidnapping?" Jason sounded exasperated, and I wondered if he'd slept at all last night.

I was so frustrated and confused that I could scream. "I don't know what to think."

"Well, if their software's causing planes to fall from the sky, I'd say they've made a huge mistake," Jason said.

David met my gaze when he spoke. "You can be certain I'll be delving into the company the minute I get back to the States."

"You should go now," Jason encouraged.

"Jason," I rebuked.

David waved his hand dismissively. "No, it's okay. He's protective of you. I get that."

Jason said, "If they're the ones who have Jenna, there's no way of—" Someone spoke to him in the background, and his sentence was left unfinished. "You sure?" Jason said to whoever it was, a bit of excitement in his voice. Into the receiver, he said, "Logan just—"

*Bleep.*

"—successfully traced—"

*Bleep.*

"—the blocked number."

*Bleep.*

Tears streamed down my cheeks. Logan may have just saved my daughter.

"Ah, Erin, I think you have another call coming in," David said. "The little tones notify you of call-waiting."

"Oh." I rarely had two calls on the go at once, and in my half-groggy state and with my full attention on Jason's words, I'd dismissed the bleeps. I looked at caller ID. "It's a blocked number. It's him." I switched over the calls, placing Jason on hold and answering Jenna's kidnapper. I'd let him be the first to speak.

"You didn't do as I asked."

I stiffened. "How do you know whether I did or not?"

"You're testing me, is that it? Does your daughter's life mean nothing to you?" With that, he hung up.

"Shit! The son of a bitch. He's gonna… He's gonna…" I clamped my mouth shut.

"Erin?" It was Jason. When the kidnapper had hung up, it must have automatically put Jason back on the line.

"He's going to kill Jenna." As I said the words, I had never been so cold in my life.

# Chapter Forty-Two

There was finally some luck on our side. Logan had tracked the blocked number, and it led us somewhere a lot closer than Detroit, but it did take us out of the city. The call appeared to have come from a farmhouse in Milverton, Ontario, a community two hours northwest of Toronto.

Jason had called in the cavalry, as he'd put it, meaning the Emergency Response Team or ERT for short. They were Canada's version of the American's SWAT, or Strategic Weapons and Tactics, unit. They were in charge of the scene, and uniformed officers were to stand down, including my brother. But he was amped up on exhaustion and adrenaline and adamant they let him be a part of the takedown and rescue. His pleas did no good, but he was afforded a comm piece and a radio so we could hear what was going on.

Local officers happily let the Toronto Police Service carry on with its investigation in the Milverton jurisdiction.

Jason was saddled with me, Trish, and David, and we were down the road, half a kilometer from the target location, in Trish's SUV. The guys were in the backseat and getting along—surprisingly.

We listened as ERT breached the property, then the farmhouse. "All clear" was shouted out a number of times. I was waiting to hear one of the officers come over the radio and say, *"Hostage secured,"* like they said in the movies. Didn't happen. With each "all clear," hope liquified into hopelessness.

"Erin, I hate to say it," Jason started.

"Then don't." I knew precisely what he was going to say. That we were too late. That Jenna had been killed.

"There is the possibility we won't find her alive." It seemed he'd felt compelled to put it into words.

I glanced over at Trish behind the wheel and closed my eyes. Exhaled slowly. "I choose to stay positive."

"Entering the drive shed," one of the officers announced.

I stiffened, imagining my sweetheart frozen inside.

David must have sensed my thoughts go dark because he reached forward and put a hand on my shoulder.

"Where is she?" I pleaded, again to any being willing to answer.

"Approaching the secondary outbuilding now," another officer said.

A few minutes later, another "all clear" came back. Would I ever see my Jenna again? The ERT sergeant had tried to prepare me for that and so had Jason, but I refused to give myself over to the statistics.

Communication came over that ERT was expanding the search to surrounding farms and properties. There was no way I could just sit here, waiting and listening. I got out of the car and ran down the road. No doubt looking like a woman gone crazy, but I didn't care. My daughter's life was all that mattered. I wanted to *scream* for her at the top of my lungs! She could hear me and yell back. But then maybe she wasn't hearing anything anymore. Maybe she was— No. No. No. I refused to become mired down in hopelessness.

*"Mommy can't catch me."*

I stopped running. There was a little girl on the road ahead of me, her back to me, and she was wearing a red and white dress.

Jenna as a little girl.

*"Mommy can't catch me,"* she taunts again.

"Oh yes, I can." I took note of my surroundings. It was familiar, just like my dream from this morning. Jenna in that dress. The deep ditches, tall grass, fences, and farm fields. All the same.

Goosebumps pricked my flesh, and I smiled.

"Erin?" Jason ran up next to me. "What are you—"

"She's in a house with a red mailbox." Ahead of me, now the girl—*Jenna*—was gone.

"Jason, did you hear me?" I yelled at my brother, who hadn't moved.

"How do you— Never mind." Jason proceeded to speak into the comm. "Officer Stone here. We have reason to believe the hostage might be in a house with a red mailbox."

I couldn't hear the person on the other end, but I imagined he'd asked David how he knew that, given how Jason looked at me. We held each other's gaze.

"Just do," Jason said. A second later, he filled me in. "They're going to look for a house with a red mailbox. If we find one before them—well, we shouldn't even be out here."

I put a hand on his shoulder.

"We'll need to hang back and let ERT handle it," he said.

I started running.

"Erin!" Jason called out. His strides struck the dirt road, scuffing the gravel, alerting me to his location.

I kept running, and I'd *keep* running until I "caught" my little girl. My lungs were starting to burn just as I came to a crossroad. Wind swirled around me, sweeping strands of hair across my face. I wiped them clear.

*"Mommy can't catch me."* Jenna's voice carried on the breeze.

"Where are you?" I cried out. At first there was no visual of Jenna, then one appeared about twenty-five feet ahead. She was facing me and holding out her hands for me to take.

"Jenna." I moved toward her. "Tell me where you are."

Little girl Jenna giggled and started running down the road. I followed her until she vanished again. I stopped, caught my breath. Waited.

Deep ditches were on the left and on the right. Beyond that, more fences and fields *for as far as the eye can see.* Then I heard it: nature's song. Breeze rushing through tall grass. *Like gentle waves breaking against a shore.*

I looked over my shoulder. A red mailbox, just like the one in my dream, across from a farmhouse. I smiled because I knew in my heart it hadn't been a dream; it had been a vision. My daughter had come to me, after all.

Jason came to a stop beside me. "Erin, you can't just run off like—"

"You can't go in that house," I said starkly. "You could lose your badge. All I have to lose is Jenna. I'm going in."

Jason grabbed my arm and attempted to yank me back. "I could lose both of you. You don't know who you're dealing with in there. He's more than likely armed."

"I can't just sit around anymore. I've got to get my girl." I shrugged out of his grip and hurried down the drive. Parked there was an old four-door sedan with weeds growing around its tires.

"For God's sake, Erin." His next words seemed to be directed at the ERT sergeant as he was letting someone know where we were.

Jason came up behind me, and gravel struck the back of my pant leg. *He's close,* was all I had time to think before he yanked back on my shoulder.

"I'm with you, but we can't be stupid." He guided me to the side of the sedan that provided cover from the house. He pulled the comm piece from his ear, flicked something on it, and stuffed it into a pocket. I looked from his eyes to his pocket, then back up to meet his gaze.

"Can't be stupid, eh?"

"Don't be a smart-ass. You follow my lead. I'm the cop."

"Yes, Officer," I teased, but I was happy he was by my side.

"I'm armed, you're not. Another reason I lead."

I held up my hands. "Now that the pecking order is clearly established, let's move." I glanced at the house, desperately wanting inside.

"Follow me." Jason started to creep along the side of the sedan.

I rolled my eyes but followed his direction.

The house had a front veranda with a door, but there was also a side door. Jason was approaching the latter.

"Wouldn't it be smarter to go in at either the front or the back?" I whispered to him.

"Shh."

*Right. Little brother, the cop, knows better.*

I continued to follow him to the side door. Its window was cracked open. There were no noises coming from inside, but I did hear voices—ever so low—coming from somewhere.

I looked toward the barn, and I saw little girl Jenna again. She was pointing inside, a grim expression on her face. "Jenna's in the barn," I said.

Jason looked at me over a shoulder. "I'm not even going to ask," he grumbled, but set out in the direction of the barn.

The closer we got, the louder the voices became. Obvious anxiety and tension. Two people—one man and…

"Please, don't do this."

*Jenna!*

I pointed animatedly toward the barn, jabbing my finger. "See?" I hissed but was careful to keep my voice low.

Jason snarled at me as if to say, *Now's not the time for "I told you so."*

"Stay put," he directed and inched closer to the barn. He put his head against the building and peeked inside. Next thing I knew, he was stepping into the open doorway, gun drawn. "Toronto Police! Put your hands up where I can see them!"

I heard screaming, Jenna's screams, and I stepped up behind Jason. A man had his arm wrapped around Jenna's neck, a gun to her temple.

*Oh God, no, please, no.*

I was flaking apart on the inside, but at the same time, there was a sense of tranquility wrapping me in its arms.

"Mom!" Jenna wailed.

"You don't want to hurt her," I said. The words were coming out of my mouth, but my voice was imbued with a serenity that wasn't coming from me.

"Her death will be on you, lady." The man who was holding her didn't look like a killer—despite the gun and the threatening hold on Jenna. But then, what did a killer look like? He had a baby face and couldn't be more than twenty-five. Dressed in a plaid shirt and jeans, it was easy to imagine him in a mall or having a beer with buddies.

"Please," I begged, "just let her go."

"I can't do that." His hold on Jenna was shaky, and I was shocked by how calm I was. *Adrenaline?* It felt like something more.

"Put the gun down," Jason barked.

More activity was coming down the driveway toward the barn. I sensed them more than I heard them. No doubt it was the ERT, and they were strategizing the best approach.

"Nobody needs to get hurt," I said.

"You're wrong about that." He pushed the gun into Jenna's head, and she cried out in pain.

"Enough people have died."

The gunman's composure faltered a bit at my words— words I was pulling from somewhere outside of myself, or that at least seemed that way. And I was getting a strange sense that he was not connected with the software company. No, someone else was behind Jenna's kidnapping. Like Trish had said, the software company would have the know-how and technology to cover their tracks.

"Who hired you?" I asked.

Jason kept his gaze on the gunman, but I saw his eyes twitch.

"I don't know what you're talking about," the gunman replied.

Someone had access to David's login with the NTSB, someone had the technical smarts to tap his phone. This person must have figured David's interest in the Texas crash had been sparked by the open case. They would have also heard everything I told David.

Techchips would have money to throw around, and they could have come after us directly, but why dirty their hands? They could have greased some wheels inside the NTSB. David had vouched for Bill Sauder, the lead investigator on the Texas crash, but he had an assistant. Ronnie. David said he'd left messages with him for Bill. The timing between then and the first threat could easily fit. Ronnie would have had time to find out who I was and about Jenna, where we lived…

One would assume Ronnie was younger, given his position. A millennial possibly—smart with technology, as Jason's sarge had pointed out about the age group. Ronnie could have been paid to keep tabs on his coworkers and take whatever action necessary to keep the company's secrets. He could be the one behind paying this kid I was looking at now. But if Ronnie was paid under the table by Techchips, why have the hacking app lead straight back to his benefactor? That part didn't make sense. Could it be another aviation manufacturer that was wanting to make it look like Techchips was behind this? David had been suspicious of an engine manufacturer.

Time passed as I thought all this through, seconds ticking off in slow motion, similar to time-lapsed photography that showed each flap of a hummingbird's wings. I was aware of each breath—mine, Jason's, Jenna's, and the gunman's.

Then there was a flicker in the gunman's eyes that spoke to fear more than anger, like someone who had gotten in over his head.

I pounced on the weakness. "I don't think you want to hurt her. I don't think you want to hurt anyone. Put the gun down, and we can talk this out."

"No, I…I don't. I didn't mean for it to go this far." The gunman was shaking, and his arm was slowly coming down, the threat against my daughter's life ebbing.

A loud boom. Red mist. Silence.

The gunman was dead on the ground. A bullet to the head. Instant death.

I ran toward Jenna and squeezed her like the world of mine she was.

"Mom." Jenna was crying.

I loosened my hold. "Sorry, am I suffocating you again?"

"No." She shook her head and leaned in for another embrace.

I ran my hand over her head. "It's okay, baby. I caught you." She didn't question what I meant, and we stood there until Jason came over, the ERT sergeant not far behind. He was a huge, muscled man and towered over my brother by a good six to eight inches. And my brother wasn't short.

"You ever do anything like that again, Officer Stone, I'll recommend you ride a desk for the rest of your career."

I stepped in front of my brother, between the two men. "My brother is a hero."

"I'm failing to see—"

"Then you're blind. I'm a civilian. It's his duty to protect me. And that's what he did."

The sergeant snapped his mouth shut, and a vein bulged in his forehead.

"And if you want to talk about screwups," I said, "your guy shot that kid when he was about to surrender."

He held eye contact with me for several seconds, then passed a quick glance at Jason and walked away.

Jason patted me on the back. "Thanks, sis."

"All in a day's work."

Jason moved to hug Jenna and held her so tight she was tapping on his back for him to release her.

He obliged. "Your mom's pretty kick-ass."

Jenna smiled. "That she is."

I had my arm back around my daughter, and I didn't have plans of letting go of her—ever.

Trish and David were running toward us.

"Yes!" Trish exclaimed and threw her arms around Jenna. She kissed her cheeks, her forehead, her cheeks again. "Are you okay?"

"Yes." Jenna laughed, but there was a bit of darkness about her.

"She will be," I interjected.

David stood there looking at Jenna and me. "Glad you're all right."

"Thanks," Jenna said, and the two of them proceeded to hug awkwardly.

I met Jason's gaze, and he asked, "I might regret asking this, but how did you know it was the house with the red mailbox?"

"Told you that you probably don't want to know."

Jenna looked back and forth between her uncle and me with a confused expression.

"I'm sure I don't, but I'm still asking," he said.

"I saw it in a vision," I replied nonchalantly. *Or was it an apparition?* Would I be seeing ghosts next? I gulped. I'd deal with that if it came to it. I was starting to manage seeing visions like I'd had them all my life.

"Pfft." He shook his head.

"Mom, you saw what in a vision?" Jenna crossed her arms.

"I'll fill you in later," I assured her. By *later* I meant at some point when she was ready to hear it. Maybe never.

Jason pointed to Jenna, then drew his finger to me. "We don't say a word about any of this to Aunt Judy. Ever."

I knew he'd bundled the visions and Jenna's ordeal together. I was fine with that arrangement for now, but one day, I might tell Aunt Judy about the visions. There was that quote: *To thine own self be true.* I just smiled at Jason, but his expression was serious as if he'd read my mind.

# Chapter Forty-Three

## Three Days Later

Jenna was asleep on my couch, her head in my lap like she was a little girl again. *Grace and Frankie* was on TV, and I was sipping an herbal tea.

Both of us had taken the rest of the week off, figuring it was necessary to reconnect and just deal with what had transpired. Turns out the gunman had been commissioned through an online forum, something found on his computer. He lived in the farmhouse with the red mailbox. He'd taken Jenna as she was leaving her apartment for school. She said he'd been rather decent to her, aside from holding her prisoner and threatening her life. Clearly, we had very different definitions for the word "decent."

He'd kept her in the basement of that farmhouse but had fed her, gave her water, a place to sleep, etcetera, to cover her basic needs. He never touched her. They'd been in the barn because that was where he planned to kill her. If we hadn't shown up when we had…well, I don't really want to know what might have happened. His phone was eventually found by investigators on the initial property that ERT had searched.

Jenna herself was a real trooper, handling the kidnapping in stride, or as my brother said, "She has cop in her blood."

Jenna had laughed it off, but I swore I witnessed a little flicker that belied her brush-off. Who knew? My girl could sign up for the police academy. A selfish part of me prayed to God she wouldn't, but as Trish had so wisely pointed out the other day, some things are outside of our control. As if she had to tell me that!

Jenna had asked for more information about my visions, and I'd obliged. She'd listened respectfully, said the right things, and seemed to offer understanding, but there was something in her voice that told me she wouldn't be believing in visions just yet. At least she didn't insist I go to the doctor again. I took that as progress. I didn't tell Jenna that I'd seen her as a little girl, like an apparition; in fact, I didn't tell anyone. Not even Trish, but she would be excited when I did.

Jason, possibly less open to visions than Jenna, still didn't want to discuss them. And that was fine. I got that it was outside his comfort zone. Boy, could I relate! Crazy how much I'd changed in under two weeks.

Jason had probed into Michael Webb's past and notified the FBI that he had been killed in a plane crash last week. He obtained the necessary approvals to access Webb's financials, and there was a large deposit that linked back to Guardian Oil Company. It would seem Ted Vega, the CEO of Howard Hayes's company, had ordered Hayes's assassination. Under intense interrogation, it became known that Hayes had intended to push Vega out of the company, near penniless. Vega must have pointed the finger at Fighters for Future America because he feared an investigation into the plane's passengers would reveal his connection to Webb. If I'd never received my visions, Vega might have gotten away with commissioning a murder. What was left of Hayes's remains were going to be examined thoroughly for any injuries that weren't congruent with the crash.

As for why Michael Webb had assumed Shane Fox's identity, that answer wasn't solid—convenience or something more? But it was speculated that Fox might have been linked to Fighters for Future America in some way, which would explain their reaction to my calling about him. What role he played for them, assuming that he had, seemed to have gone to both men's graves.

Bill's assistant, Ronnie Libberman, twenty-eight, and by definition, a millennial, had a background in computer sciences and programming. He cracked under pressure and confessed to everything—hacking David's phone, making it look like the source was Techchips, monitoring activity on the NTSB servers, and commissioning the gunman who took Jenna. Apparently, the manufacturer of the faulty engines had been padding his bank account quite well and for some time.

When I had told David to narrow his focus on the engine manufacturer, he told me that made sense. Apparently, Ronnie had been quite interested in David's progress on the older crash, and when David started asking questions about the Texas crash, it really got Ronnie's attention.

David and I had agreed to keep things between us platonic, but right after we said that, he'd kissed me again. A breath-stealing, toe-curling, sweep-me-off-my-feet sort of kiss. So, yeah, our relationship was in the screwed-up column—confusing and complicated as hell.

He returned to the States intent on finding the proof needed to go at the engine manufacturer and to ground whichever aircraft utilized their product. I wondered how he was making out but didn't want to bother him, even though he'd told me to call him whenever I wanted to. Before David had left, he asked me how I'd realized that Ronnie was being paid off, and I ran him through my thought process but emphasized it had started as a feeling.

Jenna stirred on the couch next to me, yawned, and sat up. "I've gotta go to bed."

"Okay, honey." I paused the show.

"Oh, don't worry about it. Go ahead and watch it." She smiled, kissed me on the forehead, and headed off down the hall.

I was so blessed everything had worked out okay and she'd returned to me unharmed. Some people weren't as lucky.

I hit Play, planning to watch the drama for a little longer before going to bed. My cell phone rang, and caller ID told me it was David. I answered before the second ring finished. "Well, hello there." Spoken flirtatiously as hell without even trying. I was improving now that I was getting some practice.

"Hello," David replied. "How is everyone?"

"Good. Jenna just went to bed. I'll be headed there soon." I shifted up straighter. "How are you making out down there?"

"Making good progress on building a case against the engine manufacturer, but these things still take time. And there isn't just one thing wrong with the engines, basing it on the Texas crash and the one I've been investigating from a few months ago. Both flights had slightly different things go wrong with the engines." He paused a few seconds, then said, "How did you figure it all out again? That it wasn't Techchips?"

I was pretty sure he just liked hearing my flashes of insight. "I told you. I reasoned it out, and it makes sense when you think about it. Why would a company trying to hide its faulty product have an app that led police to their door?"

"Well, you're amazing. That's all I have to say."

"Why, thank you."

"Just to think the truth's going to come out because you had the courage to act on your visions. You saved a lot of lives, Ms. Stone."

I smiled to myself. It did feel good, but I said, "You're the one making this happen."

"Not without you. We make a good team."

"We do."

"I'm so happy that Jenna's fine."

"Me too."

"When will I see you again?"

His question pinched my heart. I'd jump on a plane tonight, but with everything up in the air—or not staying in the air… "I thought we were keeping things platonic."

"We are. Friends see each other. You and Trish get together multiple times a week."

"Uh-huh." Before my heart got too carried away, though, there was a question I needed to ask. "Who's Josie?"

The line fell silent.

"David?" I prompted.

"Josie is someone I'd rather speak to you about in person. It's complicated."

"She's your ex? You were married before?" I took a stab in the dark.

"Yes."

"Okay, well, I have an ex too."

More silence.

"There's more to it," I surmised.

"Lots more, and I'll tell you in person."

His words made it clear that branch of conversation had reached an end. "Okay, next time we're together," I said.

"Agreed. And when is that again? I'm still waiting for an answer."

I was past trying to fight my feelings for him. "Why don't you tell me?"

"Let me get a handle on everything over here, and I'll be on the soonest flight up there. I'll take you out for a real nice dinner, maybe dancing."

"You might want to drive…you know, instead of fly."

"Good point."

"So, we're just friends, eh?"

"Friends eat together. Dance together…"

"Uh-huh."

"Well, I better get going. I just wanted to check in and give you an update."

"Thanks."

"Of course. Night."

He ended the call, and I was left holding the phone. David was another blessing that had come out of all this. If I hadn't been given that dream about a plane crash, we might never have connected—at least in this way. Then again, there were a lot of things that wouldn't have happened if I hadn't finally believed in my new ability. Who knew how many more planes would crash? David might never have resolved the crash from a few months ago. Or how long would the engine manufacturer have gotten away with their faulty product and how many more people would have died before it came to light? I didn't want to really think about any of that. Hayes's CEO could very well have walked away scot-free from ordering a hit. Webb had been paid. If it wasn't for the crash, Hayes most likely would have been murdered. Lily Brooks could be who-knows-where under the care of an unfit parent while her mother would have been devastated.

That dream and the visions had me examining my beliefs in a new light, and as much as I'd resisted change, it brought numerous benefits. Maybe some I hadn't even yet identified. I had been able to find the silver lining in Jenna's abduction—far easier with it in the rearview mirror and her safe. It had been enough to push me past my comfort zone again and to truly accept myself for who I was and my psychic ability.

I went to turn off the TV and inadvertently hit the input button for the cable box on the remote instead. The late-night news was on, and the tickertape read: *"Missing Newark man found buried in his garden."*

The reporter was saying, "An anonymous person called local police about missing person Shane Fox. Fox was reported by his cousin six months ago. This tipster directed police to Fox's backyard where police have now recovered his body. Cause of death is still being determined, but it seems he may have been buried alive. Police dismiss the possibility that the tipster was involved in the murder, and there have been rumors that the department may have consulted with a psychic."

I smiled and turned off the television. A couple days ago, I had another vision: I was shown exactly where Fox's body was buried. I may have called that into the Newark Police Department. After all, everyone deserved closure.

I got up, my eye catching the picture of Mom and Dad on the mantel. I picked up the frame and touched a fingertip to each of their faces. For some reason, losing them didn't hurt as much as it used to. It could be because I was starting to think they could still exist in some form—the same belief that once had hurt too much to accept now offered comfort.

Whether they went on as spirit beings or in my heart, something within me had changed. A healing had certainly taken place through all this. It could be knowing I'd had a part in bringing closure to victims' friends and family of two downed flights and prevented countless other deaths. Yes, that was definitely a big part of it.

I set the frame on the mantel and padded down the hall to bed.

I was excited about going to sleep and what would come next.

I'd just closed my eyes, and I was back on the Texas flight, Hayes across the aisle, the older woman beside me, the nose of the plane dipping down. The fear wasn't suffocating this time, but memories of the mystery woman flooded in.

She hated flying. Just like me. She didn't put faith in the afterlife. Just how I used to feel. She also had nothing to lose. A little trickier, but accepting that we were eternal beings made everything relative and fleeting. Nothing could ever be lost.

My eyes shot open. There was a reason David and I hadn't found the mystery woman—she hadn't been an actual passenger on that plane. It was me. I was the mystery woman, the observer—the point of view—all along.

I fell asleep with a smile on my face wondering what I'd dream about tonight.

# A Letter From Carolyn

Dearest reader,

I want to say a huge thank you for choosing to read *Midlife Psychic*. If you enjoyed it and would like to read more Erin Stone paranormal fiction, then please email me to let me know at carolyn@carolynarnold.net. If you want to subscribe for more book news from me, please sign up for my newsletter. Your email address will never be shared, and you can unsubscribe at any time.

CarolynArnold.net/Newsletters

If you loved *Midlife Psychic*, I would be incredibly grateful if you would write a brief, honest review. At this time, *Midlife Psychic* is the only title I have in the paranormal women's fiction genre, but I offer nearly forty published titles and five series in mystery, thriller, and action adventure. To investigate these more, you can visit my website at the link below.

Erin Stone came to me a few years ago, and she and her story hit me with such impact that I started writing right away—and I was technically just starting a two-week holiday around Christmas. The concept was so incredibly inspiring and compelling that I knew this book had to get written. It ended up taking over a year to actually finish it amid other projects I had on the go, and I was nervous about doing the story justice. Also this genre was brand-new to me and the content in conflict with my past.

Like Erin, I came from a religious background that would consider such a thing as psychics to be demonic. A lot of what is reflected in the pages of this book were pulled from my personal experience and spiritual journey. I remembered being so scared when I opened up to having guardian angels that I slept with the light on for a while. There are experiences that I had in my life that I've shared through Erin's window to the world, and I know what it's like to be cut off from my family. To this day, several years later, my choice to leave the religion in which I was raised has made it so blood members of my family who are still active have cut off all communication. Tough. Pill. To. Swallow. At first. And it took me years to reconcile and forgive. The latter really is the path to healing and forward movement. It was for me anyhow.

But during this difficult time in my life, I discovered myself— my power and the spirituality that lies within. I was free to explore thinking and beliefs that before I never would have considered. I discovered the law of attraction and redefined my relationship with God, among other things.

I say all this to share and bare my soul, hoping that if you find yourself in the same type of position—not being accepted by those you love whether it be due to religious choices or personal lifestyle ones—to hold your head up high and be true to yourself. You were born to be the full expression of *your* being, not someone else's. You are also not alone, and please trust that there is strength to be found in adversity.

Of course, I don't say any of this to sway anyone in their beliefs. They are so incredibly personal, so who can say what's right and wrong for another individual? We are all simply navigating this beautiful spiritual journey of life the best we know how.

If you feel the nudge to reach out to me either by email or through social media, I would be delighted to hear from you. (Links below.)

Namaste,

Carolyn Arnold
Carolyn@CarolynArnold.net

Connect with CAROLYN ARNOLD Online:
CarolynArnold.net
Facebook.com/AuthorCarolynArnold
Twitter.com/Carolyn_Arnold

# Acknowledgments

Oh, where to begin? There have been so many people who have helped me along the journey of bringing this book to publication! My husband, as always, is reliably by my side and supportive of all that I do. He is a shining light with whom I'm honored to spend this life.

My sister, Sherry Buikema, to whom this book is dedicated, has been an incredible presence of light in my life as well. She went through a lot of what I did, but she found her way on a new path years before me. She lovingly accepted me for who I am and has always been by my side on this spiritual journey. Sherry has helped open my mind to the possibilities in life, in the world around us, of the universe. Really, all things *are* possible. She helped me discover the law of attraction, for which I'll be eternally grateful. They say when the student is ready, the teacher will appear. Well, Sherry has certainly been one teacher I've been blessed with along my path.

Sherry also reached out to two friends of hers to clarify how to read auras. I told Sherry the feeling/mood I needed for my character, and she got the answer for me. Thank you goes out to Sherry's friends who helped with this.

Grateful appreciation also goes out to Des Ryan, a former police officer with the Toronto Police Service. I thank him for putting me in touch with the 911 dispatch center and

Pete Grande. In turn, I thank Pete for introducing me to Jeremy Fine, who so patiently answered pages of questions! Before him, I really had no idea what was entailed with being a communications operator. Thank you very much, Jeremy, for your help.

Read on for an exciting preview of
Carolyn Arnold's police thriller
featuring Madison Knight

# TIES THAT BIND

# CHAPTER ONE

**Someone died every day. Detective Madison Knight was left** to make sense of it.

She ducked under the yellow tape and surveyed the scene. The white, two-story house would be deemed average any other day, but today the dead body inside made it a place of interest to the Stiles Police Department and the curious onlookers who gathered in small clusters on the sidewalk.

She'd never before seen the officer who was securing the perimeter, but she knew his type. The way he stood there—his back straight, one hand resting on his holster, the other gripping a clipboard—showed he was an eager recruit.

He held up a hand as she approached. "This is a closed crime scene."

She unclipped her badge from the waist of her pants and held it up in front of him. He studied it as if it were counterfeit. She usually respected those who took their jobs seriously but not when she was functioning on little sleep and the humidity level topped ninety-five percent at ten thirty in the morning.

"Detective K-N-I—"

Her name died on her lips as Sergeant Winston stepped out of the house. She would have groaned audibly if he weren't closing the distance between them so quickly. She preferred her boss behind his desk.

Winston gestured toward the young officer to let him know she was permitted to be on the scene. She signed in, and the officer glared at her before leaving his post. She envied the fact that he could walk away while she was left to speak with the sarge.

"It's about time you got here." Winston fished a handkerchief out of his pocket and wiped at his receding hairline. The extra few inches of exposed forehead could have served as a solar panel. "I was just about to assign the lead to Grant."

Terry Grant was her on-the-job partner of five years and three years younger than her thirty-four. She'd be damned if Terry was put in charge of this case.

"Where have you been?" Winston asked.

She jacked a thumb in the rookie's direction. "Who's the new guy?"

"Don't change the subject, Knight."

She needed to offer some sort of explanation for being late. "Well, boss, you know me. Up all night slinging back shooters."

"Don't get smart with me."

She flashed him a cocky smile and pulled out a Hershey's bar from her pants pocket. The chocolate had already softened from the heat. Not that it mattered. She took a bite.

Heaven.

She spoke with her mouth partially full. "What are you doing here, anyway?"

"The call came in, I was nearby, and thought someone should respond." His leg caught the tape as he tried to step over it to the sidewalk, and he hopped on the other leg to adjust his balance. He continued speaking as if he hadn't noticed. "The body's upstairs, main bedroom. She was strangled." He pointed the tip of a key toward her. "Keep me updated." He pressed a button on his key fob and the department-issued SUV's lights flashed. "I'll be waiting for your call."

As if he needed to say that. Sometimes she wondered if he valued talking more than taking action.

She took a deep breath. She could feel the young officer watching her, and she flicked a glance at him. What was his problem? She took another bite of her candy bar.

"Too bad you showed. I think I was about to get the lead."

Madison turned toward her partner's voice. Terry was padding across the lawn toward her.

"I'd have to be the one dead for that to happen." She smiled as she brushed past him.

"You look like crap."

Her smile faded. She stopped walking and turned around. Every one of his blond hairs were in place, making her self-conscious of her short, wake-up-and-wear-it cut. His cheeks held a healthy glow, too, no doubt from his two-mile morning run. She hated people who could do mornings.

"What did you get? Two hours of sleep?"

"Three, but who's counting?" She took another large bite of the chocolate. It was almost a slurp with how fast the bar was melting.

"You were up reviewing evidence from the last case again, weren't you?"

She wasn't inclined to answer.

"You can't change the past."

She wasn't hungry anymore and wrapped up what was left of the chocolate. "Let's focus on *this* case."

"Fine, if that's how it's going be. Victim's name is Laura Saunders. She's thirty-two. Single. Officer Higgins was the first on scene."

Higgins? She hadn't seen him since she arrived, but he had been her training officer. He still worked in that capacity for new recruits. Advancing in the ranks wasn't important to him. He was happy making a difference where he was stationed.

Terry continued. "Call came in from the vic's employer, Southwest Welding Products, where she worked as the receptionist."

"What would make the employer call?"

"She didn't show for her shift at eight. They tried reaching her first, but when they didn't get an answer, they sent a security officer over to her house. He found the door ajar and called downtown. Higgins was here by eight forty-five."

"Who was—"

"The security officer?"

"Yeah." Apparently they finished each other's sentences now.

"Terrence Owens. And don't worry. We took a formal statement and let him go. Background showed nothing, not even a speeding ticket. We can function when you're not here."

She cocked her head to the side.

"He also testifies to the fact that he never stepped one foot in the place." Terry laughed. "He said he's watched enough cop dramas to know it would contaminate the crime scene. You get all these people watching those stupid TV shows, and they think they can solve a murder."

"Is Owens the one who made the formal call downtown, then?" Madison asked.

"Actually, procedure for them is to route everything through the company administration. A Sandra Butler made the call. She's the office manager."

"So, an employee is merely half an hour late for work and they send someone to the house?"

"She said it's part of their safety policy."

"At least they're a group of people inclined to think positively." She rolled her eyes. Sweat droplets ran down her back. Gross. She moved toward the house.

The young officer scurried over. He shoved his clipboard under his arm and tucked his pen behind his ear. He pointed toward the chocolate bar still in her hand. "You can't take that in there."

She glanced down. Chocolate oozed from a corner of the wrapper. He was right. She handed the package to him, and he took it with two pinched fingers.

She patted his shoulder. "Good job."

He walked away with the bar dangling from his hand, mumbling something indiscernible.

"You can be so wicked sometimes," Terry said.

"Why, thank you." She was tempted to take a mini bow but resisted the urge.

"It wasn't a compliment. And since when do you eat chocolate for breakfast?"

"Oh shut up." She punched him in the shoulder. He smirked and rubbed his arm. Same old sideshow. She headed into the house with him on her heels.

"The stairs are to the right," Terry said.

"Holy crap, it's freezing in here." The sweat on her skin chilled her. Refreshing, actually.

"Yep, a hundred and one outside, sixty inside."

When she was two steps from the top of the staircase, Terry said, "And just a heads-up—this is not your typical strangulation."

"Come on, Terry. You've seen one, you've—" She stopped abruptly when she reached the bedroom doorway. Terry was right.

# CHAPTER TWO

The hairs rose on her arms, not from the air-conditioning but from the chill of death. In her ten years on the force, Madison had never seen anything quite like this. Maybe in New York City they were accustomed to this type of murder scene, but not here in Stiles where the population was just shy of half a million and the Major Crimes division boasted six detectives.

She nodded a greeting to Cole Richards, the medical examiner. He reciprocated with a small bob of his head.

Laura Saunders lay on her back in the middle of a double bed, arms folded over her torso. But the one thing that stood out—and this would be what Terry had tried to warn her about—was that she was naked with a man's necktie bound tightly around her neck. That adornment and her shoulder-length, brown hair provided the only contrasts between her pale skin and the beige sheets. Most strangulation victims were dressed, or when rape was a factor, the body was typically found in an alley or hotel room, not the vic's own bedroom. For Laura to be found here made it personal.

Jealous lover, perhaps?

"Was she raped?" Madison asked.

Terry rubbed the back of his neck the way he did when there were more questions than answers. "Not leaning that way. Her clothes are strewn on main level. Seems like if sex did happen, it was consensual."

"And she's in her own house," Madison added.

The entire scenario caused Madison pain and regret—pain over how this woman's life had been snuffed out so prematurely, regret that she couldn't have prevented it. For someone who faced death on a regular basis, one would think she would be callous regarding her own mortality, but the truth was it scared her more with every passing day. Nothing was certain. And the fact Laura was only two years younger than Madison sank into the pit of her stomach.

Terry kneaded the tips of his fingers into the base of his neck. "There is no evidence of a break-in. Nothing seems to be missing. There's jewelry on her dresser, and electronics were left downstairs. No obvious signs of a struggle."

Madison moved farther into the room to study Laura and the tie more closely. It was expensive, silk, and blue striped. Her eyes then took in a shelving unit on the far wall, which housed folded clothes, an alarm clock, and a framed photograph.

She brainstormed out loud. "Maybe it was some sort of sex game that got out of hand. Erotic asphyxiation?"

"If it was something as simple as that, why not call nine-one-one? The owner of that necktie must have something to hide."

Richards's assistant excused himself as he walked through the bedroom. Madison could never remember the guy's name.

Terry continued. "Put yourself in this guy's place if things had gotten out of hand. You would loosen the tie, shake her, but you wouldn't pose her. You would certainly call for help."

"The scene definitely speaks to it being an intentional act." She met her partner's eyes. "But I'd also guess the killer felt regret. Otherwise, why cross her arms over her torso? That could indicate a close relationship between Laura and her killer."

Their discussion paused at the sound of a zipper as Richards sealed the woman in the black bag.

His assistant worked at getting the gurney out of the room and addressed Richards. "I'll wait in the hall."

Richards nodded.

"Winston confirmed you're ruling cause of death as strangulation," Madison said to the ME.

"Yes. COD is asphyxiation due to strangulation. Her face shows signs of petechiae. Young, fit women don't normally show that unless they put up a fight. And there were also cuts to her wrists."

"Cuts?" Terry asked.

"Yes." Richards glanced at Terry. "Crime Scene is thinking cuffs. I don't think they've found them yet."

Madison's eyes drifted to the bed's headboard and its black vertical bars. The paint was worn off a few of them. "She's bound, and then he uncuffs and poses her." The hairs on her arms rose. "When are you placing time of death?"

"Thirty to thirty-three hours ago, based on the stage of rigor and body temperature."

"So between two and five Sunday morning?" Terry smiled and shrugged his shoulders when both pairs of eyes shot to him.

Madison often wondered how her partner could do math so quickly in his head.

"Of course, the fact that it's cold enough to hang meat in here makes it harder to pinpoint," Richards said.

Madison noticed the light in Terry's eyes brighten at the recognition of the cliché. He knew she didn't care for such idioms, and he had proven himself an opportunist over the years. Whenever he could dish them out, he would. Whenever someone else said them around her, he found amusement in it. She was tempted to cross the room and beat him, but instead, she just rolled her eyes, certain the hint of a smile on her face showed. She hated that she didn't have enough restraint to ignore him altogether.

"I'll be conducting a full autopsy within the next twenty-four hours. I'll keep you posted on my findings. Tomorrow afternoon at the earliest. You know where to find me."

Richards smiled at her, showcasing flawless white teeth, his midnight skin providing further contrast. And something about the way his eyes creased with the expression, Madison couldn't claim immunity to his charms. When he smiled, it actually calmed her. Too bad he was married.

"Thanks." The word came out automatically. Her eyes were on a framed photograph of a smiling couple. She recognized the woman as Laura, but the man was unfamiliar. "Terry, who is he?"

# CHAPTER THREE

He sat in his 1995 Honda Civic, sweating profusely. Its air conditioner hadn't worked for years. The car was a real piece of shit, but perfect for the crappy life he had going. He combed his fingers through his hair and caught his reflection in the rearview mirror.

He lifted his sunglasses to get a better look at his eyes. They had changed. They were dark, even sinister. He put the shades back in place, rolled his shoulders forward to dislodge the tension in his neck, and took a cleansing breath. With the air came a waft of smoke from the cigarette burning in the car's ashtray.

He had parked close enough to observe the activity at 36 Bay Street, yet far enough away to be left alone. At least he hoped so. Cruisers were parked in front of the house, and forty-eight minutes ago, a department-issued SUV had pulled to a quick stop.

All this activity because of his work. It was something to be proud of.

He picked up the cigarette and tapped the ash in the tray.

Statistically, the murder itself was nothing special. Another young lady. People would move on. They always did.

It was the city's thirtieth murder of the year. He was up-to-date on his statistics. But he was always that way; he was a gatherer of facts, of useless information. Maybe someday his fact-finding and attention to detail would prove beneficial.

He wiped his forehead, and sweat trickled from his brow and down his nose. The salty perspiration stung. He winced. His nose was still tender to the touch. That crotchety old man at the bar had a strong right hook.

He rested his eyes for a second, and when he opened them, a Crown Vic had pulled to a stop in front of the house. He straightened up.

A woman of average height—probably about five foot five—with blond hair walked toward the yellow tape. But it wasn't her looks that captured his interest. It was her determined stride. And something was familiar about her.

He smiled when he realized why.

She was Detective Madison Knight. She had made headlines for putting away the Russian Mafia czar, Dimitre Petrov, but the glory hadn't lasted long. People like Petrov had a reach that extended from behind bars, and the rumor was that Petrov had gotten the attorney who had lost his case killed.

He must have hit the big-time to have Knight on *his* investigation. An adrenaline rush flowed over him, blanketing him in heat. Energy pulsed in his veins, his heartbeat pounding in his ears. He strained to draw in a satisfying breath.

*Tap, tap.*

Knuckles rapped against the driver's-side window.

His heart slowed. His breath shortened. Slowly, he lifted his eyes to look at the source of the intrusion.

A police officer!

*Stay calm. Play it cool.*

He drew the cigarette to his lips. Damn, his nose hurt so much when he sucked air in that he had to fight crying out in pain. He left the cig perched between his fingers, and the cop motioned for him to put the window down.

"I need you to move your vehicle."

Thank God for his dark-tinted glasses or the cop might see right through him. "Sure."

The police officer bent over and peered into the car. "Are you all right, sir?"

Following the officer's gaze to his unsteady hand holding the cigarette, he forced himself to raise it for another drag. His hand shook the entire way. "Yeah, I'm—" Her lifeless eyes flashed in his mind. He cleared his throat, hoping it would somehow dislodge his recollections. "Sure. I, uh…I'll get out of your way immediately, Officer…Tendum." He read the cop's name from his shirt.

The cop's gaze remained fixed on him, eye to eye.

*Can he see through me, sunglasses and all? Is my guilt that obvious?*

"All units confirm a secured perimeter." The monotone voice came over the officer's radio.

The cop turned the volume down without taking his eyes off him. "What happened to your nose?"

What is this uniform out to prove?

He forced another cough and then took yet another drag. He tapped the cigarette ash out the window. The office stepped to the side, but based on the look in his eyes, he wasn't going anywhere.

He needed to give the cop an answer. His words escaped through gritted teeth. "Bar fight."

The officer nodded. His eyes condemned him. "I need you to move your car—" he drummed his flattened palm on the roof "—and try to keep yourself out of trouble."

*Too late, Officer. Too late.*

Also available from
International Bestselling Author
Carolyn Arnold

# TIES THAT BIND
Book 1 in the Detective Madison Knight Series

**She could feel him watching her… Though every time she turned to look, there was no one there. The rest of the world thought she was going crazy—until it was too late.**

**When Laura Saunders is found strangled** in her home with a man's necktie, **Detective Madison Knight is assigned the case.** Her sergeant at the Stiles Police Department wants her to conclude it was an isolated incident and move on with the investigation, but Madison's not the type to cave under pressure. She's haunted by certain unexplainable clues at the crime scene, including the presence of a mysterious photograph. Madison believes the picture may somehow tie into the murder, but before she can dig into it, another woman's body is discovered in a local park. **Heather Nguyen** was also murdered with the same brand of necktie that had been used on Laura.

On the surface, there doesn't seem to be anything beyond the way they were killed that connects the women. But as Madison delves into the lives of the victims, **she unravels a web of deceit and betrayal and lays bare decades of deadly family secrets**. Edging closer to the truth, Madison's quite sure **at least one more woman is slated to die. But can Madison piece together all the clues in time to save her?**

Available from popular book retailers or
**at CarolynArnold.net**

CAROLYN ARNOLD is an international bestselling and award-winning author, as well as a speaker, teacher, and inspirational mentor. She has several continuing fiction series and has many published books. Her genre diversity offers her readers everything from cozy to hard-boiled mysteries, and thrillers to action adventures. Her crime fiction series have been praised by those in law enforcement as being accurate and entertaining. This led to her adopting the trademark: POLICE PROCEDURALS RESPECTED BY LAW ENFORCEMENT™.

Carolyn was born in a small town and enjoys spending time outdoors, but she also loves the lights of a big city. Grounded by her roots and lifted by her dreams, her overactive imagination insists that she tell her stories. Her intention is to touch the hearts of millions with her books, to entertain, inspire, and empower.

She currently lives near London, Ontario, Canada with her husband and two beagles.

### CONNECT ONLINE
CarolynArnold.net
Facebook.com/AuthorCarolynArnold
Twitter.com/Carolyn_Arnold

And don't forget to sign up for her newsletter for up-to-date information on release and special offers at
CarolynArnold.net/Newsletters

Printed in Great Britain
by Amazon